Haight St.
Posse

Token Jackson

Cast:

Aaron
Angelo
Bear
Belue
Brandy, aka Moonflower
Kathy & Moon
China Mike
Dready Christy & Osiris The Dog
Fozzy
Grasshopper
Gretchen & Der
Hetzel
Honduras Allan & Kristy and her son Harley
James, aka Sparkle
Jason Nance & Mariam
Jengo & Erica
Jim Minchow
John & Lucky
Josh & The Spinners
Junebug
Katie Moon
Kelly aka Kelly Belly – Kells Bells
Kevin
Laura & Arien
Lauren - Tuscan, AZ
Little Bear
Little Mikey
Mark Brantly
Maria & Cheese
Mike Kyte
Mike (Thin Black Hair – Virginia Beach Crew)
Michelle Gibby

Morgan
Mouse & Beth
Patches
Phil Lisi
Ragin' Rob
Raven
Rhonda Roy
Roach & Kim
Robert Philips, aka Funky
Smiley Rob
Spooky Rob
Stephanie Robinson
Stoney
Tim, aka T-dog & Beth
Wess
Zen Jim

The Wrecking Crew:
Artie
Fast Eddie
Ira
Jackson
Marlina

1988

I remember…I'm still there…somewhere around Waller or the Panhandle in San Francisco, California. It all started in the fall of 1988 for me. I was a high school student swinging singles of LSD (Windowpane was the name). There were pictures of album covers on the print. I would score them from some bro in Gaffney, South Carolina. It was enough to open the door and unlock the journey.

Like most kids in high school, I wanted to be accepted. I, of course, did what most kids do and hung out in the smoking area, which led to drinking alcohol and whatever. I failed my tenth grade year as a result of too many unexcused absences. David Carter was my best friend. He had come from another school, and I met him in the smoking area. By the end of that year, we were both failing, because of skipping school. We ended up walking out together at the same time, officially quitting school. Too many good times, I suppose.

I lived in Clifton, South Carolina at the time. I was fifteen years old, and I just started playing on my father's acoustic guitar. I used to go to DawGone, a pub in Spartanburg and, yes, I was under age. There I met people who were into acid and The Grateful Dead. Among these people were Mike Kyte, Funky Philips, and Mark Brantly. I looked up to Mark and Funky because they were older, and I was a "newbee."

I just bought a Volkswagen Sirocco, and Mike K. was like, "man we gotta go to Philly and see the Dead." (He had one of those Grateful Dead stickers that you could stick on and then take off.) So, we headed to

Pennsylvania. I was told I could get a hundred hits for fifty bucks, so I said let's go. I was selling doses in South Carolina, spending like two and three bucks a hit.

I hadn't even really listened to The Grateful Dead, in fact, I don't think I cared too much for them. Anyway, we gassed up and off we went. Mike was a cool soul, he was an excitable guy with positive energy. The whole time, on the way up there, he insisted we listen to these fucking bootlegs that sounded like pure shit to me. Smoking weed seemed to help the grinding sound of these awful bootlegs. But he insisted I get a taste of these guys before I go, a painful experience to the closed mind. Driving is always fun, ya know, so I soon adjusted ...I do that. As I think about it, I remember the song "Crazy Fingers."

We had about a nine to sixteen hour drive, and we did it in good time. I had never been to Philly or "Philthy-delphia." I loved the drive. There's nothing like the tollbooths and sunshine. Truthfully, it was pleasant, and we rolled in the scene on a bright beautiful day. The Spectrum has a lake across from it and this is where they were directing us.

Fuckin' awesome site: hippies everywhere and bettys, bettys. bettys...yummy! It was September '88, and there was full on camping. We finally parked. A couple of guys rolled up next to my VW in a Honda Accord. We got out and did the typical stretch. Cars were steady being parked, so Mike and I took off on foot heading toward the Shakedown. For those who are not aware of this term, it is the busiest and most congested of all isles in whatever venue The Boys play.

This particular Shakedown was one of my all time favorites. There was a lake with a sidewalk right next to it and tents all around. Grills were set up cooking everything from falafel to grilled cheese. People were walking by, selling everything you could want. Mike and I eventually made it back to our spot, and we proceeded to set up our tent. It was a five person tent. Not the easiest to set by no means. Of course, we finally got it set up.

Our neighbor was also setting up his tent. Phil Lisi was his name. He had one of those easy to set up dome tents; however, his friend didn't seem to be helping much. I walked over to them, and we officially met. Phil was older than I and he had curly brown hair like a small afro. He was twenty-four or twenty-five at the time, I believe. Phil was a mail order type of guy who always had his ticket and weed. Phil showed me his tickets for both nights. A beer was usually attached to his hand throughout this journey. Mike was on a mission, and as soon as he saw our campsite was secure he was off and running in search of tickets.

I myself wasn't concerned about getting in. I just wanted to score a sheet with what little money I had. My plan was to sell single hits back in Spartanburg and keep some for my head. You must remember, Mike persuaded me to be here. He offered to pay for gas and assured me I would get my acid cheap. Going inside wasn't a priority, especially after he made me listen to this band on crappy tapes all the way up here.

The fucking scene was overwhelming. I wanted to hang outside and save my money. Looking around, all I could see were tie-dyes and tour shirts on all the guys. I wandered up to the Shakedown, checking out all the shirts for sale. By this point, I did feel a bit out of place with what I was wearing.

I found a white t-shirt with a river flowing to a building with columns. It caught my eye. I sure wish I still had that shirt. It was my favorite. I think I paid eight to ten bucks for it. I went back to my car and put it on, feeling I would now fit in. Classic story for most kids at age sixteen. Mike showed up shortly after that, and he showed me tickets the he scored. He tried to convince me to buy a ticket, and I once again told him I couldn't afford it. Phil and his bro next to us were smoking some weed, so we wandered toward them.

Well, it was getting closer to show time and everyone around seemed to have a ticket, except me. I just walked around, window-shopping up and down the strip. As it started to get darker, I was offered marijuana for the hundredth time that day, and I decided to take a look. It started with the typical statement as you walked by, "kind buds." It looked a bit wet still, but it smelled very sweet.

I bought it and went back to my car to pack my pipe. At age sixteen, I really didn't like beer, or any alcohol for that matter. I was into LSD and marijuana. So spending the money for that was a priority. It was my ticket, at that moment, you know. Eventually, dark thirty was creeping on as well as my high. Mike and Phil had already gone inside and I was left to wander around the lake.

Bumping around from circle to circle, I met up with Phil's friend. He was feeling good from all the beer he'd drunk. There were about four or five of us in no time, and somebody had an acoustic guitar. Phil's buddy asked to play the guitar. The first thing he did was strum the harmonics. This was quite beautiful. If you've ever heard the band "Yes" and I believe the song is called "Roundabout." The intro was what he was playing. He struck a few notes....da didi dala ... followed by harmonics ... pling. At this point he had our attention completely. Once again the notes ...da didi dala …..pling. The moment of awww, and each one of us was very quiet waiting for the song to take off. Just as you thought he was going to start the song he fucking played it all again, and, with a smile, he said, "Uh, that's all I know," …we all laughed. With that our circle dissipated.

I wandered towards the Shakedown; it was now almost completely dark. All the venders had their oil lamps and battery powered lights on. The smell of sage and incense was in the air. To me, this is a smell of "beauty"…of heaven you might say…our heaven. Getting something to eat was my next move. On tour, the cheapest meal on the lot was a grilled cheese sandwich, and that's what I ate. One dollar was its going price.

One of my memories that stuck with me, was how open this particular show was towards illegal drugs. Yes, there were cops on the outer brinks of it all, but they were not hassling anyone. In the middle of it all, in the dark of the night there was even a man holding up a large sign made of cardboard with blinking lights that read "LSD." I chose not to purchase from him. Maybe I should have, who knows?

It was at this first show I tried heroin, or so it seemed. It was Soapium which was popular. There was also this crystal stuff which was a yellowish orange color that actually broke down like crack cocaine. The Soapium was a head shop drug, which was just opium incense that looked like the real thing. The crystal shit actually had a small cut of heroin, in my opinion. You would break off a small piece and place it on top of some bud. It would melt down into whatever you placed it on. It tasted quite good. It did taste like opium, yet it was more likely heroin. I was just sixteen, so it's hard to say.

Somewhere along the way I did connect with the product I was looking for. I scored a couple sheets of "L." I say "L" because that is what I call it now. Back then I called it acid, hits, blotter, ect. It wasn't until Philly that I started calling them doses. Mike called them "Zodiacs" because there was a zodiac sign on each hit. Hell, I could be wrong; could have had a different astrological sign per hit; however, I believe it was all the zodiac symbols. Those who were there would recall. At a young age our minds are affected differently from all toxins, aka: drugs, whatever. It could have been a double set batch, and I may have had a good time from it. However, it was family "cris" so I believe it was cleaned up quite well. As I recall, I did try it out that night. As long as I had weed I would trip, and I had weed.

Being this is my second attempt in writing this book, I've lost some enthusiasm, to a certain degree. In the initial writing, I did go into more detail as far as the acid trip in Philly. Pretty simple, I would drop a hit to make sure it was quality, and I got through the night.

What I remember, that was cosmic, was the come down the next morning. Mike showed up after the show, around 11:30 pm, raving about how they opened with "Let The Good Times Roll." I didn't really care. In fact, by the second day, I was ready to bail. Going back home to sell this acid seemed more exciting after I had run out of money. Don't get me wrong, I was into being there; however, I had spent what little money I had on buds and doses.

Like I said, I did drop a hit and it kept me up all night. Sometime around noon the next morning I was still sleepless. Mike had his glass graphix bong, and he had scored some actual opium. This was not Soapium or violin resin …it was "the shit." All that was left was just the residue in the glass stem. He heated it as I inhaled. The effects are hard to explain. The trip went from bright to darker. That's about right, with a wave of "ahhhhhhhh," and a lot of tension relief. That was foreshadowing, in my opinion.

Man, what a site to watch the sun come up from our view in Grateful Dead land. I was a car length and a half from the lake. The grass had a nice coat of morning dew. It just doesn't get any better than that. It sounds like a bad beer commercial. My first show was a typical one for the 80's. I didn't get in any of the nights. Well, moving right along; I got my doses and my bud and I was out of money. Meanwhile, Mike's got hella money and running around buying up all kinds of shit.

Phil Lisi and his buddy were doing their thing at their car … the infamous Honda Accord. I broke out my zodiacs and Phil busted out the shit he'd scored and we compared our products. There was a big print of a skeleton head (Oxomoa type) on all one hundred hits of Phil's doses. He had eaten it as well, so he knew it was straight too. I'm sure he was going back to Ocean City, New Jersey to swing to all his friends as well. Phil called it "Ocean Shitty," which I visited four years later. We finally picked up our ass and got moving homeward bound for Spartanburg, SC. I don't remember the drive home; I have a selective memory.

I got home, sold all my shit, and off we went to New York. Mike had a surprise for me though. He had scored a twenty pound tank of nitrous, which he planned to sell and we did. I must say putting that all mighty dollar in your pocket, at any age, will make you feel better, and I was more than ready to re-up. Now, I don't mean to make this seem like a smugglers freak scene. Yeah, we were small time drug dealers, if you look at it with a shallow mind. Truth be known, I was having a great time just going through the motions. While millions just sat around, we were on the move, and it was exciting.

The New Jersey turnpike is expensive. You must keep money on hand if you want to get through all the tollbooths. Of course, this being my first time to New York, Mike made sure we were ready. I don't know if he'd been there before; however, he knew to have the change. Going into the city of Manhattan for the first time is a trip, this is where you experience the Lincoln Tunnel. It was $2.00 in 1988 for the fall tour, and by the time you got there, you'd easily spent $10.00 in tolls. The multi lanes of one-ways were shocking to me as a first timer.

Eventually, we made it to Madison Square Garden, and as we rolled in Mike said, "hey, look at the top the garden!" Perched at the very top of MSG was a stuffed gorilla in a tie die t-shirt.

Finding a place to park was crazy. The Park & Lock across the street was a very tall parking building, and it was also going to be our motel. Basically, the vans and buses were best in these circumstances. We were of course in my VW Sirocco. We pulled in, took our ticket and up we went looking for a spot.

The sixth level is where we ended up. The first thing we did was take another hit of gas from the twenty-pound tank; we had been hitting it here and there on the way as well. Five bucks a balloon is what we sold it for. Immediately we started selling nitrous balloons. "Hippie crack," as we called it, was flowing on our side of the block, and there were others selling n20 close by too. Mike shut it down because the valve was freezing up, and we both needed to check out the scene. We walked down the levels of the Park & Lock, which were flooded with VW's of all makes. At the very bottom was a small pizza joint which served super thin crust pizza.

All around the Garden were swarms of people. Everyone was on a mission of some type: anything from buying a shirt to scoring some LSD. I myself was out to score more acid. I did have more money for this venue because I got rid of the shit from Philly. There's nothing like driving eleven hours to buy product from a complete stranger. The fucked up thing is I was just going to get a few sheets. You would think I would have had more money to invest, but at sixteen, what do you expect?

Mike went off somewhere looking for a ticket. Next time I saw him was back at the car, and he had a ticket for me. The date was September 18, 1988. In passing, in the lovely Park & Lock, some bro sold me a couple sheets of brown paper with dancing skeletons. I ate a couple hits in the car, and then we headed toward the Garden. Mike was wearing a graduation robe from Spartan high that he had tie-dyed. The colors were quite bright, and this acid was kicking in quick. The tickets were on Jerry's side. I was starting to really feel the LSD kick in.

The Boys opened with "Feel Like A Stranger," and let me tell you, I sure did. I've taking quite a bit acid before this moment, so a couple of hits didn't seem like too much. Mike next to me was having a grand time. Through all the shock, I was trying to enjoy the show. "Goddamn this acid is strong," I thought to myself.

My sides started to vibrate. The song changed suddenly to a happy melody. This guy in a graduation robe next to me was having the time of his life saying "Franklins Tower."

"Dude, I gotta get the fuck out of here; I'm having trouble breathing. Fuck, my hands, I can't feel my hands, everything's fucking vibrating. I'm not enjoying this. I'm leaving now. I can't fucking breathe, and my heart is racing beyond enjoyment." I thought and before I knew it, I was at an exit door having a conversation with the staff.

He told me, "If you leave out these doors, you can't come back."

At this point my arms, face, and especially my jaw was a steady vibrating grind. So I was on the streets in no time thinking the fresh air would slow everything down. It sure as fuck didn't. Things just became different with mass confusion, and the primal instinct to go back to the nest. What madness, I didn't know where the fuck I was. I sure as hell didn't come in this way. I did know where the Park & Lock was. I could find it if I was at the same gate as I entered. Fuck it, I knew it was right across the street, somewhere around MSG.

So I continued on, sporadically breathing, with the electric butterflies at my sides churning. The air seemed tight in my lungs, with a chill. Pulling on each breath as it was my last. All I knew was I had to get to my sanctuary. My car was the savior in this mad world that was trying to kill me. I circled anther block … no sign of the tall parking garage. Wandering like a broken fool, I turned another corner and I could see it was at the other end on my left. I made my way toward the entrance, step by step.

Almost immediately, upon entering the building, the stench of urine overwhelmed everything. "I don't remember it smelling so strong before." The lights in the building had a purple glow…to say the least. "Where is my car? God, where is my car? Shit!" I kept on walking. "There's so many damn VW's, surely I didn't pass it. Were we not on the fourth or fifth floor? Or was it fifth or sixth? Fuck, Fuck, Fuck…. alright, calm the fuck down Brad. Ok, here we go third level. I don't think it's on this level."

"Buds, Doses," some bro says as I walk by.

Yeah, that's what I needed. "What I need is my fucking car. Getting close, I know I'm getting close, seems like I recognize that. Yeah, ok, breathe. God help me. Shit, I'm not gonna make it. Killed by acid in New York, no fuckin' way. If I can just get to the car, the sanctuary." The palms of my hands were covered in sweat. I kept moving my mouth and jaw. Finally, there was the car in its green beauty.

"Keys… I got keys, it's cool, as I reach in my pocket, here they are. The car, thank you god, I'm home." My hands fumbled the keys out of my pocket and inserted them into the door lock. As I opened the door, that familiar VW smell you only get from the interior of Volkswagen, entered my nostrils. It's a heavenly scent right up there with frankincense and myrrh.

I climbed in the seat looking around at the wreckage we had accumulated. All I could think to do was ball up into a fetal position and pray. At that time, I'm sure I was asking Jesus for help, as well as God. The family I was brought up in had those teachings. I hadn't been exposed to a lot of culture yet. What I knew was when you're about to be hit by a truck you cry out for help. I believe this is where people find God at the last minute. However, in that state of mind, help carries no name. I could not shut my eyes for shit, in fact, that made it worse. At least I'm back in my sanctuary safe from all the evils of the world, but fuck, I had to get out here.

"Arrrrrrrrg! maybe if I throw up, and get the poison out I'll feel better. I must go out side for that. Man, I'm in hell. I need some air…anyway, here we go." A blast of air hit my face as I stepped out of the car bewildered. A couple passed by and one of them looked my way. They knew … I knew they knew.

I walked to the front of the car, and put my finger down my throat. Gag reflex followed by pain. "No, that sucked…that sucked hard. What the fuck do I do? I want my mom or my dad. I'm never taking acid again. God, get me through this and I'll never trip again." In desperation, I climbed back in the car waiting for some relief. My hands had a different feel, it seemed.

I turned on my side. The sweat on my forehead was cold. "Ok, I don't think I'm going to die. Get me through this and I'll do right, I promise," just the usual spiel. I was adjusting slowly. Somebody opened his or her car door next to me. I just sat there in a fetal position. Time was slow. The vibration had decreased as colors began to flow. Slowly, but surely, I was adjusting to the alkaloids in the acid.

Mike showed up eventually with the weirdest look on his face. That look of, "what a pussy." How could he know what I'd been through? I explained to him I took too much, and what I took wasn't very clean. As he listened he started taking nitrous hits. Of course the tank was calling others, as expected. A line of people soon appeared at our car. All of this was a bit overwhelming considering the circumstances. I did stay by the car, from this point until I got right in the head.

Sleep? Well you know how that goes ... it doesn't. Sometime around noon the next day I wandered down towards the street. If you remember, there was that new style of pizza being sold on one side at the bottom of the main opening. I walked my tweaked out self over there and ordered a slice. It was heavenly, super thin with the right amount sauce, not too much not too little. I believe today this is why I love thin crust pizza the best. I finished half of it in a matter of steps. I was tempted to go back and get more.

"Doses," every other fucking step. Shit, why didn't I wait. I probably would have gotten some cleaner acid. Oh well, "wait until that deal come round," is what the song said; however, I wasn't listening yet. High above us, the gorilla wearing the tie-dye t-shirt sat perched at the very top of the Garden watching over us all as we wondered about. Being spun out in Grateful Dead Land is priceless, especially at some of your first shows. Anyway, I walked around what seemed like an hour before I went back to the Park & Lock. Mike was still busy swinging nitrous. It looked inviting, so I had him fill me up a balloon.

We got some tickets, thanks to Mike again, and he found us two bettys. The one with him was obviously pretty, and her friend had a great personality. The friend and I hung out right along side of them, which was very cool. Having a girl to kick it with is always nice. It was awkward since she wasn't really my type and vice versa. We made the best of it. I don't remember shit really, all I recall was Mike, after the show, ranted and raved 'cause they played "China Doll." This was the highlight of his evening. The gas was almost gone, and Mike was about $1500 richer. The bastard didn't even cut me in on the take. I stand corrected, he may have kicked me something, but I don't recall profiting too much since it was his tank.

In one of the random conversations, from circle to circle, one girl told us Eric Clapton was playing the off night in another venue somewhat close by. This may have been hearsay, I don't know. Mike and I were not truly interested.

They played many nights, nine to be exact. My first show was on the eighteenth, and on the nineteenth I actually got to see the whole "movie." All I knew was I had my shit, I sure as hell didn't have as much money as Mike, and I was ready to go. Leaving New York isn't much different than entering it. They both suck, if you're not used to it. And with my South Carolina plates, believe you me, I was honked at by many frustrated cabbies.

I lived with my parents in a house across the street from "The Beacon." They served the greasiest burger with onion rings that you can imagine. It was in a fairly good neighborhood. Growing up in my family meant moving from city to city for years. We lived in a lot of shit holes, so this location was definitely one of the better places.

I still had some pieces of the yellow and orange crystal that were supposedly opium. Like I said, I believe it had a tiny cut of heroin in it. I say this because of my reaction when there iy was all gone. It basically smoked like crack, and it melted down into whatever substance you placed it on top of. The classic chrome colored metal pipe with a kitchen faucet screen was what I used to smoke with. Glass pipes, other then Graphix water bongs, were not prevalent yet. Of course, you had your soapstone, Minnesota pipestone, marble, and wood pipes, but all I had was my metal pipe.

I remember breaking up the last pieces of wannabe opium and/or violin resin (or whatever hell it was) over some kind bud. It tasted pretty good, and I had a good nod as a result. Mike and I were smoking this shit pretty much throughout Philly and NY. I slept well that night just like so many nights before.

Come the next day, mainly evening time, I started feeling the pain from the lack of something. All of a sudden my teeth started to chatter together. I was thinking to myself, "it's nice outside, and it's not even chilly," but I kept getting chills up and down my back. At age sixteen I didn't drink beer because I thought it tasted like shit. If I'd have drank some alcohol, maybe it would have helped. However, I started feeling shaky and down right cold.

I jumped in the bathtub, and, in a crouched position, turned on the hot water then the cold. With my hand, I cupped the waterspout making the water shoot towards my head. The water ran down my neck and down my spine. This felt glorious. The chills stopped, and I felt better for the moment. Leaving this spot was never going to happen. It was pure bliss, forgetting all about sickness, almost. As the water started to get cold forcing me out of my hibernation. I felt the empty void creeping back in.

Fuck, I'll just get pajamas on, and wrap up in a blanket. That's what I'll do. In no time, the dreaded shakes returned. This only lasted fiercely for a day then tapered off by the next day. It could have been my age. It's hard to say.

My parents are hippies who lived their lives as chameleons to pay their bills. They took me to my first show, technically, in '73 or '74 when Donna was with them. They said I would bob up and down to music.

Anyway, being that I just got back from Philly and NY, I had product. Selling it, plus keeping some for your head, was the name of the game. I laid out about twenty Triscuit crackers, and dropped a couple drops of liquid LSD on each one of them. I wrapped them all up in tin foil, and stuck them in the fridge. Mom and Dad were out of town, and I didn't expect them for a day or two. I figured they were safe for a night.

There was this girl I met as a result of selling some "L" to her brother. Tripping and seeing a movie sounded cool to me, so I asked her if she wanted to go. She agreed, so I drove us to the Regal 7 Cinemas. This was the dollar show, and it was closer to us compared to the other theatres. We agreed to see "Naked Gun" because we heard it was funny. I talked her into dropping a couple drops of liquid on her tongue. We both did it together. The vial had a yellow cap and it was some of the best "L" I ever had. The trailers were quite exciting especially since the shit started to slowly kick in. Finally the movie started. The beginning was quite stupid, funny and we both were laughing our asses off. About twenty minutes into the film, my brother-in-law, Mike, showed up out of nowhere, tapping my shoulder, just as I was peaking on the acid.

He said, "Hey Brad, your mom and dad are at my house tripping out bad, they ate some crackers in the fridge."

With that said, I looked at the girl I was with for the last time, and said, "hey, there's something going on in my family. I gotta go." Like an asshole, I bailed with my brother-in-law leaving that poor girl tripping alone in the theater.

When we got to my sister Michelle's house, my Dad was saying he was going to kill me for doing this. He kept saying, "I'm alive, I'm alive!"

Mom was tripping real hard right along side of Dad and telling him, "It's all right, it's ok, we're gonna get through this." My father had a partial for his missing teeth, and he wound up throwing up in the toilet, and it got flushed. I was speechless. All I could tell my folks was how sorry I was, and that I'd never do drugs again.

Eventually, we all made it back to the house, and took our drama away from my sister's life. Back home, I was finally coming down. It was around two in the morning. Lying in my bed I could hear my parents finally starting to enjoy themselves after a long four hours of "why Brad" and "never again." Dad was playing his guitar saying and shit like, "I see the notes" and Mom laughing. These were wonderful sounds that were long over due. I was funned out, and ready to sleep. They had a little more than me. They were going to be up for awhile.

The thing is, when my parents went out of town, I ate every fucking thing in the house except the crackers. So when they got home after driving for hours, they decided to eat some crackers. They were stoned, and had the munchies on top of fatigue from the road. (Yeah, if I didn't mention it, they got high back then. They hadn't done any LSD for fifteen years though. I felt pretty bad about all this.) I took a sabbatical until spring tour.

Chilled out on the whole scene, I did, and I got a job at U-haul in January. It was next to the Regal Cinemas in Spartanburg, SC. For the most part, it was one of my favorite jobs I'd landed. Spring tour was on in no time, and I was giving them notice in advance for the shows in Atlanta and the Greensboro shows, back to back.

Jim Peacock was my manger and he wound up hiring his girlfriend's son at the same time as me, and he eventually cut my hours back. The kid drove a supped up Camaro with nitrous in the trunk. He would race it in Cherokee county. The tank was industrial n2o with sulfur added to increase combustion. I heard the sulfur scars the walls, and it isn't as effective as it could be. They put the shit in there just to keep us kids from enjoying it, in my opinion.

I put in a request for the up coming shows, and Jim gave me shit of course. I could see I wasn't gonna be able to get whole lot of time off as long as he was manager. Brad West was our assistant manager, and he was hella cool. Working along side of him wasn't painful, by any means.

My car was a piece of shit. It was a gold, two-door Chevette. My Sirocco had fallen apart as a result of the Philly and NY trips the previous fall. On the Chevette's gas lid cover, I painted the "steal your face" on it, since it was perfectly round.

1989

Finally, the shows came around, and I was very excited. Ever since the shows the previous fall, my heart just hadn't been in the right place, you know. It wasn't all about coppin' some doses and bailing on this spring tour. I had been listening to the Grateful Dead religiously and thus entering into the "realm." In the town of Spartanburg, SC, your music enjoyment was reduced down to 101.1 classic rock and all the other country stations. No, I'm just kidding it wasn't that extreme. You did have 95.7 "The Rock."

Incidentally, 95.7 was the only station at that time that played "Dead Air" hosted by David Ganz. This was a one hour show that came on at 10:00 pm Wednesday nights. The damn station was in North Carolina, unfortunately, so the reception wasn't perfect. So what I did was steal a car antenna off a vehicle in a junkyard, and then I cut the end off putting the two wires on the back of my stereo antenna inputs. Basically, I half-ass mounted the antenna outside my bedroom window and poked a hole in the screen running the wire through it. Yes, every Wednesday night I would kneel in front of my stereo alter taping whatever was played.

At this time, no one was trading tapes with me. Mike and I didn't hang out at all anymore. The only Dead heads I knew besides Mike Kyte were Mark Brantly and Robert "Funky" Phillips. Mark was cool, and he basically did everything he could to keep me from excelling in the Dead head click. I did look up to Mark, to a certain degree. He had been to a lot more shows, and he was older. He knew this so he was still cool to me; however, he wouldn't come off any fuckin' Dead bootleg tapes. So I was reduced to buying most of my music at the malls in town and taping off the radio. This is how it was for a long time. I had the typical mind set as a novice taper, writing fancy on the tape's covers, as I recorded them. Arranging them from store bought to "Dead Hour."

Before coming to Spartanburg, I lived in Tryon, NC. It was there that I first came in contact with Funky Philips. I was young as fuck and had the little brother syndrome. Not to get off track, but my sister Michelle was hanging around Rose, who was hanging around Funky. Rose worked at "Rax" or "Arbys" with my sister. I remember they all came up to Tryon a couple times.

Anyway, back to the story. David Carter and I were pretty much the same. We both loved Pink Floyd, and everything else most people like when it comes to stoner music. I told Dave about the shows coming up in advance, and I asked him to go, he agreed.

Why we took my car, and not his, I don't know, but we did. I would swear I went to Atlanta as well in '89; however, I don't remember shit about it except bits and pieces of stuff which I can't tell weather it was from '89 or another year. Greensboro is what really lays heavy on my mind, as a result of the events that happened.

Dave and I rolled in around four or five o'clock to Greensboro. We both had tickets. They were my first mail order tickets from GD merchandising and tickets. The thing is I had no weed, and, like a dumb ass, I traded my first night ticket for some nugs. If you live in a swag town you usually break down easier, and I lived in a swag town. Turned out both nights were good, so it wasn't a total loss.

They parked us in the main parking lot on the asphalt with the chain link fence surrounding us. And yes, it was 1989 with camping and vending. We had to set up our tent. It was one of those dome tents, so it wasn't too hard to set up, considering we were on pavement. Once we got it secure, we took off towards the Shakedown.

I didn't feel too good because my head had been hurting. I was taking Tylenol for the pain and it seemed to be helping. I already had it in my mind to trade a ticket for some kind bud since we were out of pot. You have to have weed for the show or no show at all.

Eventually, some bro walked past us saying, "buds for a ticket." I got his attention and took a look at it. It was nice. I've seen nicer, but it was a lot better than the shit I'd been smoking. We traded and I went back to our tent to puff. It was tasty. It seemed to help my head. The time was passing by fast, just like it always does when your having fun. I got out of the tent feeling better. The Tylenol I took was going well with the nugs.

Across the road was a smaller parking lot, and the staff was parking people there. Up in the sky were a lot of dark clouds blocking what little bit of light we had left for evening, and it was getting darker. Dave and me walked around the asphalt jungle for a while, and then decided to check out the lot across the street. As we were walking out of the gated parking, we had to cross the street to get to the gravel rock lot, which to me seemed more like the "grovel" lot.

Upon crossing the street, there was a girl with a beautiful tan wearing a sundress. She held a cardboard sign with flowers on it that read, "I'll do anything for a ticket." The show was just about start. When we got to the other side, almost immediately you heard the n2o tanks. Standing in line is where I was next. I got me a big ass punching balloon filled with gas. Dave got one too. We walked on a few paces away from the tank line and started to inhale the love.

Dave started laughing in a low demonic voice, "Ha ha ha ha…" (n2o makes the voice low while helium makes it high, but most people already know this.) Anyway, my knees started to buckle. I reached out for an imaginary railing as I went down. I hit the gravel hard face first. My balloon did its classic whining noise, as it sped away. Apparently, I was "fishing" according to Dave. He said my body was contorting and shit. Hell, I believe him, I've seen it before.

When I got up, my forehead was bleeding, and it was pounding. Dave was laughing hysterically, but trying not to. Embarrassed, I was, no doubt. I got up and shook the dirt off myself. My head hurt. I needed to take another Tylenol. We checked out the scene a little more before we decided to walk back across.

Things were moving right along. Some people were going inside while others raged the lot. I personally loved hanging outside, as long as I had my provisions. The wind had picked up in the last ten minutes, and I felt a couple drops of rain. Dave and I headed back to the tent. He said he wanted to hit some whippets. Yeah, I brought some nitrous charges and a canister. I had bought them from Brendle's in Ashville, NC. I wanted to save them, and bring them inside. Why? Because I also had a hand held dispenser I could sneak in the show.

Oh well, it started to sprinkle lightly, and the wind was blowing harder. I grabbed a couple more pills out of the Chevette to ease my head.

It was really hurting now. The bump on the head across the street didn't help matters. Jumping back into the tent, Dave was filling the canister with a fresh charge. All of sudden it started raining cats and dogs. Dave handed me the whippet canister. I took in the gas. At that moment, the wind started blowing mad and, at the same time, I held the structure of the tent with my arms on my side while Dave did the same. The wind had taken on a hurricane effect. Outside you could hear commotion, mixed with yelling. Rain was seeping through the material.

Someone shouted outside, "Hey, someone help!" I unzipped the door just in time to see an identical tent blowing past us like tumbleweed in a desert. Now that's something you don't see everyday. It seemed like pandemonium had set in. What was once a peaceful and cheery Dead lot had transformed to a dark and gray tropical nightmare. If you were there on the thirtieth of March in '89, then you know.

It was like something out of a Hollywood movie, and in a second's time, the wind stopped. Almost a dead stop. The rain ceased as well, and before you could blink, what little light we should have, appeared through the clouds. All this happened, right around the beginning of the first set, I figure. Only the lot people experienced it, meaning kids without tickets.

Well, this was supposed to be home for the next two days, and the inside of our tent was soaked. I wasn't going to sleep in this mess, and my fucking head was killing me. I just wasn't feeling up to hovelling out in a wet tent. I decided to go to my other house… the Chevette. Dave tried to sleep in the dome of water. He showed up in the car in the passenger seat a couple of hours later. I kept dozing on and off for hours in between the delirium.

I was awakened by Dave, in some fucking panic state, accompanied by screams outside of our window. Apparently, our neighbor's tent was on fire. Dave rolled down the window and started throwing water at the inferno. Ok, if you haven't figured it out yet, this was a bit crazed. A few other people joined in throwing water. Eventually the fire was put out. While all this was going on, I just sat there hoping I could fall back asleep to escape the sickness and I finally did. Keep in mind, I was deathly ill, or I would have helped as well.

Waking up stuck to the vinyl in the Chevette accompanied by the afternoon sun was just peachy. (Peachy, what a word, the ultimate sarcastic term.) I pulled myself together and exited the vehicle. I walked over to the tent, Dave was there and he handed me a whippet. I would swear I felt a little better. You know that feeling you get right after a rough night of flu like symptoms, and then you actually feel better? That was me at the moment.

I went ahead, and took the canister pulling the trigger. My head exploded, and I swear I heard something break. Wow, wow, wow my head pulsated painfully. Fuck, there's aneurisms in the brain. Somewhere up there was a vein spewing blood like a garden hose on full blast that got away. I let out a cry of pain.

Dave said, "Are you alright?"

"No," I said, and quickly sat down before I hit the fucking pavement again.

I had tickets for that night. I knew I was going to have to nurse my health back until show time 'cause dude, I was gonna enjoy this show if it fucking killed me. And it just about had killed me, in my opinion. I don't know what the fuck I ate for brunch. I'm sure it was grilled cheese or stir-fry cooked by some fucking drainbro. I'm kidding. But anyway, the boys played a good show.

My dad says I can't write. He says I need to read more novels from great writers. I said, "what, like Ernest Hemingway?"

He said, "yeah, have you read any Steinbeck?"

I hadn't. If you've read this far, you may agree with Dad. I'm not a writer; I'm just trying to tell a true story, mentioning a few names of those that have died just so they live for another moment, at least in your minds.

We picked up our bones, and headed back to Spartanburg, SC. It seemed like nothing was going on except work. Mike contacted me shortly after we got back home. He wanted to know if I was going to Louisville, Kentucky (4/9/89). I said no, due to the fact that I had a job, and I was lucky to get the time off just for Greensboro. I don't know how the fuck he did it, but for a lousy fucking vial of LSD, he talked me out of my car.

Mike drove my Chevette to Louisville all right. Yes, that's right, he took my fucking car without me to the show in Kentucky. I didn't hear anything from him for a couple days, which wigged me out. I mean, hell, they only played one fuckin' night.

Finally, I got a call from Mike. He said, "Dude, your car broke down in the mountains up in North Carolina."

I'm all like, "What the fuck? You just left my fucking car?"

His response was typical.

Now I had a problem. I lived with my parents right next to the Eagle Chip factory. They had moved from the Reidsville Rd. house. U-haul was not too far; however, I wasn't trying to walk to work. I talked my dad into driving me up to NC to get the car. When we got there, we found it on the side of the road. We called a wrecker to have it towed, which cost over two hundred dollars. So not only did Mike fuck me out of all the n2o money we made in New York, but he left my car to rot on an off road between Asheville and Hendersonville. Like all good fathers, my dad bailed me out, and we made it back home.

When we got home, the mechanic we took it to told us the water pump went out. Mike's punk ass overheated it and did the classic number...blew a head gasket as a result. It was my only ride, so I had to fix it. Plus, I still owed some money on it.

Anyway, I spent three hundred or so for the head job. You hear that Mike? Somebody's in debt. Lets talk about the one fucking vial that bro kicked me. I remember it well because it had a red teardrop cap. It was trashy "L" and dirty as a mother fucker. In fact, it was my first experience with liquid that was not clean. The funny thing is this was one of the last times I ever saw Mike. He kind of dropped off the planet from our little click. For what its worth, I miss him. Mike was fun.

It was business as usual for The Boys, but summer tour, I didn't do. They came to RFK in DC, but I was a working man and would not budge. I did like my job. I was going through a dry spell of sorts. No girlfriend to speak of. I believe I was too stoned or tripping all the time to notice anybody. That summer I scrounged day to day always looking for more weed, more weed. My parents kept me up as much as they could. Fortunate I was to have my particular Mom and Dad. However, I spent a lot of time looking for buds for myself and my parents.

The high life for me was taping the Dead Hour every Wednesday night at 10:00 pm and building my pathetic tape collection. I think this was the year I started to realize how I could sound very much like Jerry on lead guitar. Playing my electric guitar to David Ganzes Dead Hour, I believe I may have agreed to take his place. What I mean by that is, I started really enjoying playing lead, and I did tell the devil I would take his place. However, fame is a part of the equation, and this hasn't happened, of course, so I rest at ease.

I chuckle at this statement, and I'll be damned, at age 33, I must say I'm a dead ringer for Jerry, in comparison to others. Now don't get me wrong, I'm not bragging, just amused that's all. Ok, I've said it, or written it, I sold my soul for fame and fortune; however, I asked to take Jerry's place specifically. Meaning, I did ask for personal gain, as a musician. Even at a young age, I loved how Garcia brought the passion into my musical abilities, and I simply wanted to carry the torch, if the torch went out, that's all.

Fall dates came rolling around, and I was itching to be at a show. The closest they were coming to the good old south was Charlotte, North Carolina on October 22 and 23, 1989. I did what any deadicated young man would do, I smoked some crack to celebrate. I'm kidding...well maybe not.

I mail ordered tickets from GD merchandising. I can't remember whose credit card I used. No, wait a minute, I sent money orders to San Rafael, California, yep, that's right. Oh, and when I got them in, they were so crystally funk nugget like with their sparkly sparkles. Yeah, I was excited. I had my tickets and, once again, I asked Big Dave to go.

I'm gonna be straight with whoever reads this. This story isn't to glorify the Grateful Dead lifestyle; it's to share the story that hasn't been told. In the fall of '89, to live in the south as an outsider, like I did, was just what it was: being an outsider in the south. So when culture came to town, I went.

Charlotte Coliseum is where it was located. These shows, in the beginning, were fun; however, talking about the bullshit we did doesn't appeal to me as much as getting right down to the point of why I'm writing. A wonderful time, I did have. There were no major events at this venue. The major fucking event was the lack of events. This was the first damn tour where they cut out camping and vending. Vending was still happening, you know, the grilled cheesers, stir fry guys, ect. Also, kids were still walking around swinging t-shirts.

No fucking camping at all! That was hard to deal with, even though I hadn't been touring for years and years. I was there at the end of it at least. I believe Dave and I went to the campground. Yogi Bear was the name of the place. We also stayed there again in '91. Yogi Bear was like all campsites at a show, you listened for the tanks and huffed nitrous all night. Well, I did. Yeah, these were great shows. I added them to my belt, figuratively speaking.

I wish I could tell you more, but I don't really want to. Not a whole lot to tell. Bought some doses, saw some shows, raged, and went home. And, of course, going back to Sparkle town trying to fit in with the rest of the click we had. Acceptance was my goal, it seemed.

Like most of us, maybe the fact I hadn't landed a Dead head girlfriend yet, at this point, brings no life to the story. That is the ultimate goal. From my first moment in Grateful Dead land, I saw all these beautiful sisters in sundresses and a lot of them with their boyfriends. Shit, I'd be lying if I said I didn't want exactly that. Dave is still close to me to this very day, but he's no betty, not that I wanted a summer tour betty. They are just the summer tour girls that drop off when school starts back up. No, I wanted a long term, till death betty, and I still feel that way.

Back in U-haul land, Jim Peacock was getting harder and harder to deal with. The son of a bitch started cutting my hours back more and more so his girlfriend's son could get more hours. He wasn't going to fire me. His plan was to reduce my hours so drastically I'd wind up quitting and I did just that, like a dumb ass. I don't know what the fuck I did, as money goes. I probably sold doses, and finagled deals here and there, until I went to work at the Regal 7 Cinemas right next to U-haul. I still had to hustle, believe you me. I was working for five bucks an hour, I think.

I landed a job at Cineplex Odeon on West Blackstock Road. It was a rage working for a movie theater, in every way. The pay was shit, of course, but the perks were sweet. You basically served the customers popcorn and drinks as fast as you could, then the movie started, and you'd sit on your ass until the next crowd. I worked with a pretty cool crew. The assistant manager was the typical geek type. He was kind and good to be around. The main manager was pleasant to work for too.

Yeah, spring tour was on, and I had to give these guys notice. Atlanta, Georgia at the Omni on April 1,2,3,1990. I asked for the time off, and they gave it to me. When I got back from the Omni shows, my co-workers were dead. They were robbed at gunpoint, shot and killed. This would have been me, if I wasn't such an obsessed Dead head.

They closed it down shortly after this, and demolished the building. I have a fond memory of tripping balls on some nice liquid watching "Childs Play." In fact, all three of us were the first people to watch it. I wouldn't have guessed that job would have killed both of those guys. Fucking tragic. It seems people around me tend to die. James and Mike were their names, I think. I knew them well, and for the likes of me, I can't quite remember everything; I've shut them out. It was traumatizing, so shutting it out and acting like it never happened is my way.

1990

Spring Tour '90 came around. I don't think I got mail order tickets, or maybe I did, I'm not too clear on that. What I do remember is the craziness. Dave agreed to drive his car to the Omni in Atlanta, Georgia. He had a silver Mazda Rx7 with these stinking sheep skin or wool seat covers. It fucking stunk like a lamb's ass, but mixed with my patchouli oil, it was heaven. Anyway we got on the road, and half-way into the journey to Atlanta, the Mazda broke down. As soon as we both realized that the car wasn't going to start, I immediately stuck my thumb out. In no time at all, a blue VW bus, with a new paint job and brand new Goodyear tires, pulled over. I remembered the tires well due to the fact they were fatty wide-like, and looked fuckin' cool. The kind of cool a JC Whitney catalog couldn't touch.

The bro at the wheel was named Brian. He was as cool and kind as his ride. Now picture this, dude was a real Dead head, from the looks of it. His hair was long and accompanied by a beard. Alongside of him, riding shotgun, was his girl. Not the run of the mill sister we all had grown accustomed to on tour, she was straight-laced to the tee. What she saw in Brian, I don't know. Don't get me wrong, Brian was a good-looking bro; however, it was odd. She was a model type, and the two of them together seemed strange.

Anyway, off we went toward the big city of Atlanta. We reached our destination in good time. Brian parked his bus in the gravel lot, basically under and on the side of the Omni. Nether one of us wasted any time. We got right out and perused the lot.

I, of course, was on a mission. I wanted to cop some doses, and sell them back home. We wasted no time and scored a sheet of "Blue Unicorn." Being that we rolled in right about show time, Dave and I ate some of the shit. I'm not too clear whether we had tickets or bought some; however, we were in line making our way in the coliseum.

At this point, it hadn't been fifteen minutes since we dosed, and I was already feeling something, that was for sure. Blue....that was the color things started to shift to. Dave looked at me with a crazy smile, the kinda smile of lunacy, for sure.

I got that feeling of cattle being prodded towards the gate. I wanted to let out a yell of "Mooo" and "Bahhh." But this was back when we actually sat in our fucking assigned seats. So yeah, we found our seats, and the show began.

The opener was "Stranger" then "Mississippi" and they played "The Weight" ...pretty hot first set. I don't think we actually heard the first couple of numbers though. We were running late, from what I remember.

Man, this fucking acid was heavy shit. I continued on dancing like I was shown and what came naturally. The doses we ate were hella dirty; however, from experience (New York) I kept on dancing and sweating, thus giving me a better chance of survival, I hoped.

Dave, on the other hand, wasn't doing so well, it seemed. He made it through the first set. Intermission was craziness, like all Dead shows when you're tripping, good or bad. Bright lights in the halls mixed with the confusion. Once we walked out of the coliseum into the surrounding hallways, Dave looked at me and said, "Dude, I'm outta here."

I felt pretty twisted, I must admit, but I was gonna hang in there. Come to find out that product we ate was super toxic, and there were rumors of fatalities. How I got through it is a mystery. Well not really, I knew just being outside wasn't any fucking fun on a bad trip. I made the mistake of going into the over crowded bathrooms attempting to relieve my fuckin' bladder. I probably had to shit, though I wasn't about to do it. Eventually, I got out there, and the lights went down as the second set started.

The Boys fuckin' jammed. They opened with "Foolish Heart." If you were there, you would remember well. Why? Not because it was phenomenal or anything, but because right as Jerry was reaching that peak in his solo, it just didn't quite get there, and the crowd let out an "Awwwwww" of sadness that is burned deep in my memory.

I remember three songs mainly from this show "Death Don't Have No Mercy", and I would swear "Last Time." On a crappy dirty hit of acid or rat poison or whatever the fuck it was, these tunes can be crazed. I know they ended the night with "Black Muddy River" and there was some sketchy guy to my left that looked like a cop. Yeah, I was ready to fucking bail, no doubt. I was holding a felony even though it was swag crap. Can't say it was bunk, it wasn't blank.

Now, Dave, during all this inside, was puking his guts out in the parking lot. Brian was inside the show of course, so Dave climbed under the bus, and curled up in a fucking ball. This is some heavy shit, and by no means filler. I do apologize for the statement; however, he lived through it. Like so many others that did live, they did shit like get religious and suddenly find Jesus, swear they would never drop "L" again, etc, ect. Dave, on the other hand, was Dave, and a year later he was sitting next to John Teter, our boss, who also obviously loved The Boys, in the Charlotte Coliseum.

If this shit ever gets read by anyone, I'd like to say this: talking about the crap that went down along this journey, like what you just read, is filler to me. I really would like to talk about the kids. I continued on the next two years with similar shit and countless shows until I truly started to get to the heart of it all. The people I lived with day-to-day and watched slowly die away, as a result our life style. I really want to jump to '92, but I won't do that just yet.

That summer was a rage. In July they came to Raleigh, NC. It was fucking great. The power went down during "Promise Land" in the first set. Tapers remember, I'm sure. During "Bird Song" every time Jerry sang "Snow and rain" lightning struck right behind stage. Pretty Crazed.

Finally, I landed a girlfriend right before fall tour in '90, and I talked her into going to Madison Square Garden. This was some fucked shit. I had my first VW bus, and it broke down outside of Durham, North Carolina.

Somehow we made it back to Spartanburg, and I talked her into taking her car.

Now she had a Ford Escort. Yeah, that's right, the best car in the world. Her name was Katie Moon. She was special, and I was a shit. She had the prettiest eyes and lovely brown hair. If I knew then what I know now, I would have never let her go. Lessons we learn along the way, I guess. So being that I have the ability to persuade people, we took her car up to MSG. Katie's mom kicked her down a Texaco card, so we raged it. We made it about 300 miles, and then the car stopped shifting properly.

There we were, on the side of the road, and in '90 cell phones were not in everyone's pocket yet. We managed to make it to a phone, and get the car towed to a service station, a Texaco, no doubt. They replaced the filter in the transmission, and gave us brand new fluid. Basically the trans was throwing shit in the filter, and every three hundred miles it would completely plug up. We learned this rather quickly, and the card became vital.

My karma has been horrid for years and this is just one of the reasons. Poor Katie's mom had a bill of about $2000 as a result of this venture. Can you imagine stopping every couple hundred miles from South Carolina to NY and back, replacing the same fucking transmission filter plus fluid? Not to mention the food and cigs we put on the card.

Well, we finally made it into Manhattan in one piece. The city was the same as it always was, of course. Gee, I wonder where we were going to park? The Park & Lock maybe? Right, right, so we found our way to the Garden. (Did I go last year?) Katie and I walked around together, she had that classic look on her face like so many tourists do every year. There wasn't a gorilla on the top this year.

We walked around hearing brothers and sisters chanting about needs for tickets or whatever. We eventually wound up in Penn station. (This is under the Garden, if you didn't know.) There are all these shops like a mall. A tall, dark headed man brushed by us and said, "tickets."

I asked him how much and he replied, "Forty Bucks" with a very thick New York accent.

I said, "Man that's a bit steep eh?"

He stated that they were press box seats; however, on the fucking tickets it said, "Obstructed view." This guy assured us both they were well worth it. Problem was neither one of us had the ducats to invest in spendy tics, but I broke down and bought them.

We had no time to lose, so we rushed off to go inside. Katie really didn't dig the band like I did, and I attribute our break up later as a result of this. Anyway, we finally went inside expecting bogus seating with an obnoxious obstruction plainly blocking our view. To our surprise, on Jerry's side (front right side) was a complete row of eight-cushioned, fold out seats with an actual table in front. You could fold your arms and lay your head down on the table, like you were in high school, and pass out if wanted. Fucking sweet... I never saw this before. And the funny thing is that's just what Katie did. Now I didn't mention the fact that we scored some boomers from the guy as well. (Boomers are mushrooms...cubenzie.) We split the bag right before we got in.

I would say 'shrooms are the only way to fly, even to this day. Wasn't it Garcia who said, "They clean the cob webs out?"

I looked at the set list online last night, but I don't remember the show, really, at this moment. What I do remember is Katie passing out right there on the press box table, after she came down. It was the "drum/space" that did it.

I looked over at her, as they were coming out of "Space" into "The Wheel," and said "Hey, what gives? We just drove all the way up here, and you're passing out."

Her reply was, "You just have a good time."

That did piss me off. I danced, I tripped, blah blah blah...the show ended. Even though Katie wasn't big on the scene, she was big on me. That was my biggest mistake in life, or at least one of them. Dedication she had for me like the dedication I had for the Dead.

We had purchased about twenty cartons of cigarettes, and after the show we walked around selling packs for one dollar. Now, in New York, that's fucking crazy. This town, where gas is hella expensive and cigs are too. So there we were, walking around, and swinging death for a dollar. It didn't take long before word got around that we were doing that.

We sold almost all of the cigs, and got back on the road, stopping every three hundred miles, changing the transmission filter and fluid. By the time we got back to South Carolina, both of us were exhausted.

Katie and I decided to go to the "Texaco" on main (Hwy 29 next to Hillcrest shopping mall). Sitting outside on the pavement was this bro' Kevin with the all too familiar Guati clothing and Guatemalan bag as well. Being we just got back from GD land I said, "Hey, what's up bro?"

Kevin replied like the typical hippie. Come to find out, he had hitched all the way from Manhattan. Why? I'll tell you why, a girl. Not just any girl, a Dead head sister. "Sister" is the slang term for a betty within our circle. Anyway, they obviously connected, so dude was gonna look her up. He just got in actually, and we had been back for a couple of days. Kevin showed me the number he had written down. We walked over to the pay phone together. After he hung up, he had directions, and I offered to help. Christy lived in Converse Heights with her mom.

We found the house without much problem, and watched as they reunited. This was a very cute scene. She was dressed in a sundress with the appropriate sandals to match. As soon as she directed her attention towards me our eyes locked. She knew at that moment, as well as I did, we had to hook up. This was unfortunate for Katie Moon and Kevin, aka "Shaggy" though. Passing soul mates in time hold no rules.

As our conversations went from one thing to next, it was finally revealed we were the dollar cigarette kids. We all had a big laugh, and agreed what a small world it really was. I don't want to go into detail about how I sabotaged my relationship with Katie, just so I could get with Christy. No matter how you looked at it, I was a shit. To this very day my family still mentions Katie.

Yes, I am the fool. Yeah, yeah, we hooked up eventually after the fall, only to find out we weren't as compatible as we thought. Karma I suspect. I was left alone without any girl in my life for a while. During this dry spell for love I started smoking "hubbas," better known as crack rock.

1991

The Boys went to Europe to tour after all this. The year '91 came around and, of course, spring tour. This memory, I'm very fond of. They were gonna play Greensboro, NC again, and they were selling tickets at the Camelot (CD's & tapes). Camping out for GD tickets was the shit, no matter where it was. No different from the lot to me. This particular episode was at the Hillcrest Mall off of 29. Of course, all of the Spartanburg family was present and counted.

There was a new face in the crowd though, and her name was Rhonda Roy. She was the ultimate, and my drunk ass has no right to grieve. I'll get to that soon enough. Hanging out, raging, and bouncing from one circle to the next, I finally bounced into Rhonda. She had dark brunette hair and the most beautiful smile you could imagine. (Oh how I wished I wouldn't have fucked that up.)

Had a good time, all of us did that night, and I scored her phone number. We did evolve into a relationship of some sort. She had friends coming down from Connecticut. Nate and Kevin were among the group. There were a couple of others; however, I didn't click with them. I would see Kevin later down the road on tour. In fact, it was summer tour Charlotte '91 when I got to kick it with Kevin. I remembered that well due to the fact Rhonda made her appearance, with a laugh, while Kevin and I were hanging out in the bleachers. She was with one of her friends looking at me with laughter while Jerry was singing "The sailor, coming out again, the lady fairly leapt at him."

Now, I may have been high on "L," come to think of it. However, at the time, I would swear Jerry was saying, "Lady fairly laughed at him," and, like I said, this all happened simultaneously. That did hurt by the way, and I took it personal.

I understand Rhonda's decision to break it off with me, after all I did give her crabs. Why? Because I was a dirty fuckin' hippie, and I was drunk when some random woman knocked on my door and seduced me. I take it that's where the crabs came into the mix. There's no fuckin' excuse for my actions. I lost one the best girls as a result. Sorry, so sorry, I am in every way. I play this over in my head and wonder what the fuck I was thinking, drunk or not. I've been known to sleep with girls I shouldn't when I drink too much.

After the Charlotte show was over, Kevin and I waited for all the people to leave the coliseum. We started from the top, and worked our way down the coliseum in search for the big "Ground Score." I found a few articles and Kevin scored a fatty. This was my first experience working the arena for lost possessions. After that incident, I religiously kept my eyes pointed downward.

I went to New York again in the fall... mainly for business. I collected some money from "Jimbo" and headed off. Jim Minchow was his name. His brother and I went to school together, Mick Minchow was his brother's name. Jim is vital part of my story due to the fact he funded my journeys from time to time.

I believe Jimbo was the first to clue me in on some of the spiritual education. He made the statement that, "The Grateful Dead culture is in the same bracket as Danzig." He was correct, a heathen is a heathen. However, the moral system of most hippies on tour was quite different from that of Danzig kids. I believe this separated us from the dogma he preached as well. When I got back from MSG, I had some white fluff, in which I kicked down to Jimbo. Not a very profitable journey, I must say …it's irrelevant though.

> GRATEFUL DEAD: The motif of a cycle of folk tales which begin with the hero coming upon a group of people ill-treating or refusing to bury the corpse of a man who had died without paying his debts. He gives his last penny, either to pay the man's debts or to give him a decent burial. Within a few hours he meets with a traveling companion who aids him in some impossible task, gets him a fortune or saves his life. The story ends with the companion disclosing himself as the man whose corpse the hero had befriended.

Hero? Hmmm… this is a concept to fight with. Delusional thinking can bring you to the question. "Am I the hero?" Only the Deadicated that still live shall ask this very same question of themselves. The fact that so many kids have died as a result of the lifestyle on the Grateful Dead journey brings me to this point.

Now if every person that died of a heroin overdose, in our circle throughout the years, intentionally did it … then that would be different. However, what if there is a place of dedicated souls waiting for the hero? Their deaths were unjust, and they were surely cut down before their time. As a result of these fatalities, I myself feel obligated to help. By no means should I be writing this, but I'll get to that later.

My parents were moving back to Missouri, and since I didn't have my life together completely, like usual, I moved with them. There sure wasn't a girlfriend keeping me in the south. We actually moved to Overland Park, Kansas.

My dad was working with Champion Air Views, same as I. The boss had flown over Kansas, taking aerial photographs, and that is a lot of flat lands, believe me. I was crazy about CB radios, at the time. My dad and I bought some so we could communicate while we were on the road working because we would go out at the same time. My handle was "Belue" from the Jungle Book. I sure as hell wasn't as big as the fictional character, but I stuck with it. Dad's handle was "Black Eagle" on account that he drove a black Eagle Talon.

Basically, my job was to show residents, farmers and businesses an aerial photo taken from a 172 single engine Cessna. It was my job to convince the prospect that having one would be nice, and then simply sell them whatever size they wanted.

Well, one day in March, while working out in the field, somewhere in the flat lands of Kansas, something happened that changed my whole life. The sky had darkened considerably, and it was getting darker. I was going door to door, not paying much attention to my surroundings. I was singing along with The Boys, looking down and studying pictures. I looked up at the last minute only to realize there was a stop sign. I slammed on my brakes and uncontrollably went sliding through a three way stop. The surface underneath me was a dirt and sand mixture. In this particular area, you could exit a major interstate and find yourself on a dirt road. And there I was, skidding on a dirt road, heading straight for a number of trees.

The first collision was a deep ditch about ten feet from the trees. I hit it hard and was thrown into the windshield. I heard a loud snap followed by a gush of blood from my nose. This first impact broke my nose. The car still hadn't stopped and was driving right on through with a ferocity from hell. The car finally smashed into a tree hurling me face first once again into the windshield. The force was so strong I bent the steering almost flat. This last impact shattered my entire nose. My face looked like it had been hit by a flat shovel, crushing the bones into pieces.

I stumbled out of the car, and I managed to drag myself to the closest house. Everything around me seemed surreal. Standing up straight was a chore at that moment. Eventually, the door opened with a scream. The lady in front of me was holding her mouth and crying out for her husband.

The next thing I remember, I was in an ambulance looking up at the ceiling. This was all too familiar to me. They rushed me into the ER. There was so much commotion around me, and I couldn't focus on anything very well. You know that hazy blurred look you've seen from movies trying to depict the actual vision from the person ... well that was me. A nurse or doctor was trying to tell me they were going to administer a sedative, and I was scheduled for surgery. I remember them asking me if I was allergic to anything to my knowledge. That was the last thing I recall, as I slowly faded out.

I awoke violently, pulling out IV's and cussing out the nurse in some drunken rage from the anesthesia. Crazy as it seems, I actually do recall this. I was sedated again, and woke up with my parents at my side.

The car I was driving was my mom's Honda Accord. It was a burgundy four door with all the extras. Why her car that day? I don't know. It was the fact I was in her vehicle that had something to do with the actual bill being covered. My rhinoplasty cost about twenty four thousand dollars. They even corrected my deviated nasal septum. In other words, one of my nostrils was bigger than the other. The surgeon cut off some of the tissue of the smaller nostril hole, and this did even it out a little more.

For the next month, I stayed with my parents to heal from it all. They had placed a shunt on the bridge of my nose. Unfortunately, it fell off, and, as a result, my nose didn't mend exactly straight.

This is the not my first scare as a result of the Grateful Dead lifestyle. As it is written … "Steal Your Face" is a part of the whole journey. Now that to me has a lot to do with drinking and drugging, as the close-minded would say. You stay up, break your body down, etc. Thus, losing some of your natural beauty as a result of your actions. Years of that will no doubt steal your face - the lines come sooner. However, it's when you dedicate yourself so deeply that you lose sight of the obvious.

1992

I was still working for Champion Air Views when I decided to sneak out my window one late evening. My bedroom was on the second floor of this apartment building, Arrow Head Apartments located in Overland Park, Kansas, to be exact. To this very day I don't have a fucking clue why I decided to climb out my bedroom window like some twelve year old. I do

I remember I prepared my car for a journey, and all I had to do was get to my car. I made an escape rope with my bed linen. You would think I was eloping or something. I climbed down the side of the building, as quietly as I could.

My car was a blue two door, Honda Accord with all the Deady stickers to go with it. Being that I was in Kansas City, I was obviously going to take the northern route. What possessed me to go west is a mystery. That is what I actually did... I got on the road and left. (If you've ever driven 1800 miles by yourself, not knowing why, maybe you will relate to this story.)

It was February '92, it was terribly cold outside, and not the greatest road conditions. Taking the southern route is always best no matter what the season. However, I didn't have that option. Things went pretty smooth until I got to Nevada. Going through the Rockies is no joke. Don't get me wrong, I did make it through, but Colorado and its altitude change made me sick.

My Honda was a strong horse. Try the Rockies in a fucking VW bus. Anyway, there I was with zero visibility, well I'm exaggerating, you could see the taillights, kind of, in front of you. The snow was coming down really hard, and I was tired of driving twenty-five miles an hour.

When I started seeing signs for Wells, Nevada, I knew I would take the first train smoking and that's what I finally did. I pulled off of the main road onto the Wells, Nevada exit, heading for a place to lay low. I was feeling quite ill. So here I was, in Nevada, feeling like absolute hell and stuck in a fucking blizzard. The only thing I saw right off the interstate was a casino. I pulled in and parked. I laid the seat down, fluffed my pillow I'd stashed for the journey, and attempted to lay down.

My fucking head hurt really bad, so I propped back up to get more Tylenol. What I really needed was relief from this pain with some hot tea, and I needed to get the fuck out of this car. The snow was still coming down hard when I opened my car door. The parking lot was a blanket of white accompanied by the other vehicles, either of gamblers or those just seeking shelter. I wobbled back and forth, working my way to the front entrance.

Upon entering the casino, I was showered with lights, and the smell of smoke. I went to the bar, and they lobbied me into the restaurant part. I ordered some tea and took some more Tylenol. In about twenty minutes, I was feeling somewhat better. The waitress serving me had jet-black hair and brown eyes. She looked to be about forty.

I must have looked haggard and tired sitting there drinking my tea all by myself, which can be a conversation starter anywhere in the US. Before my tea was even gone, this random woman had revealed to me that she was Wiccan, and she invited me back to her place to get some rest. This was very tempting, no doubt. She told me to hang around for another four hours, and offered to drive me to her place. If I hadn't been so fucking sick maybe I would have, but I didn't.

I hovelled back to my car and as I lay there, in my front seat curled up as much as I could, I pondered the idea of going with this stranger. I finally drifted off. When I awoke the storm had passed, for the most part. My headache hadn't passed, and I had definitely had a fever. Like clockwork, I took more pills and headed for the gas station across the way with a mission for coffee. Coffee, Tylenol, and I would be on my way.

I felt absolutely horrible. Breaking down, oh so hard, I remembered my uncle lived in South Lake Tahoe. That became my new goal, even though I didn't have a fucking clue as to where in Lake Tahoe he lived. My parents, I'm sure, were worried about me. I mean, shit, I just blew out of their lives with no note, no clue why or where I was going … hell, I was worried.

Being that I was on the edge again, I did need to recoup. I had to at least make it to Tahoe. Where the fuck was I in relation to my uncle's town? I checked the map. Wells, Nevada is one the first places you can stop once you enter the state. So, unfortunately, I had about four hundred miles to go. That is six hours of driving under feverish conditions. Thank god I was going to attempt this during daylight hours. Feeling like dog shit in the light of day is a plus, comparatively.

Even though it sounds mad as I write this, I miss the pain, so to speak. Nevada is quite beautiful, and the drive across its desert beauty is well worth it. I was about fucking broke and I was eating on the supplies in my car that were growing smaller and smaller. I didn't eat in the casino as a result of my money situation. For those that don't know, Tahoe is like Wells in that it is one of the first cities you hit, as you enter California.

Interstate 80 is what I was on, and once you get to Tahoe, 50 takes you to Sacramento. Fuck, all I knew was I was broke and running on fumes. Once I finally got close to my destination, calling my parents was the next step. Now that isn't easy, like most kids know. However, I needed some help.

As miracles go, I did make it to the "sky town," and found my way to a pay phone. I remember the sun was shining, the air was crisp, and I was relieved to finally be in California. Now, I had no plan, granted, and I knew nothing of what I was to do. I asked the operator to call my parents collect. My mom answered, and I told her everything. Like all conversations that start out with, "where the hell are you," it ended like most, "and I need money."

Mom and Dad wired me some money, Western Union, and contacted Uncle Ronnie. Ronnie is my mom's brother, and he lived in a nice trailer in a retirement trailer park. His roommate was about hundred years old, and smelled like a hundred old people rolled all into one. He was a nice fellow indeed, but I knew, even then he wasn't going to last long. On top of that scenario, I was going to stay with these two briefly while I figured out what hell I was going to do.

South Lake is the shit. The sun was shining with patches of snow on the sides of the roads here and there. It was like seventy-two degrees that day, and, as shitty as I felt, the atmosphere around me brought me to a higher plain.

Back to the trailer though, Ronnie's roommate did not like the fact I was gonna stay with them for any amount of time. He met me at a gas station and I followed him back to their place. I was dead tired, but I couldn't sleep. I needed to pick up the money that Mom and Dad had sent, and get some real fucking food in me.

Ronnie picked up on the fact that I was another Dead head kid, immediately upon seeing me. He told me about the local bar where a lot of "my kind," as he stated, hung out. It was called Hos Hogs, and he was correct, a lot of kids kicked it there. They had a jam/open mike night there, and Ronnie let me borrow his acoustic to play. In fact it was that very same night that I came. I remember playing two tunes in particular "Little Red Rooster" and "Going Down The Road Feeling Bad." It was a lot of fun. Some bro out in the audience yelled "Go Bobby" while I was singing "Rooster." After the performance, I met a few kids, and they invited me to go hiking with them the next day. I was told to bring my acoustic.

I gave the bro a call the next day, and met up with them at a house these kids shared. For the life of me, I can't remember the name of this place we were to hike. However, if I researched it, I'm sure it's one of the tallest peaks in the city. There were four of us. One guy had red hair, and, like myself, carried his instrument, a violin, to the top as well. The hiking trail was snowy and rocky at the same time. Oh, I almost forgot, like all hippies, we did some mushroom tea before we started out on the journey. I remember looking down at the snow-covered landscape as I walked towards the top. With each new step, I could feel the boomers creeping in.

When we reached the top, the wind was blowing fiercely and it seemed the temperature had dropped considerably. The first thing we did was gather twigs and whatever wood we could find. There at the top of the ridge, was a spot on the ground, you could see where a number of fires had been started. The wind was making things hard for us. Putting all our resources together, we eventually got a fire started.

The mushrooms were in full effect at this point. After the fire mission was accomplished, the dude with the red hair pulled out his violin, and started to make some noise. I, of course, followed suit, and got the acoustic out as well. I wouldn't swear on it; however, I believe we played, "Cold Rain and Snow." The wind was stinging every piece of skin that was exposed. Playing under these circumstances was a challenge, especially when your fucking fingertips are numb. It was just awesome that we did make it to the top, started a fire, and played music. It was time to go, so we made our way back down.

Eventually, I found myself back at the house these kids hung out at. At this time of my life, I was very obsessed with collecting Dead shows. One of the kids had an audience recording of Charlotte '89. Somehow, I managed to tape this either at my house or theirs.

Now, it was February of '92, and I finally got a copy of a fucking show I was in years before. Dude, I was so happy. It seemed on the east coast most of us kids would have the shows from the west coast, and vice versa. That's coming from a time and era when I was limited. In fact, the bro that kicked me down this show, I later saw at my second JGB show, which was in San Jose, California at Keizar Stadium.

Outside of all this shit, the bottom line was I needed some income from somewhere. All this was fun and all, but I was crashing at my uncle's pad, and he was living with an old geezer who didn't appreciate me crashing on the couch. In less than a week I knew I had to go. Fuck it, go somewhere. Mom and Dad sent me money, and I had already depleted that. I wound up looking around this old man's place for something of value to pawn. Outside the old man had a shed with a lot of power tools. (Its not like I wanted to rape him, I just needed a little extra cash.)

I took a drill, I believe. When I got to the pawn shop, they said something like, "We got a lot of those in the back," followed up with, "I'll give you twenty dollars if that will help."

Like a crack head I said, "I'll take it."

I'm kidding, he didn't say that. He gave me forty dollars, and I bought some nugs. I actually think that is accurate. Not very kind of me. I hope I'm forgiven for such shit. Maybe, I used the money for gas…I doubt it.

Well, I'd scored a couple new Dead tapes, played a small set at the local "head" bar, hiked on boomers, and overstayed my welcome on a couch. It was time to move on. Now this is the weird fucking thing. Yeah, I'd been seeing shows for a few years, and all that; however, no one had ever told me I need to go to Haight and Ashbury in San Francisco. The fucking crazy thing is I just woke up one day, and there I was. Yeah, I know, it wasn't quite like that; however, let met tell you what I know.

I got on the 50 heading west. Before too long I got off on a random exit, and called my Dad. Before I left, I had an argument with Ronnie concerning my stay in South Lake Tahoe, and this motivated me to leave. I explained my situation, and Dad finally got around to suggesting an aerial photography gig. He told me he would call Lee Champion, and ask him if we have any work in northern California. I called him back about twenty minutes later, and he said there were pictures in Matador County, mainly around the town of Spring Valley. This sounded good to me. I believe my mom researched this as well, and told me of a campground I could stay at in the Spring Valley area. I had a plan, so I changed course, and headed full speed ahead.

When I got to Spring Valley, I located the campsite. I paid them some money, and found me a spot to park my Honda. Now I didn't have a fuckin' tent, just a pillow, a couple blankets, and my clothes. So, obviously I was sleeping in my front seat. Oh, how fucking comfortable that was.

Dad had the company overnight me four rolls, general delivery to the Spring Valley post office in my name. I picked them up the next day. Every fucking picture was the perfect home and garden type. The entire community was based around this fancy, dandy golf course. So a lot of these people were never home, or could care fuckin' less. Well, I had my maps and film, and I needed money so I went to work.

Door to door in these types of community is always a challenge. Door to door in any fuckin' community is a challenge, what the fuck am I thinking? Anyway, I wasn't getting the response I would have liked, of course. Being that I was trying, Dad was helping me and Mom sent me more money Western Union until I made some with the company.

The good thing about this time in my life is that I hadn't crossed over into the realm of consuming alcohol everyday. All I needed was ganja, and that was completely a mental addiction. However, I was just about out, and Dad wasn't around to give me more. I wasn't sure how I was gonna re-up, but I had the motivation.

How and why the fuck I decided to drive to the city of San Francisco to cop some nugs is beyond me, still to this very day it's baffling. I could have scored some swag from some random esse in Stockton, California. I believe it would have been a shorter drive. I'm telling you that throughout all the shows, I've been to up to this point no one ever told me that "Haight and Ashbury in the bay is where you need to go." I'll shut up about this. I realize now it's common knowledge among most people, but I must have lived a very sheltered life for a Dead head.

I got on the 5, heading south, which eventually becomes 580 going into the San Francisco bay area. If you just keep following the route always going forward (not straight…never go straight, just forward) you'll eventually get to "The Bay Bridge" in which you'll cross over water touching the little island of Yerba Buena, which means herb is good. (I was later taught, by the family, that if you have nugs, you must puff them while driving across the bridge.) Anyway, this was my first experience crossing this bridge, and I was literally driving blind, not knowing anything. I just kept on driving forward, and I wound up in the upper Haight. I was guided by a force much greater than luck. From '88 to '92, I had no idea this was where all the family of the Grateful Dead lived … on and off tour.

I don't have a fucking clue where the fuck I parked my car the first time, to be honest. It could have been anywhere, ya know, and who fucking cares, right? I do remember the first kids I met on the Haight, in my endeavor to score more weed. Their names were Laura and Arien. I believe Laura was the one who actually hooked me up with a twenty bag of kind bud. Laura didn't have dreads and neither did Arien.

Laura had long brown hair. She had acne really bad, and you knew she would have been much prettier if not for that. Arien was much shorter than her, with a beautiful smile she always seemed to wear, no matter what the occasion. I had a small crush on Arien in no time. These girls were priceless in every way.

After we introduced ourselves, and I'd given Laura the money for the twenty sack, they hugged me like no other sisters had before. Back in South Carolina, the kids growing up around Grateful Dead Land weren't known for their genuine hugs. I felt the heart and kind energy within their embrace. As I type, this I truly do remember, how it was in Laura's arms. You know that hug? It's the one you never forget. It fits like a glove or a favorite pair of pants.

I didn't stick around long that first day. I was still currently working a job, technically. It was a lot like living on the east coast trying to work a 9 to 5, and do Dead tour at the same time. You go to the show, you get your fix, and you go home back to the grind to bring in the money to do it all over again. However, living so close to the shitty, you're dangerously close to brothers and sisters that live a lifestyle that eventually engulfs you. What

I mean by that is: if you were like me, always trying to be at every show and every fucking gathering, or whatever the kids were doing, eventually you'll have ropes (dreads) hanging off your fuckin' scalp. And, of course, there will be another kid looking at you with the short hair and never enough Dead tapes. I think you get the point.

I drove back to the campground in Spring Valley with my twenty sack, with the delusional plan of being an aerial photography salesman living outside the bay…in my car. That night I picked up a six pack of some swag beer at the local store. I drank a couple beers, smoked a couple hits of this beautiful tasting flower, and I nodded off in my front seat.

I woke up a couple of hours later in a pool of smoke. This was smoke of a different kind. The car was filled with an acrid burning stench, and there was smoke billowing out from under the dashboard. The smell was unbearable. I quickly rolled down the windows, and opened the doors. My water bottle on the floorboard was the only thing I could think of at the moment. I grabbed it and started pouring it on the fucking dashboard. I could see the fire was under the dashboard, so I splashed the bottle at it as best as I could. It eventually went out. There I was, standing in the middle of a fucking KOA, next to a fucking smoking car. When it finally smoldered out, I sat there next to the car, dazed.

The next morning, the dash lights no longer worked, nor the blinkers, nor anything inside the car, really. The headlights, brakes, and the blinkers outside all miraculously still worked. I re-wired the fucking radio, got it working and called it quits. That day bumping around from door to door in the community of Spring Valley was a chore. The car had a smell of burnt plastic and rubber. This was not pleasant, I wasn't selling shit and I was getting discouraged.

Now, quickly let me explain to you that a "sample proof" is the picture that you show the customer. It is a five by seven inch, black and white copy of the aerial photo of their property. You are not allowed to sell the sample proofs, but I broke down. The next day I drove to Stockton and found a wholesale place that sold picture frames. I bought a dozen of them. They had mahogany and a light oak, so I purchased both types. When I got back to the territory, I started swinging the proofs in the frames for twenty bucks each. Sometimes I got $30, depending on the customer. I wasn't selling shit like I was supposed to. Once in a while I would luck out, and a customer didn't want that small of a picture, then they would buy the company's painted portraits.

I was running out of bud. A twenty sack from the Haight doesn't last that long, so I went back to re-up. When I got there, I found Laura and Arien. They both gave me a big hug. Laura quickly asked me if I needed more. She called me by "Brad" which felt good that she remembered my name. I bought another one.

As I was roaming around Haight St., I met this Indian bro, and he seemed cool. He was looking for a ride out of the city, or as we called it "the shitty." I could afford to give him a ride since I was leaving in just a bit. I'll call him "Chief" because I don't remember his name.

On the ride out of the shitty, he let me know he was houseless (that was the term we liked to use) and didn't actually have any particular place to go. I told him of my situation, and let him know he could crash on my campsite. He did have some gear with him so I figured he had a tent or something. The first mistake I made, hanging out with Chief, was picking up beer. We bought a twelve pack of Keystone beer. It tasted like shit to me, but it got you drunk.

We decided to gather some wood and start a fire. The fire was at a good roar when Chief started showing out. This guy was the classic Indian. Cool as fuck and very fucking hard not to like. Somewhere around the fourth or fifth beer, good ole Chief started to get talkier. Granted, this was one of my first lessons in getting shit faced with a full-blooded Indian.

Chief started jokingly punching me in the arm and freaking me the fuck out. All of a sudden I was no longer having a good time, and the realization that I brought a crazy fucking Indian back to my campsite set in. Yeah, this guy had to go. That quiet Indian had just blossomed into the "I drinkum firewater." I decided to call it a night, and retreated to my car-house.

I was awakened a couple of hours later by Chief tapping on my window asking me if he could crash out in the passenger seat. What was I to say, no? Of course, I said ok. Come to find out he did have some gear but not a tent, just a sleeping bag. If I didn't mention it, this was a fucking tall guy, not a small man. I slept very little that night.

We went back to the shitty the next day. I told Chief, when we got back to the Haight, I was gonna have to go my own way. As a sober man he was very reasonable, and he knew what was up. I roamed around with very little money in my pocket; however, I bought another small twenty from some random runner. I didn't see Laura and Arien, and with that, I went back to my campground.

The next day, I finally sold a fucking aerial painting to a rich doctor who lived in a Spanish style house. I sent in what legitimate business I had done to the company for that week. Somehow I knew that was going to be my last report for a long time. I checked the fuck out and drove back to the shitty.

Finding a spot to park on the upper Haight is always fun. Now, I didn't drive an international school bus or anything, yet it's still not easy. In the spring of '92, the majority of kids would park around the panhandle, and this is where I found a spot. I walked up Masonic towards the street since I parked at that end of the park. It was a bright, sunny day and the bay breeze to go with it. These are the days we live for, with business as usual on the street. There's nothing like the feeling of having nothing to do but peruse up and down the strip.

At the moment, I was soaking up the scene, and seeing just how things work. It's pretty simple, from Masonic to Clayton is the main strip. Relatively spaced out brothers and sisters would stand around as people walked by. When the potential customer (custy) strolled by you would say, "buds" or "doses" or "dirty needles" …just kidding.

Being that I'd done tour for the last few years, I was no stranger to this. It was basically like this on the Shakedown of any Dead lot in the US. Anyway, the kids were doing their thing … well working anyhow, and I didn't have fucking shit to do except soak it up.

Some of the first people I did meet, outside of Laura and Arien, were the "Wrecking Crew," and these guys were veterans of the Grateful Dead Land. There was Fast Eddy, Jackson, Ira, and Artie (it might be Marty.) Fast Eddy was 5'9" with brown hair and a thick beard and always wore a tie-dye accompanied by a leather jacket. Jackson was a little taller, he was the musician of the bunch, and also had brownish hair with a beard. Artie was the short guy, without a beard, with blond, straight hair. Artie was from New Jersey (upstate somewhere), and we related to each other right off the top. Ira was the aggressive one of the bunch. He was definitely the tallest, and he was full-blooded Indian. He had the typical Indian complexion and dark hair. I believe he was Marlina's brother. Who's Marlina? Aw, she was just a sweet older Indian lady who used to terrorize us kids. She was a permanent fixture, or "furniture" as we called it, on the Haight in '92. (Not to associate Marlina with the Wrecking Crew but she was a real character, and Ira and her would get hostile when they drank.)

That morning Artie was working more so than the rest of the crew, and he was in full gear walking up and down the street saying, "buds." The

Wrecking Crew spare changed (spanged) to make a living, most of the time. They were famous for "spanging" the locals on and off of tour. Now, in the beginning, I'm sure it wasn't all about panhandling, but after you get "knocked off" by the police a couple of times, you might rethink your actions. Also, alcohol has a big affect on your occupation, and alcohol was what these guys preferred. Jackson and Fast Eddy were sitting down on the corner of Haight and Masonic. Jackson had a brand new Dobro, and he was attempting to play it.

I walked up to them both, and commented about the shiny chrome guitar. Jackson handed it to me, and took a swig out of a bottle wrapped in a brown paper bag then handed it to Eddy. All the strings were lifted and designed for slide playing, and this was not something I could do. However, I attempted to make it sound. I gave it back to Jackson, and introduced myself. They did the same, and I walked on. They were sitting more on Masonic than Haight and closer towards Page Street.

I walked to the corner, and took a right on Haight and walked past "All You Knead." At that point, I hadn't eaten there yet, but it would soon be a favorite, for the money. We used to call this place "All You Bleed" and it was famous for the hairy potatoes. You could get two eggs scrambled with twelve grain toast with home-style potato squares for a dollar ninety-nine. I guess because they left the skins on the potatoes it gave you the impression of hairy potatoes. Fuck, I don't why the kids insisted on calling them hairy. I personally liked them. Fuck, for that price you don't fucking complain, and it had a wonderful atmosphere.

I walked on towards Ashbury, and I saw Laura and Arien. I tried not to run towards them even though I was excited to see them. Arien walked up to me first with that big, beautiful smile, and said, "Hey, what's up?"

I replied with, "Nothing much, just hanging out."

Laura looked at me and said, "You need anything?"

I said no, and told her I still had a little left.

She said, "That's cool Brad, but if you find a custy, I'll give you a twenty sack for fifteen bucks and a eighth for forty-five." Either way, I'd make five to ten bucks. This was my first experience, on the Haight, as a runner. (The definition of runner is a person who gets buds, doses, or whatever fronted to them, and then runs up and down the Haight looking for customers.)

Laura said her and Arien were going to hang out on Ashbury near the clock, and she suggested I go down a half a block towards Haight St. Music. This was a music store in between Ashbury and Clayton. She handed me a twenty sack, and said if anyone wants an eighth to come get her. I said ok and walked on.

As I was walking, I was checking out all the people strolling by me. One by one I inventoried each prospect, in a seconds time, contemplating whether I should let them know I could help them with there ganja needs. I walked on past the music store, a few feet past their awning, and propped myself against the building wall. A couple of kids walked by wearing skater gear and carrying boards. Not usually the type to option with nugs. A few minutes passed, and a definite candidate walked by. He was dressed in common college attire, you know, the Izod shirt type, but you can tell they like to smoke herb.

As he passed, I said, "buds," and with a jerky stop he turned around. He said to me, "how much?"

I said, "twenty."

He replied, "cool."

I told him to follow me, and we walked towards Clayton then took a right. As we walked past the front entrance of the Haight and Ashbury Free Clinic, I handed him a very small, sealed, square, zip-lock baggy with outdoor grown marijuana inside. He opened the seal to smell and took a whiff. He lifted his head with a smile and handed me a twenty dollar bill. The kid kept on walking down Clayton towards the panhandle, and I turned around heading back towards the girls. Walking past more people on the way I continued on with my sales pitch, "buds."

When I got to the corner of Ashbury, the clock said it was ten after four. The clock was mounted on the corner edge of the building directly above our heads. The building it was connected to, on the famous corner, was a t-shirt distributor which sold tie-dyes. I gave Laura the twenty, she smiled and asked if I wanted another. I nodded yes, and she handed me another accompanied by a five-dollar bill. Laura looked up at the clock, and said, "Hey, it's almost 4:20, let's go puff," and off we went to find a kind spot to huff some delicious nuggies.

Arien said, "Lets go to 710." Laura agreed and we crossed the street. We walked past "The Gap" heading towards the house where it all began. For those that don't know, 710 Ashbury is where The Boys used to live, in the sixties, of course. "The boys" meaning the band members of The Grateful Dead. (The terms "The Kids" and "The Boys" I attribute to Marlina. She is the one who taught me the terminology.)

So we walked up on the left side of Ashbury until we reached 710. Arien said, "The owners are cool. As long as we don't throw our cigarette

butts down on the ground, they don't mind us hanging out on their steps."
And this was true. The owners, at this time, were kind individuals who
definitely knew the history of the house and embraced all that came to visit.
Not to say that they publicly announced all to come and smoke pot on their
front steps. You get it, I'm sure.

Laura opened one of her twenty sacks, and loaded Arien's glass pipe
with it. She passed it to Arien, to her left, and then Arien passed it to me. It
went around a couple of times then it was gone. This was a momentous
occasion for me; however, I didn't let on that this was my first time visiting
710, and one of my first times smoking with tour family. A couple of
people walked by as we were puffing, but it was just another day in the bay.
Once the bowl was completely "kicked," Arien ashed the remains in her
hand then she wiped the soot onto the interior of her sundress. She put the
glass in her corduroy pouch, and we headed back to the street.

Laura had a couple more twenties, and eighths to swing, so I agreed
to help her. The street is like any retail business, you have your slow days,
and you have your good days. Today was like hump day, a Wednesday, I
guess. You didn't exactly rage nor did you go home without selling
anything. A while passed before I had any bites. Finally this semi-sketchy
dude reacted to my repetitive squawking of the words, "kind buds." This
guy wanted more than just a gram of dank, he wanted an eighth. I told him
wait right there, and I went off to find Laura.

She was in the middle of a deal when I approached her. I quickly told
her I needed an eighth, and she gave me one. When I got back, some
drainbro was trying to snake my deal. I told the bro, "I got him," and, like
most strung out hippies do on the Haight, he started going off telling me this
was his "custy." I let the dude know I had what he wanted, so we walked to
Clayton, once again, and took a right. I wasn't sure how long he had been
coming here to score so I tried him. I said, "The bro I got this from wants
fifty-five. Could I get sixty so I can make five bucks?"

Dude was not happy about this; however, after showing him the shit,
he agreed. Once again, another happy customer kept on walking down
Clayton. I turned around and headed back to Laura. She went ahead and
gave me an eighth to hold after I gave her forty-five bucks. I went back to
my spot. I got restless, so I took a stroll down our strip and back. While
doing this I called out, "buds" a few times. I found myself back at the music
store in no time, of course. Five minutes later, I sold a twenty sack to an
Asian kid.

Eventually, the daylight started to dissipate showing signs that night was coming. Laura came up to me about thirty minutes later, and said she was out of nugs. She asked me if I wanted to hang out with her and Arien, which led to the next question of where I was planning on sleeping. I told her I had no plans, and I was gonna crash in my car on the panhandle.

Laura said, "I'm gonna round up some kids to go in on a motel room in Oakland, are you game?"

I said, "yes." I was starting to get hungry so I walked across the street to Cybell's Pizza. There I ordered a fatty slice and eagerly ate every bite. When I got done, I met up with the girls on the street, and we all walked down to the Panhandle where my Honda was parked. There were also two other people, that Laura found, who followed us.

I had to move shit around in my car to make room for everyone. Finally, I got things situated, so we piled in and headed for Oakland. I asked Laura if she would pack a bowl. She said, "Brad, let's wait till we get to the bridge."

I said, "ok." Now, this was my first drive over the bridge with family, so I didn't realize that it was a must to puff while you crossed. Apparently, the kids have been doing this for quite awhile. Maybe this was how it has always been. Fuck, I sure as fuck didn't know. I was like, "whatever, let's get high."

The traffic was different at this time of day. It wasn't terrible, granted, but it was more congested than earlier. Not more than twenty seconds had passed when I smelled the sweet aroma of love. These particular nugs she had were very nice, Humboldt outdoor, I believe. Now, I'm not just saying that to fuckin' say it like, "ooh, Humboldt," no, it was truly the mother fucking shit. Humboldt County had only the best dank nuggies, no doubt.

I could see in the distance the small little island called "Yerba Buena" coming closer. The whole fucking car was filled with smoke, and one of the randoms in the back was packing another bowl. Laura looked at me; she was in the front seat. She said, "Do you know what Yerba Buena means?"

I said, "Fuck no."

Laura said, " It means herb is good."

I was like "Right on," and no, I didn't have a fucking clue. After we passed over the little island of Yerba Buena, Laura pointed out to the water where you could see another island of sorts. She let me know that was Alcatraz. Which had been shut down for a while. This city was a definite historic journey. As we crossed into Oakland from the bridge both the girls were giving me directions simultaneously. That's all right with me cause my vision sucks anyhow so I truly don't mind back seat drivers.

The motel we were going to was the Easy Eight better known as the "Sleazy Eight" to the kids. It was either that or Motel Six, aka "Motel Six Up," unless you wanted to spend big money and stay at the "Travel Lodge" at the lower end of the Haight. We like to call it "The Hovel Lodge." Although I wouldn't say it was hovelling by any means. The reason kids called Motel Six, "six up" was because of a rumor that it was run and owned by the cops. Like there would be cameras behind the mirrors and shit. So if you were planning on laying down some LSD to paper you might want to rent a room somewhere else. Fuck it, the majority of people who would break down and stay at Motel Six Up (towards the end) usually were not in the "L" business.

We pulled in the parking lot of the Sleazy Eight, and Laura volunteered to put the room in her name. Having a valid fucking ID is a big fucking plus in this cold ass world we live in. Why? Well, for starters, in the game of motel hell, the guy or girl who rents the room usually gets to sleep in a bed. While the rest of us losers kick five to ten bucks for floor space.

But hey, I was the driver; shouldn't I get bed space? Well not just yet, being that I was new to the family, and I was cool with that. Floor space is wonderful, especially if you've been sleeping in the front seat of a goddamn Honda for a month. Shit, I'll just grab all my blankets and pillow and enjoy. The other kids Laura rounded up to go in on this room hadn't showed up yet, so we sat around in the parking lot waiting for them. About ten minutes later they showed up. Laura told them what room we were in, and we all got out, grabbed our shit, and headed inside.

The reason the other people took longer was because they wanted to stop at a store and get some beer and cigarettes. I didn't know these other guys for shit, but it didn't matter really, this wasn't a party. We needed a place to lay our heads. A fifty dollar room split eight ways works out real good, not to mention the hot shower you get. Speaking of… the smart ones went for the shower right off the top. By the next morning, hot water was always hard to come by.

That night it worked out like this: Laura and Arien paid ten bucks a piece, and the rest of us kicked five dollars each. This is a grand total of fifty dollars. It's amazing isn't it? This is how I lived, for a couple of years, until I got my own place on the upper Haight after spring tour '94. The fucking crazy thing is that it's still cheaper to go in on motel rooms.

Laura and Arien plopped down on the bed. I threw my shit in the corner, and claimed a spot on the floor. The rest of the crew did the same. The TV was up and running in no time of course with the standard surfing until something worth a shit came around. The nugs were being packed in all types of pretty blown glass, and were being passed around to the left as much as possible. Our room was filled with smoke in no time.

Two of the people, who kicked in for floor space, were already passed out. Yep, mission accomplished, no doubt. I myself did not feel like nodding off yet. Laura was a good controller for the remote. Well, for the most part, the sisters I've met on this journey had good judgment for a lot of things, including television programs. So I just sat back and enjoyed the ride. I eventually fell asleep, and I slept well.

The next morning was like any fucking morning when you wake up in a motel room with eight fucking bodies. It's all about the shower. And if it ain't, then you're a fucking grime wigger. There weren't too many kids, that I was close with, that actually stank, and if one did, we threw his rainbow ass in the shower. Now, when you enter the crack zone and/or the drainbro department, things do change. I can't really talk. I had my share of crack hovelling without the bathing.

Enough about that, I'm supposed to be talking about the kind wake and bake we hippie kids do when we arise. Ok, that did happen. One head awoke, thus another awoke, and so on and then we puffed hard watching whatever bullshit was on the motel TV. If you're lucky, you awake among kind hippies to be smoked out right off the top. That didn't always happen, and, like I said earlier, it's all about having a warm comfortable place to sleep, mainly. Getting high is just a perk and form of anti-depressant, in my opinion, or maybe if I wrote this book sober, I'd feel different.

My favorite part of the morning was when the manager called on the phone or banged on the door telling us to check out, or the desk clerk yelling at us for having dogs in the room. All of the above usually would happen. I call it the "Check out time … you must leave … thank you come again" syndrome. It's about like that every time.

Well this particular morning was quite calm there was no, "Get the hell out … thank you come again." We had to be out by noon and we were. Everyone got their shit together, had bathed either last night or this morning, and prepared themselves for the street. Laura had re-upped the night before we left the Haight, and her and Arien were breaking up nugs, stretching a seven-gram quarter out as much as one can.

From the looks of it they made three "heighth's" (less than two grams), and a couple of twenty bags from it. It was fluffy outdoor as well, so that makes it easier. I'd made a few dollars last night; however, I didn't have the ducats to buy a whole quarter. My plan was to run a few more bags and capitalize on the fact that I had wheels. We were on the road heading back to the street. Once again we were on the bridge puffing nugs.

If I didn't mention it before, I'd better do it now. In the beginning, I noticed the majority of the kids lifted the glass bowl or chillum upward after they puffed and then passed it to the left. You know the saying, "when in Rome" and I was ...so, I too started to do this too. This was more prevalent with the dready kids. Apparently huffing nugs, and raising the pipe upward after you just puffed it was an act of praising Jah, the everlasting provider. I see it as simply a thanking the provider for the opportunity to smoke ganja, however the opportunity arises. Hopefully that isn't hard for anyone to understand. I believe this can work for anyone if they so choose. I liked it, and my friends did it so there you go, and yes, I too would soon have fucking ropes hanging off my scalp.

We found ourselves looking for a parking spot around the Panhandle. There was none to be found, so I decided to turn right onto Central. I climbed the hill, looking left to right for a fucking spot. There wasn't shit to be found. When I reached the top of the hill, I was on Haight St. so I turned right. There it was, a half of a block up the street on the left, a parking spot. I turned around and parallel parked. We all got out of the car, and did the stretch thing.

There's a little market on the corner of Central and Haight. Laura, Arien, and I walked in. I saw the girls grab a muffin, so I did the same. I got a blueberry muffin and chocolate milk. After smoking all that morning ganja, the muffin tasted good as fuck, and I was sure glad I got the chocolate milk. I noticed the girls didn't buy any milk. I wondered if they were vegan or something.

They glanced over at me as we were walking down the Haight. Laura asked if there was anything left, and if so, could she get a drink. Well that answered my question. I said yeah, and handed it over. She took a sip and gave it back. The street was moving at a slow pace from the looks of it, but we were looking at it from Masonic. Being that we were on the left side of the street, I decided to cross the street to the other side where all the action was.

Before I could, Laura said, "No, don't cross, let's go to The Coffee Zone, I wanna get some java." When the traffic allowed us we walked across Masonic. Right on the corner of Masonic and Haight was the coffee shop she was talking about. We walked in. There were small round tables on the left and the right. On the right, after a couple tables, was the main counter, and behind the main counter was a huge chalkboard with all kinds of writing on it. The girls lined up behind some dude waiting for his coffee.

Eventually they got waited on. I don't know what the fuck it was she ordered particularly. I just finished my nestle quick, and I wasn't dying for a cup of coffee. I did want one, though. I was standing by the table of condiments facing the main counter. On my left, was a stairwell leading up to somewhere. At the top of the stairs was some girl with black boots sitting down. Then someone walked by her, and she got up. He was obviously coming downstairs towards us. I assumed that's where the bathroom was.

Arien came over to me, and asked me if I was gonna get some java. I said no. I was sticking close to these girls for several reasons. Number one, they new their way around more so than I, and two, Laura did have work. That being nugs, which were bagged, tagged, and ready to sell.

The Nestles had me awake anyway. I wished I would had held out. I wondered why they didn't get anything to drink at the market. They only bought one muffin and one coffee. Underneath the stairs, on the left, were a couple tables. Two of them had chess games set up on them. I didn't know how to play chess, so I didn't care really. There were two people playing chess on the right side of the stairs on a table on the back wall. This place was a haven for many, and all it cost was the price of a cup of coffee, well their cup of coffee, which was more than some. But it was worth it. The cup was your hourglass. The smart people who came to enjoy the atmosphere would slowly drink their java in order to completely enjoy their stay.

We walked outside. Laura was nibbling on her muffin while Arien sipped her coffee. I was getting a little antsy just waiting around with nothing to do. I leaned over to Laura and said, "Can I hold one of those bags?"

She looked at me kinda funny then said, "a twenty?"

I said, "No, let me hold one of the eighths." She kicked me down one, and I crossed the street. There were a lot of kids swinging nugs on the main strip. That would be on the Haight St. Music side, on the right side facing the Golden Gate Park, between Masonic and Clayton.

Competition sucks anyway you look at it, but stepping on toes is not something you do. If you snagged a custy 'cause you approached him or he approached you, then that's obviously your customer. If a mother fucker tries to snake your deal (as a runner, you might have go get a bag from someone) you gotta handle it properly. Yeah, even on the streets it's important to have tact. Being political and tactful is very important. We all had to get along and survive together. The Haight has always been one big happy family. A family that changed every few years as a result of the game.

On the corner of Haight and Ashbury, Artie was hanging out in front of a white, vacant store that had covered steps. It wasn't a set of steps, it was just one big four foot by four foot slab in front of the entrance door to an empty store. It was across the street from the clock, and, like I said, it was covered, so on rainy days you could duck inside there for shelter.

Sitting down on the step was a bag lady, of sorts. She was more like a hippie bag lady. She was dressed in a white and pink dress with a sash thrown around her neck. She wore white sunglasses which were quite tacky, in an Elton John kind of way. She was drawing on the sidewalk with chalk, making flowers and a big heart. Artie was a few feet from her wearing a tie die shirt with a bandanna around his head, saying the word, "buds" to every other person.

The sun was shining very brightly, and the hipster bag lady appeared to be the smartest of us all with her protective sunglasses. I decided to keep on walking across the street. I passed the clock and an empty store, soon to be a T-shirt distributor. I was hoping to score a custy. There were a lot kids working today.

As I passed by people that looked like prospects I chanted, "buds." I passed the music store, and, as I got closer to Clayton, I slowed down. On the corner of Clayton and Haight was an oriental store that served food and sold food off the shelf. A few feet before the entranceway I leaned against the building wall. There was no awning above me, and the sun was starting to let me know of its presence. "Buds," I said as another random walked by.

A tall man dressed in black was standing on the corner selling bumper stickers. They had a black background and the wording was white letters. It read:

George Bush
The Only Dope Worth Shooting

I got a kick out of that. I believe the bro actually made them himself. I wish I would have had the ducats to purchase one, now that I think about it. "Buds," I sound off as another possible passes by me.

The dude turned around and said, "buds?"

I tell him to follow me, and we do the Clayton shuffle. After we passed the clinic, I showed him the heighth I had.

The dudes said, "cool" and gave me a fifty dollar bill, and turned around heading back toward the Haight. He did this so quickly I didn't even get a chance to put a word in edgewise. I do believe he was a regular. I needed to re-up, so I headed back to the clock. When I got there, I didn't see Laura or Arien anywhere. Some skater kid was sitting on the trashcan that's on the corner of Ashbury. He was swinging buds as well. That's a pretty good spot I guess...for the fearless. I personally didn't like making a spectacle of myself. You are perched above head level for those that pass. It's a sketchy position to sell illegal shit, in my opinion. I crossed the street to where Artie was still hanging out. The bag lady's artwork had expanded tremendously. It stretched from the doorstep almost to the curb. She had added more flowers, and made the heart more elaborate with psychedelic colors.

The sun was directly above us now. I walked past the lady, looking in both directions for Laura. She still was nowhere to be found. By the time I got to Masonic, I made up my mind to ask Artie if he would front me a sack. I turned around, and went back to Ashbury. As I came closer to Artie, he automatically propositioned me for buds.

I said, "I'm no custy man, but if you let me hold one of your bags, I'll swing for you."

Artie said, "No, I'd rather not do that, I've been burned too many times by the crack head runners. If you find anyone who wants an eighth, mine are damn close to weight. They're not two gram heights."

I said, "cool," and went back to the oriental store. I stood there for about ten minutes. While I was spacing out on a sign across the street that read "Buffalo Exchange" a guy walked up to me, and asked if I had nugs.

I said, "yes" and told him to follow me and we headed toward Artie's spot. When I got to Artie, the guy was practically up my ass. I looked at him, and said, "Wait over there" I pointed down Ashbury. He walked over to the general area I pointed at, and waited in the sun.

Artie said, "What's he want."

"I believe he wants an eighth."

He handed me one and said, "If you go down a half a block there's a place in between two the houses you can duck into. It's where that gray car is."

I said all right, and took his advice. As I approached the custy, I told him to walk with me. Like Artie said there was a place to duck into. He followed me in between the buildings, and I showed him the bag.

The guy exclaimed, "That's a nice looking sac."

I replied, "Yeah this is weight, so I'm going to have to ask sixty."

"I don't have sixty on me. I just brought fifty."

I said, "Alright; I'll take a little out." And that's just what the fuck I did. I went back to Artie, and gave him his money. He was singing along to a tune that was coming from a tape player propped against the empty store. It was "Lazy Lightning" a fucking great Dead song. I asked him if he had some tapes to trade.

"I gotta a couple on me I could trade you," he said.

"Great, let me grab a tape or two out of my car, and we'll swap if you want. I don't care. I've listened to these same tapes a thousand times I could use a new one." I walked down the Haight towards my car. I looked through my collection for a couple of tapes he would be willing to take as trade that I myself was tired of. I shut the door and walked back.

When I returned, the music was still playing. I showed him the two cassette tapes I brought. He said he was really into Pig Pen shows and neither of the tapes had Ron McKernan on them. Anyway, he picked one of them. I asked him if I could have the one in the tape deck, and he said yes. The show he kicked me was Glen Falls, NY 1982, I believe. Artie went to the box pushed stop on the player and handed me the tape. "Thanks man, I appreciate it. I don't have any shows with Lazy Lightning and I fucking love the Supplication Jam."

"Right on!" he said.

"Your name is Artie right?"

"Yeah, what's your name again?"

"I'm Brad, we met when I was checking out Jackson's Dobro."

"Oh yeah, that's right," Artie replied. The new tape started.

"That's sounds pretty good," I said.

"Yeah, it's good quality. I've enjoyed it." Across the street under the clock I saw Laura and Arien.

"Hey man, I'm gonna holler at my friends. Artie, I appreciate the connect and the trade."

He replied, "Right on Brad, if you need another, I'll be right here."

"Cool, I'll do that," and with that I walked across the street to meet up with the girls. "Where were you guys?"

"We went to the park to puff, and try to get rid of some of this bud. Did you get rid of that?"

"Yeah, I did", and I handed her a fifty. She gave me ten bucks back.

"I'll give you that for forty," then she smiled at me. It was like an involuntary action when we both reached out and hugged. Some things just are. Laura said, "Alright we got to rage one more eighth. You wanna hold a twenty sac?"

"Ok, that's cool," I replied. She slipped it to me real cool like. Both of them walked across the street heading towards Masonic. The skater bro was no longer sitting on the garbage can. He was attempting to play a drumbeat of some type on the top of the square lid. "You play drums?" I asked.

"No, not really, but I've sat in on a few drum circles," he said.

"Right on," I replied. About the same time he said this, I noticed a relatively short kid, walking up from Page Street, carrying a big red drum. This kid had very curly brown hair, and he was wearing a black leather jacket. It was pretty warm, and the sun was shining at its peak. He made me feel hot just looking at him. I looked at the bro at the garbage can, and asked, "is that the type of drum you're used to?"

He replied, "I wish, that's a nice one." The bro carrying the drum sat down at the wall about twelve feet from me. You could see sweat on his forehead. I walked over to him, "hey, what's up?"

He looked up at me, smiled a big, friendly smile and said in a witch-like, crackly voice, "what's going on?"

"Oh, nothing much, just hanging out. That's a pretty big drum you just carried up the hill. What's up with that?"

"Its my drum. It goes everywhere I go," he replied.

"Wow, that's awesome. You're a better man than me. My name is Brad, what's your name?"

"I'm Patches," he said.

(When I'm driving down the road listening to Jerry, in one way or another, I'll think about Patches. He was a close friend of mine, and I miss him a lot. Loved him like a brother, I did. Patches was one of the coolest, kindest, and nicest brothers you could ever meet. I love and miss you very much bro. I say this with tears, as a result of what has been told to me through the grapevine.)

Patches said to me next, "You know where I can get a shower? Where are you staying?"

I said, "I crashed with some friends of mine last night in Oakland. Probably gonna do that again. Catch up with me later, and I'll let you know."

Patches was like, "Right on," in that high-pitched, crackly voice mixed with that lunatic smile of his, it was priceless. I kind of felt sorry for him as I was walking away.

I was wearing a long sleeve tie-dye I scored on tour, and I was quite proud of it. When it was cold I wore a dark green poncho with gray stripes. In March of '92, this attire was what most did wear.

Patches seemed a bit out of place, and, to be honest, his whole get up sketched me out a little. I wasn't being a hundred percent genuine towards him, as a result. I didn't go out of my way to make sure he had a solid place to crash that evening. That was pretty shallow of me. If Patches was wearing cords and chuck tailors, I probably would of kissed his ass, and cut a double flip backwards just to make sure he was in my family. (My family being Laura, Arien, and whoever they trusted.) Or maybe not… just a thought.

The day was coming to an end, like most, and working after dark thirty only meant you didn't sell enough and you were trying to sell your last, or you were smoking hubbas. Those that were (smoking crack) usually didn't give a fuck about going across any bridge to any motel. As long as you stay in the shitty, you can get your rock at any time. Not that you can't in Oaktown; however, you can do late night, and work the people that do come out. It's not like you can sit outside your motel room, and say, "buds" all night to passing buyers. So staying in the city does have its advantages.

We got another room that night at the same place, but a different room. There were less people, and I had to put in ten bucks. I wasn't complaining, though. There wasn't a whole lotta smoking going on. There were just five of us. I didn't have any nugs either. I did have almost a gram that I pulled out of one of Artie's bags, but I'd turned around and sold it for twenty bucks an hour later.

Now, I was up to a hundred dollars. My plan was to hook up on some weight first thing the next day. I wished I could have scored before we left the street, but I didn't have enough money until after the "weight man" left for the day. That is how it goes working your way to the top. Trick is not to spend shit till you re-up. The same thing happened to Laura and Arien. They didn't have shit left, but they had double the money they had the day before. What little herb they did have, we puffed.

We were back on the Haight by one o'clock pm. It was much grayer because the sun was hiding behind the clouds. As a result, the temperature was ten degrees lower than the previous day. The nug man was nowhere to be found. So I perused the street to see who was working. Fuck it, I'll run a bag or two until I can get my own. Some work is better than no work. Once in awhile, the sun would cut through the clouds and give us its warmth.

While I was hanging out on the corner, talking to one of the kids that did have some buds, a skinny hippie, wearing overalls and a tie-dye, came up to me. He said to me, "Hey check this out." He reached in his pocket, and pulled out a handful of perforated blotter hits. "I found all this on the ground down the street!" he exclaimed. I found that hard to believe, but crazier shit has happened on the Haight. "You want some?" he said.

"Sure why not," and he handed me a couple of ten strips. Why I even took them, I'll never quite understand. In the back of my criminal and dishonest mind I was probably contemplating bunking some poor bastard. So, for that, I should have been schooled and punished.

The bro standing next to me that witnessed the scene looked at me and said, "that's Grasshopper, he's well known for selling bunk." As he was saying this, Grasshopper was skipping away towards Clayton. I say skipping cause he was not walking but more like trotting.

"So all of these hits are blank?"

"More than likely," he says.

"Right on." I should of put them in the garbage right then and there.

I got with Laura about an hour later and asked her if she had re-upped. She said no, and told me she still waiting. I sold one heighth for that dude that told me about Grasshopper. I hate when I don't ask someone their name, or I just fucking forget.

A couple of hours passed and still no connect on the weight. The sun was now shining, and the day had blossomed from coldish, gray to warm and beautiful mixed with a light breeze. I was very content to be hanging out. As I was looking around, in a daze, two very large dirt bikes came out of nowhere. They were both white with SFPD on the gas tanks. They were both cops, obviously. These were guys that patrolled Golden Gate Park, for the most part; however, they were known to ride on the streets at any given time.

The first officer had a mustache and sunglasses. He asked me for ID. I pulled it out and gave him my driver's license. He proceeded to run my name. The second cop kicked out the kickstand, and got off the dirt bike. He said, "You don't mind if I search you, do you?"

I knew I hadn't re-upped, so I said, "yeah, sure, I got nothing to hide."
The officer asked me to raise my arms while he padded me down, and began
his search.

"You got any needles or knives, of any kind, on you?" he asked.

"No, absolutely not," I replied. He pulled out all my belongings in
my left pocket. Then he went to my right pocket. There he found a couple
ten strips of black blotter paper.

"Oh, look what we got here."

I was fucking terrified. I'd forgotten all about that shit. I
immediately told him it wasn't real. As the bike cops looked it over, I kept
on with, "It's not real. I found that on the ground," I told him.

"We're going to have to run you in regardless, to test it."

"Come on man, it was wrinkled up in my pocket, it's not real."

The officer looked at me in a casual manner said these very words,
"It's bunk?"

"Yeah, it's bunk alright," I repeated. I was surprised to hear the cop
say "bunk." The San Francisco police department, especially on the upper
Haight, knew the fucking lingo, no doubt.

The officer with the mustache said, "Well, you check out with no
warrants; however, we still have to take you to park station." This was
located at the end of Haight Street, to the left, technically on Waller, I
believe. It's been there forever, it was mainly built as an out post for
officers on horses back in 1910. They went ahead, and called for a squad
car, which showed up promptly. I was put in the back and driven to Park
Station.

Across the street from this remote police station, along side of Golden
Gate Park, was a prime area to park a school bus. A lot of people would
park there. I was taken out of the squad car and escorted inside. I was put
in front of a window where I was instructed to empty all of my pockets.
Every article I had on me was inventoried. After they bagged and tagged all
of my shit, they handcuffed me to a railing along side of a waiting bench. I
sat there as the fucking handcuffs cut into my wrists.

I waited there for an hour as more people were brought in. Finally,
one of the jailhouse officers came over and unlocked my cuffs. Without a
word from the key holder, I was then walked towards the holding cells. He
put me in the last cell by myself. All the walls were covered with metal
sheeting and it wasn't exactly warm in this mother fucker, by the way. This
holding cell was as typical as they come, a shitter and a sink. I nervously
paced in a circle several times.

After hearing absolutely nothing for another hour, I began to get restless and bored, of course. As I looked, around I noticed writing on the walls. Now it was not markers or ink, by any means, all of it had been scratched into the metal surface. Eventually, I ran across a loose nail that was holding one of the metal sheets in place on a corner. With nothing better to do, I began working on it. It came out in about two minutes. I believe this actual nail was the culprit for a lot of the writing already there.

By the corner of the door, on the right side, I began scratching my name, with a brief message after it. When I was finished it read, "Token Bradcliff Jackson was busted for bunk doses," with the date after that. I replaced the nail from where I got it, and just sat there waiting. I was a little nervous. It was possible those doses were real or had a small amount of product in them. Twenty minutes later a random key holder came up to my cell.

"Can I go now?" I asked.

"Yeah, they checked out. They were bunk." Once again, one of the officers used the hip lingo. I was escorted to the property window, given my stuff and released. The outside air never smelled so lovely. I walked down the street towards McDonalds, which was on the corner of Haight and Stanyan, across the street from Cala Foods.

I was fucking hungry so I got something to eat. When I got done eating, I walked back to Ashbury. By this time, news had passed that I had been "swept up." So when I got closer, a few bro's that saw it all were questioning me. Laura came running up to me with Arien by her side. I filled them in on what happened. Everyone agreed I was lucky. I mean, shit, I was less than five minutes away from hooking up with some nugs, according to the girls. Fortunately, they did give all my money back, so I was back where I started. Shaken up a little I was, but I still needed to score a quarter. Laura suggested she pick one up for me, and we could go ahead and break it up back at the motel.

They were ready to bail, and I wasn't arguing. I didn't feel like working. I wanted to smoke some herb and go chill out in Oakland with them. When the driver of any family gets locked up, with his keys, it's no picnic. We all rely on that bro or sister. So everyone in our little crew headed down to the car to go across the bridge to Oakland. No one ever told me the golden rule concerning writing on walls. Ninety percent of all people who write their names on jail walls, come back to see it.

The next day, when we got back to the city, it was business as usual. I had four heigths bagged up and ready to sell. Yeah, four bags, all resembling an actual eighth. That's two hundred dollars I'd make from ninety bucks. I sure as fuck didn't wanna hang out on the corner of Haight and Ashbury so the cops could sweep me up again.

I decided to go swing outside that oriental food market close to Clayton. I hadn't really eaten yet so I walked in the place. On the far left side as you walk in is the counter, and behind that they prepared a varied selection of dishes. The menu was mainly of the healthy type. They didn't fucking serve pork fried rice here, no sir. I ordered their version of a vegetarian burger. It was made from a tofu patty with purple onions, cucumbers, tomatoes, alfalfa sprouts, and much more. This was one the first moments here on earth I realized how good it can be to be a vegetarian, but I'm not one. Experiencing as many things as I can, is what I've been known to do.

I stood about six feet from the entrance, against the building wall, eating my burger. In my left pocket were two heigths. I had left two more hidden in the car. Eating food in the general area of the place you bought it was a pretty good cover. So I ate slowly, as I savored every bite. In between bites I said, "buds" to the passing buyers. Eating my last bite, I repeated my word, and a guy looked back at me. We did the shuffle, and I was fifty dollars richer.

Walking back to my spot, I felt relieved I had started the day off with a sale. I stood there for about a minute, got squirrelly, and decided to walk down a block or so. Not to the left towards Ashbury, but to the right going towards Cole. I went as far as Sharader and turned around. I was wearing my Milano Birkenstocks and corduroy pants. I noticed all the people that walked by me, and I automatically took their inventory. I was checking out their garments, seeing who was wearing corduroy pants and that type of shit. It made me feel good to know I was wearing the same thing as the majority of the family.

Before I got to Clayton, I was selling my other heigth to a semi-sketchy, random guy. We crossed the street, and I walked him up Cole heading to Waller Street, instead of down towards the panhandle. You definitely don't always do the same pattern.

After ducking into a doorway to make the exchange, I went back to Ashbury. I needed to grab my other sacks in the car. When I got to our corner, I looked at the clock, and it said it was two thirty. A bunch of the kids were standing around the trashcan under the clock, and by the small tree planted in a square of dirt less than a block down. Among them was a bro named Spooky Rob, who I'd met the day before, and one the most beautiful girls I ever saw on the Haight. As I came closer to them both, she walked up to me and asked, "Do you have any buds?"

I said, "Yeah, I'm on my way to get my last two."

"You got weight?" she said.

"No, there heigths, but they're beefy," I told her.

"Cool, go get them, I got a custy waiting. Will you give them to me for forty a piece?"

"I can't, I'm selling them for fifty or more if I can get away with it. I'll do it for forty five," I said. She agreed and off I went, practically running, down to the Panhandle where we parked. When I got there, Arien was sitting on the grass next to the car. "What are you doing?"

"I couldn't find you on the street, but I remembered you telling us earlier you was going to leave half your nugs in the car. So I figured you'd have to come back to the car eventually. I did the same. I gotta get it out my backpack," Arien said. I unlocked the car. We both got our shit and walked back up Ashbury together. The girl with the customer was still standing in the same spot when Arien and I reached the street. That walk is all up hill from the Panhandle by the way.

She quickly came to me, and said, "Go ahead and give me both of them." I handed them to her. They walked down the hill together, and cut around the corner. Arien had already disappeared by the time I turned around.

Ten minutes had passed, and there was no sign of her. "Fuck, I don't even know her name," I thought to myself. The last fucking thing I need is my last two bags gaffled. And right about the time I was thinking all of this, there she was coming around the corner. She motioned for me to follow her. We walked across the street to the other side and climbed to the top step of someone's front porch. There we sat down. She handed me four twenty dollar bills, and a ten.

"That guy was a regular of mine, so I couldn't tax him too hard. Thank you so much ... that was some real kind bud. He really appreciated it. My name is Brandy, my rainbow name is moonflower, what is yours?"

I sat there for a milla-second thinking to myself how surreal this all was. She was so damn beautiful. I just couldn't figure how someone so pretty could be a swinger kid. She had blond hair with blue eyes. She was wearing a very thick, handmade, Guatemalan wool sweater with corduroy pants accompanied by Birkenstock sandals, the covered style (Boston). She was a dream. I said, "I'm Brad," that's all I could say for that moment. I paused a second, and then said, "Oh yeah, you're welcome. That was some kind bud no doubt, I hope he's got more of that."

She reached in her pocket, and pulled out two little nuggets. "I took a tiny little nodule of bud out of each sac. Here, I gotta a glass, you wanna puff with me?"

"Sure," I said. Brandy fished out of her pocket small blown glass pipe that had nice color. Apparently she didn't have a pouch for it. The wind started to pick up.

She scooted next to me and said, "You don't mind me getting close to you do you?"

"No, not at all," and with that she cuddled close to me to light the bowl.

I believe I fell in love with her at that very moment. The wind kept blowing the flame out so she got even closer. We were huddled so closely together. I could have stayed cuddled next to her just like that for eternity. Finally, Brandy got it lit, took a small puff, and handed it to me. I could see she didn't even huff much of it. Like the kindest people do, she lit the very edge of the green only, to make sure there was a green hit for me. I tried to return the favor, but I wound up burning up half of it like an asshole or a novice player. Once again she huffed very, very little and gave it back to me. I said "Brandy, go ahead, and get a decent hit. I got a good one… maybe too good of a hit."

She said, "I'm good, I want you to have most of it, you hooked me up."

"Whatever, that was nothing. Just doing what any other brother would do for a beautiful sister," I replied. She smiled at me, and gave me a big hug. I felt her wool sweater brush against my face as we embraced. Brandy looked up at me with those blue eyes of hers that had a timeless innocence. I knew something happened, but we were both powerless to do any thing about it.

As the wind picked up, the moment passed. We both had to go back to work, since we were essentially on break. Yeah, it's like that for the swinger kid on the Haight. There was just no paper work for the job.

The life expectancy, for the majority of all those who enter the Haight and Ashbury scene and become full time swinger kids, is five years or less, and that's pushing it. Brandy died three years later. The homeless of the Tenderloin family had a parade on Market St. in honor of her. I regret every day for not doing something when I could have, and at the very fucking least, not being there to march with all the others that fell in love with her too. I was in prison three thousand miles away, and this may be the only reason I wasn't buried with her.

I walked back down to the Panhandle to re-up. The Panhandle has a small building in the middle of the park. That's the bathroom, which was always locked. For those that don't know, it's an extension of the Golden Gate Park that runs in between Fell and Oak Street. The actual park is the size and shape of two city streets and three or four blocks long. (Refer to picture.) Over to the right of the bathrooms, is where our family would hang out, and swing weight.

Let it be known, for the record, that nobody in our circle would sell cheeva or coca (heroine or cocaine), or anything outside of marijuana, in the parks. Maybe a couple city kids that raged our product may bring death from the Mission or the Tenderloin (TL), but for the most part it was just kids swingin' nuggets mainly to family.

Very rarely did you see street custys coming down from the Haight to cop unless some bro dragged one down, sat him on a bench, and finagled the money from him in order to walk over to the bro selling weight. Then once you get the weighed out seven gram quarter you gotta tax it, and give to the customer. That's a lot of Johnny-spot working, and nobody appreciated that shit. It kept things separated with more structure when you had your life together enough to buy it, and have it already bagged. However, if you knew where to go, you went to the Panhandle.

There were city custys that started buying heigths on the Haight, then later found what they were looking for from the kids in the park. Those types you knew by name, and, as a weight guy, you appreciated their business just the same. Our street clearly functioned better when Haight family and street swingers went through the motions of breaking down the weight into smaller bags.

This gave SFPD job security as well; they also had their "nut to crack." Comfrey and Goff were the head honchos that patrolled the street in my time. They would come in and sweep the mother fucking streets, and bring a handful of workers to their jails and probationary system. That's a lot of manpower, and money, money, money. If you had one bag, most officers just dumped it out and rubbed it in the pavement. If you carried two or more, that was intent to sell and then you went to Park Station. And just remember, if they focused on the kids holding weight, it would devastate the amount of money spent in the shops all up and down Haight Street, meaning, if you take out the big guy, then there's no work for anyone… at all.

There were a lot custys from all over the world that came to the Haight and Ashbury to get high grade LSD or marijuana. Hell, at about 2:30 one night, the big guy from the show "Parker Lewis Can't Lose" showed up while me and Angelo were hanging out playing acoustic guitar. Kobiac was looking for LSD, not buds. He said to me, "I don't need kind bud, I got plenty of that. I need some doses." I recognized him and he walked up to me with a buddy of his. They had pulled up in a truck and parked it right there on the side of the street on the Haight. At dark thirty you have a better chance finding a spot. Anyway, as they walked toward me the big guy says, "You got Doses?"

I replied, "No. You won't find any at this time of night, not any that's real." As all this took place, one of the late night hubba heads overheard this. He was on my right; I saw him duck into a shop opening, and it was there he attempted to make a matchbook look like a book of LSD. I'm no fucking savior; however, through all this I picked up very quickly that this guy had a well-known face. In less than thirty seconds it came to me, "Hey your that guy that plays Kobiac on the show Parker Lewis Cant Lose."

He hesitated a moment, then broke down, and admitted it. "Yeah, so there's nothing here at all?" he replied.

Then dude with the matchbook hits walks up to us.

"Yeah. man, I got doses."

I looked at him, and said, "No, dude I know this guy. This is not a sale," and with that the runner backed off. The actor saw all of this go down without the knowledge of the bunk hits in the runner's pocket next to me. "Man, I love that show," I said. "It's a fucking pleasure to meet you," I reached out to shake his hand. Kobiac takes my hand in his and gives me a firm shake. I was speaking clear English out loud, and yet none of the others cared at all. Others meaning: tortured souls forced to stay awake as a result of the coca lifestyle. All they could see was a late night custy slipping through the cracks seeping back into good life they don't have. Both of the guys waved at me goodbye, and got in the truck, and pulled away. I tell that little story once in a while, in the right company; however, that company doesn't surface much.

I do apologize to the reader for the memory outburst of that tale. It isn't supposed to be talked about, well, not yet anyway. Not quite in line with the story that's later. Anyway, the next day, after meeting the girl of my dreams, Laura, Arien, and I stayed at a motel somewhere other than

Oakland. I don't fucking remember exactly where, and I should say, we stayed there off and on. It was in the shitty, I believe.

Haight St. was gray as fuck that day. Just the way I like it, without that annoying sun beating down on you, and all that. The day was uneventful. I sold a lot of nugs, smoked a lot of nugs, and blah blah blah the day ended and we took off toward Marin. As we were driving to the Fireside, Laura was telling me about the studio the boys would go to, and how you could see them go in and out from the motel room. I'm not sure if we went to the Fireside that particular evening, or if it was just in the conversation.

Once we got there, you immediately saw kids in the parking lot with dreads, most of them wearing corduroy pants and ragged earth tone t-shirts. There was a nice looking dog hanging out with one of the bro's.

We walked in the motel room. Inside there was no walking room really. The fucking place was loaded with hippies. Laura smiled real big when she saw a couple of her friends, and she walked carefully through the bodies on the floor. When she reached them, she hugged a sister sitting on the edge of one of the beds. Arien joined her shortly after in the hugging ritual.

I didn't fucking know a soul. A lot of these kids didn't hang out on the Haight, or I didn't recognize them. Like I said earlier, less colors (tie-dyes) in this bunch, and more browns and earth tones. One bro was sitting in the corner with a wild look in his eye wearing white overalls with no shirt underneath. I had a tie-dye on and it stunk. All my clothes were filthy, and I needed to shave, well spot shave. I have a patchy beard with lots of bald spots so if I trim the topsides it doesn't look so bad. Now, in this bunch it didn't really fucking matter anyway; however, I do look better when I maintain my shit.

That wasn't on my mind that second, but hitting that glass pipe being passed around was. While the girls were doing their socializing, I was waiting for that dank bud to come my way. Just about everyone that hit it would lift the pipe in an upward gesture after getting his or her fill. Finally it came to me, and it was just about cashed. I eagerly hit what was left and passed it on. The bro in the white overalls kept looking at me from time to time, and I noticed a frown on his face. I am paranoid at times, I can admit that, but it seemed he didn't approve of my looks. I tried not to notice or let it bother me.

I looked around for the girls in hope of an escape. They were in there own world chatting away with some hippie chick. A couple of the floor spacers were passed out. They were awake when we got there earlier. I saw a small space over in the corner. I decided that was where I was gonna crash. The vibe in the room wasn't super friendly. Hmmm... what do I do? Walk outside, and just grab my shit. Well considering I didn't have a fucking thing to do with getting this room I didn't feel too confident throwing my shit down, and claiming a spot. I mustered up the courage to walk outside and get my shit. Coming back was fun. Balancing a couple blankets, and pillow throughout the maze of bodies. Thank god no one was in the little spot I planned to call home for the night. I pitched a tent, and passed out.

The morning came early for me. My fucking back was killing me. When it gets like this theirs no fucking sleeping. It nags at me second to second until I can't take it anymore, and I finally get the fuck up. I smelled like hell. All my cloths were dirty, and I hated the fact my patchy ass beard was looking so goddamn patchy.

That morning, I don't know what came over me. I had to get my fucking clothes washed, and trim up this fucked beard of mine. Laura and Arien were passed out on the floor to the left of me. I was on a mission. There was a girl walking in and out of the bathroom. She was the only one up besides me. I walked over a couple people and made my way to the door. A black lab lying on the bed raised his head as I opened the door. Light poured in the room for a brief moment, and it was gone. When I got to my car, I went through all my clothes sorting them in two piles, one pile to wash now and one for later. After I got everything sorted, I started the car and took off down the street, hoping to spot a laundry mat.

I drove by a Safeway, and then I found a little laundry mat. I turned my blinker on, and drove into the small parking lot. The clothes I had on were filthy, so I took them off. I found a pair shorts that were tie-dyed. They were once very large jeans that were cut off. They were clean 'cause they were ugly. I found a shirt just as ugly to match.

Now the weather outside was actually brisk, so this was not suitable attire for such day. I had to have jacket or sweater at least, and my fucking legs were freezing in this get up. I just happened to have a long trench coat in the car. Where it came from, I don't fucking know. So I put it on got out of the car and grabbed my clothes to wash. I loaded a washer, and put the soap in I bought from the machine. I closed the lid, and walked to my car.

When I sat down in the front seat, I looked in the rear view mirror at my patchy beard. That's when I made up my mind to get a razor. I already owned a Gillette razor; however, the blade was dull. I started the car and headed towards Safeway. I spotted it on my left, and turned into its entrance. I pulled into a parking space, turned the car off, and got out.

I looked rather sketchy, I must admit. There I was walking across the parking lot, in a long black coat made from wool, and wearing a pair of Birkenstocks. The coat just barely covered my knees so you could see my naked legs. I walked in the store, and quickly found what I was looking for. I couldn't just buy one cartridge; I had to purchase at least four. Which meant spending more money than I wanted. Why I didn't just take a pack of four, and go directly to the counter, I'll never know. I opened up one of the packages, slipping one cartridge in my pocket. Briefly looking around as I did it. I started walking towards the door. Well, so far so good, I thought to myself. Right as I stepped outside the exit, a man approached me from behind. He said, "You need to step back into the store, and come with me."

"What are you talking about" I said.

"Empty out your pockets please".

"Oh you mean this? Here I'll pay for it." I gave him a five-dollar bill and kept walking to my car.

He shouted, "I'm calling the police!" I started up the car, and raced to the exit. The tires squealed, as I quickly turned right on the main road. There, a couple blocks up, was the laundry mat. I pulled back in frantically looking for a place to park that would hide me. I saw two cars with a space between them, and I parked my Honda. I immediately pulled on the seat handle, and laid down out of site for about ten minutes. When I thought the coast was clear I got out, and went inside. I put my clothes in the dryer, and sat down. There was no activity outside that I could see. I picked up a magazine next to me. Time was passing way too fucking slow. After thumbing through the pages, and looking at the pictures I walked back to the dryer. It read eight minutes on the LED. Butterflies in my gut were going off. How in the fuck do I get myself in these messes? Ok, I'll just sit back down and calmly wait, and that's what I did.

When the clothes were finally done, I folded them on a table, put them in the basket, and headed for the door. As soon as I walked out the door, on my left were two cops in blue uniforms. One of the officers quickly drew his gun and shouted, "Freeze! Get down on the ground."

I was stunned. As I slowly set the basket down they bum rushed me throwing me to the ground shouting "Get down on the ground!" I could feel the cold steel of the gun on my head. My arms were violently place behind my back, and cuffed tighter than needed in seconds time. "Do you have weapons or needles on you?"

"No," I replied, and with that I was hauled off to the Marin County jail.

Marin County jail system is very sweet. It's still a goddamn jail, but with cable TV and even Showtime. There's a schedule on the wall, like a TV guide, of what's on. After I was booked, and my shit was inventoried, they put me in a four-man cell. The cell was split into two different sections. The sleeping area was on one side, and the TV section, complete with metal table and chairs, on the other side. The chow hall was up the hall and it was a complete cafeteria of sorts. The Club Fed of county jails. I sat there long enough to be let go; however, they impounded my car. I didn't have enough money on me to get it out, unfortunately, so I called Mom and Dad.

The conversation ended several times with, "No, I won't send you money." My father's conclusion to it all was to personally come out here and get his car and his son. This is exactly what he did. When they got there, a week later, they parked on the Panhandle, and found me on the Haight. Dad needed some nugs for the trip back. My dad actually put me on one last mission before we left.

I don't know if it was the lack of car that took all the fight out of me, for that moment, or just needing a break. Whatever it was, I decided to bail with my parents. Oh boy, off to Kansas City, but we needed buds for the journey. I went looking for Laura, and Arien to tell them bye, and cop some nugs. I ran into them almost immediately and told them the deal, and we all walked back down to the panhandle where both Mom and Dad waited. I introduced both girls to my parents. I believe Mom took a couple shots from her camera. The sky was very gray. I was dressed in a green and black hoody. I said my goodbyes and we left.

On the way back, through Flagstaff, Arizona Dad hit somebody. He gave the dude his white Fender Stratocaster because it was his fault. We made it back to KC in good time. I went to work at Sonic down the street, and the movie theaters a couple block up from that. I wasted no time. The Grateful Dead was going on spring tour in about a month. All I needed were two paychecks and off I would go.

Working at Sonic is a good thing if your like me, someone who loves tater tots smothered in cheese. Their Coney dogs, and corn chips with chili on top are the shit too. I would dip the corn chips in the chili, as I steady worked. Ahhh…the good old days. The movie theater job was very brief, a week and a half, I think. I was the guy that tore your ticket.

While I waited, working these two jobs, I made copies of all my live Dead tapes on these multi colored Memorex's my mom had. They were recordings of college classes she had no need for anymore. Mom gave me all of the class tapes, so one of my ideas was to sell each tape for a dollar, and I had over thirty tapes to swing, once I finished taping. Between that and swinging grilled cheese, I figured I'd bring in some decent money.

Spring Tour '92

When I got my second check from Sonic, I purchased a Greyhound ticket, and took off for Atlanta. The Omni was the second stop for spring tour '92. Once I got to Atlanta, the first thing I had to do was find a grocery store, which, in the downtown of any major city, is a chore. By locating a phone, and checking the yellow pages, I found what I was looking for. I called a cab and went from there. No, that's not what I did. Being the cheap bastard that I am, I walked from the Greyhound Station to the nearest store. I'll remind you, I had a backpack complete with a fucking Coleman stove.

Anyway, I walked my ass half way across town to buy some cheese and bread. Once I bought all the shit I needed, I then took a cab to the Omni. I set up in the gravel parking lot just outside the under part of the Omni. You could walk from that lot, through the belly of it all, and go up the stairs into an entrance. It was a beautiful day. The sun was shining, and all the hippie freaks of the south were there.

My main gig was selling grilled cheese sandwiches and swinging these live Dead shows. As soon as I put my blanket down, set up the grill, and laid all the tapes out, the custys came a runnin'. In less than an hour, my hands were saturated in butter from cooking; I had sold half of the tapes, and at least twenty sandwiches.

As I was turning over a customer's grilled cheese, a familiar face walked up to me on my right. The sun was shining directly above him and behind him at the same time. He moved his face where I could finally see him clearly. It was Phil Lisi. Same old Phil accompanied by the short curly brown hair, wearing a worn out tie-dye he probably bought back in '85. "Hey Phil, what's up?" I said.

"Nothing much," he replied. "Hey, do you think I could hang out here with you, and sell beer?"

"Fuck yeah, dude. That would be awesome," I said.

"Cool, I'm gonna go to my car, and grab my cooler," and with that Phil headed off to his car. By the time Phil got back, I had sold a couple more tapes, and grilled cheeses. Phil was still living in Ocean City. Not a whole lot had changed for him in the last four years. He had mail ordered his tickets, as usual. I hadn't, so I would be looking for some. That's if I can justify it. Selling all of my shit would justify it. I knew I wouldn't even start looking till the third day.

Phil had a round cooler filled with Bass Ale and a couple of swag beers, which he drank. I asked him if I could have one, a couple of hours later. After Phil sold all his beer he went back to his car and put away his cooler. He then grabbed what he needed for the show. Which usually was a couple of pre rolled joints and his tickets, of course. As it got closer to the show, people thinned out up and down the rows of cars.

Phil walked back to my spot where I was selling. He had put on a flannel. The temperature was starting to drop. Probably the same fucking flannel he wore in '88. Being it was time for the show to start, people were heading toward the gate, including Phil. Phil said, "Hey Brad, I'm gonna go on inside."

I replied, "What are you doing after the show? Where are you staying?"

Phil said, "I was planning on going to the campgrounds."

"Right on, can I catch a ride with you?"

"Yeah, sure, I'll catch up with you after the show," Phil said. "You gonna be here?"

"Yeah," I replied. And with that Phil left.

The sun was no longer in the sky and the city of Atlanta was dimming down. Lots of people were parading towards the entrances. My selling had slowed down considerably. The tapes were almost all gone, except three. I had two sandwiches on the side, already made, waiting for a customer. That customer wasn't in any hurry. However, it sure was good seeing Phil again. I had managed to bump into him a couple of times in these last four years since Philly '88, and, like I said, it was usually under the same circumstances.

This was my first time kickin' it with Lisi as a vendor. He always sold beer at every fucking show. That way he drank for free. I didn't drink all that much, really...well not yet. I didn't know where his car was. I was too busy swinging. I hoped Phil would show back up after the show or I'd be hitching a ride with someone. What the fuck was I thinking? I did leave Kansas City knowing I'd have to sleep somewhere. I did have a fucking tent I bought at K-mart in my backpack. I suddenly thought I might have made a mistake. If Phil doesn't come back, I'm fucked. Well, not entirely, I'm sure I could catch a ride from someone. That wasn't a very appealing thought, having to bum a fucking ride. A guy came up to me at that moment, and asked me for a grilled cheese sandwich. I hand it to him he hands me some money.

The sky turned to a dark blue as the night slowly consumed the day. I need to fucking take a piss. There's no one around I know to watch my shit. There were porta-potties on the backside of this gravel lot, which was about four rows over from me. I'm gonna have to risk it. I've waited all fucking day. I decided to leave all my shit, and head to the porta johns. When I got there, all of them were full with a line of people waiting. I got in line and waited as well.

While I stood there in line, it dawned on me how fucking sober I was. I hadn't inhaled any fucking nitrous balloons, and I hadn't smoked any weed all day. I had managed to drink a beer Phil gave me and that's it. When I finally relieved my bladder, I walked back to my spot. Nothing was touched thank god, but I was still tired of hanging out in the same fucking place all day. Getting high had become a priority. It was a Dead show after all. That didn't fucking matter, I just needed to get high. Unfortunately, I wasn't a free man yet. I had a Coleman grill to tend to. The thing is when the show lets out there's a lot of hungry fuckers. So I had to stay put.

The show let out an hour and a half later. As people were coming out, the parking lot scene came back alive. Alive: meaning money exchanging from one hand to another. I was selling in no time. A lot of the people that did buy from me asked if I had any thing to drink. I didn't, and it made me think of Phil. Where the fuck was Phil? I started to give up on the idea of him coming back. Then, there he was, right on time. The congestion picked up pronto. There's nothing like the late night Omni crowd of the Dead: high, hungry, and thirsty. Well, this was mainly the kids that didn't do so much acid that they lost their appetite.

"How was the show?" I asked.

"It was good," Phil replied.

"What did they open with?"

"Jackstraw," he said, and then followed with, "They did a Scarlet Fire that was cool."

"Right on," I said.

"You sell much?"

"Yeah, a good bit. I can go ahead and break down if your ready to bail." Phil nodded his head, and I packed up everything. I had a frame backpack with tent, sleeping bag, and clothes. Fitting the Coleman stove meant throwing the propane tank out or stashing it in the car. Living on the road, with everything on your back, limits you. I was very grateful Phil was there. He had parked his car on the other side, so we headed that way. Once there, I put my shit behind the passenger seat, and we took off. "Stone Mountain is where every one is tonight."

Phil nodded again and drove towards the interstate. He knew where to go. Every year, most heads wind up at this campsite. When we got to the campground, you knew you were at the Deadhead haven. Lots of VW Buses, and cars with hella stickers just like any dead lot. You did have to actually drive up a paved road like a mountain. On each side were vehicles parked with their tents. Most of them were playing Grateful Dead music from whatever player they had. We kept on driving upward until Phil saw a spot and pulled in. We just barely fit with room for the tents. I wasn't sure if he wanted to set up his or just nod out in the car. I had my tent and gear, so I went ahead and set up. Phil didn't seem too interested in setting up anything. He just leaned against his Honda, and drank a beer that he had grabbed out of his cooler. "Hey Phil, will you get me high?" I asked

"Yeah, in a minute," Phil said as he took another sip from his beer. My fucking hands still had butter residue on them as a result of my hard work. I could hear, off in the distance, the familiar sound of a nitrous tank filling a balloon. Phil produced a pre-rolled joint he had in the car. "This is one I rolled for the show and didn't get around to smoking."

I thought to myself how in the fuck can any one in a dead show not get around to smoking every last piece of weed. The joint was lit, and we puffed. "Hey man, lets do some nitrous," I said, and we wandered off into the campsite. Both of us went from tank to tank, hopping around, and eventually we found our way back to the car.

Phil didn't set up shit, he wound up drinking at least three more beers, and crashed out in his front seat. I climbed into my little dome tent and passed the fuck out. Tired, I was. Worked, I did, with no room for LSD or Mushrooms. You could tell the majority of Stone Mountain campers were up for the night. As I nodded away, the joyful sounds of Grateful Dead Land danced in my ears.

The next morning we wasted no time getting motivated. There were others, just like me, quickly breaking down their tent. I packed it all up and put it behind the passenger seat. Phil already had on a new shirt. He had gotten up before I did. The car was started, and off we went.

The traffic sucked getting back into Atlanta. I couldn't tell if this was everyday traffic or what. It didn't matter, what did matter was setting up my grill and raging the lot. I asked Phil if I could set up at his car, and he said yes. And then I asked him to stop at the nearest Wal-Mart. He did, and I re-upped on cheese and bread, and Phil re-upped on more Bass Ale.

We got in early enough to get a decent parking space on the same gravel lot. After the majority of vehicles piled in, we were a row or two from the Shakedown, on this side of the coliseum. That was good for me. I had sold all of my tapes, but I still had grilled cheese sandwiches to swing. As a result of being in a prime spot, I raged and I was up to two hundred and fifty dollars. That was after I bought bread, cheese, and propane for both nights. Tomorrow night, I'm gonna get in. Fuck working all three nights. I'll break down early, and crank it back up in Hampton.

The second night was like the first, except that I got to work with a car at hand. The irony of it all is it's a fucking Honda Accord just like my old one, despite Phil's was gray and mine was blue. Also, Phil's Honda wasn't taken away by his Dad and given to his sister. Anyway, because I got to stash my shit in Phil's car, I also had the ability to get high while cooking. I knew I was getting itchy to get inside. I had many chances to get a ticket, but I didn't have the money till now. The first night was a better night; however, I didn't know that.

The day was coming to an end. The show was half way over, and I was outside selling to whoever wanted a fucking grilled cheese. When all the people started coming out, business picked up, as usual. I still had over a hundred slices of cheese left and bread to match. This was plenty enough for tomorrow. I sold another ten or so in the next thirty minutes. Phil immediately broke out his cooler when he got to the car. Like usual, the beer sold well along side of the cheese.

From the corner of my eye I noticed four or five men dressed in dark blue with red embroidered tags on there uniform. They were walking alongside each other on the outer row. The bro in front of me buying a beer from Phil said, "Those dudes are called Red Dogs. They've been shutting down all vending." They kept on walking, and didn't turn up our row. That wasn't the first time I'd heard the term "Red Dogs." Someone had mentioned it earlier. They looked scary enough to me from a distance at that. I decided to break down. Phil carried on without blinking.

The thing about Phil is that he never said a fucking word. A lot of kids swinging beer would sit on their cooler yelling shit like "Ice cold beer . . . two bucks." Not Phil, he just stood there (maybe holding a Bass Ale sign but usually not) with his Afro like curly hair, and flannel over a Dead shirt in blue jeans with Pumas. And sure enough some thirsty kid was handing him money before you know it. Seriously, you've got competition on tour. The squeaky wheel gets the grease. There are some that work hard, and some that don't. Phil had seen a couple "rodeos" so he knew how to go about it.

After selling a couple more, Grateful Dead security showed up on their white golf carts and yelling out of their bullhorns, "Leave! Go Home! It's Time To Go!" On the carts, were two guys. A gray haired man that looked like Michael McDonald with a haircut, and a shorter fellow with brown hair. They kept on shouting, and it was effective. Both Phil and I were ready to bail anyway. Before we got in the car, Phil would always make a huge effort to pick up every piece of trash in our area. I can't say that I was always as good about it. I watched him walk several cars down picking up trash, bottles, and cans. When he was satisfied we would go. I'm not exaggerating, it was like this every night, if you rode with Phil Lisi. I respected him a great deal for this outside of all the other redeeming qualities.

Once we were on the road, we decided to go back to Stone Mountain. The price was right, and it seemed like the best thing to do. "Spent a little time on the Mountain, spent a little time on the hill." The "hill" could be Boulder, Colorado (where you cop nugs) or the top of Buena Vista Park in San Francisco. Or it could be any other swing spot, USA. It's a metaphor, ya know.

Phil set up his tent the second night. We raged a little, crashed, and got up and went back to the Omni. The third night was March 3, 1992. I was already tired of grilled cheesing. I wanted to run around, and have fun, but no, I had a nine to fiver. It separates you from the many. Being a consumer rocks in Dead Land. I managed to get my groove on for thirty minutes or so, and then I set up shop.

We were parked in a different place than the other nights. Still we were in a good spot, but not close to the Shakedown. Phil decided to walk around with his small cooler 'cause he wasn't selling as much here. I dealt with it. I sold about thirty sandwiches before I gave up. I still had more of everything, but fuck it, I'll be ready for Hampton.

Just as I was about to break down, a pack of Red Dogs walked up on me, four deep and in all plain dark uniforms with only a Red Dog patch on them. "You gonna have to break down. Vending is prohibited," one of them said.

"Ok, no problem. I'm breaking it down now." As soon as they saw I was obeying their order, by putting everything away, they continued to walk on. That sucked, but it could have been worse. Hell, they could have taken all my shit. I've seen it more so with n2o tanks, but I've heard that venders get shit taken all the time. I was done anyway. I hadn't even gotten a ticket yet. I was on a mission. I put away everything and locked the car. I knew I couldn't get in without a key, but I sure as hell wasn't gonna leave it unlocked. I headed toward the Shakedown. Upon entering the main stretch of venders and heads I smelled that oh so familiar fragrance of sage, ganja, and "us."

"Who's got my miracle ticket," cried out a young girl in a sundress holding up one finger. I wasn't asking for a kick down, I had made some money. I kept my eyes, and ears open. Looking around at the same time.

"Doses," some bro said as I walked past him. When I reached the end of the Shakedown, I decided to go towards the Omni entrances. Walking, walking, walking, so much walking. I'm exaggerating, but when you're constantly looking left to right, and scoping in all directions, it makes it less enjoyable. Needless to say, once I got closer to one of the many entrances, I saw several people with tickets in hand. One was definitely a fucking scalper. The other one looked like a bro, so I approached him.

"Twenty Five Bucks," the dude said.

"Fuck, Yeah!" I said, and gave him his money. Well that's that, but I wanted to get up with Phil. He's still roaming around with a fucking cooler of beer for sale, and that nigga got some weed. All the years I'd known Phil, that mother fucker always had fucking weed. And it's always good fucking quality swag, like heady swa'.

Anyway, I needed to find him, so I walked back down to the Shakedown where I saw him earlier and he wasn't there. I walked back through it once, and then headed for the car. As I got closer to our particular lot we were in, I saw Phil in the distance. He was standing at the back of the car with the hatch up. Either he was putting away his cooler or just getting a beer. I was relieved to see him. I wanted to get high for starters. "Hey, what's up? How did you do?" I asked.

"I sold out, I'm just getting one for myself."

"I got shut down by the Red Dogs, but I was done anyway. But hey, I got ticket. You got some rolled for the show?"

Phil said yes, and said he was going in. I told him I was ready, so we locked up the car and walked toward the Omni.

The coliseum inside was as full as it could be. My ticket stub said I was in upper seating on Jerry's side. Phil's was lower level Jerry's side, so I just followed him. I never fucking went to my seats. There was limited seating all around the section we were in, and the ushers were checking. However, no one was sweating me for the seat I was claiming next to Phil.

The lights went down. The crowd got excited. On the stage, Bobby was making noise with his guitar, "chinck, chinck," sounded from his amp. Then a couple drums rolls followed by a chord on the keys. Sounded like a minor chord. Phil lit up a joint next to me, and passed it to me. I hit it a couple times, and passed it back. Right then the band kicks in full force with "Hell in a Bucket." The sound was quite nice, not too loud yet on the verge of loud. "Fuckit Bucket" was a common opener back in the day. Some called it "Puke in a bucket." Those were the same kids that would beat up new tunes like "Corrina." They would call it "Velveeta" but all in good fun. I was so fucking glad just to be inside, and not cooking in the "grovel" lot. And yes, my fucking hands still had the stink of butter, but whatever, I was inside. I'm not gonna go into detail on how great Jerry's notes were or how Bobby fucking whaled. I was just grateful to be there.

The next tune was "Sugaree," and it was sweet. A very nice show, by all standards. I danced my ass off, standing next to Phil. When they slowed down by going into "Walkin' Blues" I stopped waving my freak flag and quit dancing. I suddenly realized I hadn't taken a fuckin' piss for hours. I didn't need to go urgently yet, but I knew I wouldn't be able to last too long. I sat down and chatted with Phil. They went through a couple more numbers, and by the time they started playing Tennessee Jed my fucking bladder was telling me I had to relieve it. I looked at bro, and said "Hey man, I gotta piss. I'll be back."

Phil was like, "yeah, yeah, do whatcha gotta do." Being that I was only stoned, the bathroom wasn't such a bad scene, compared to others. As I stood there pissing at the urinal, I could still hear the band. "Better head back to Tennessee Jed," the crowd sang right along with boys. I walked outside the bathroom, and got in line at the water fountain.

Then, from behind me, someone grabbed me. I turned around, and there was Arien shouting out my name, "Brad! Where have you been?" she asked.

"I've been at my parents place in Kansas City getting money together to be here."

"Right on," Arien replied. "Brad, come with me to the Phil zone. I'll puff you out." I said ok and followed her. They just ended "Tennessee." Even in the hallways you could hear the magnitude coming from the crowd.

We walked all the way around towards the left side of the coliseum. She was taking me to the top, left, upper level on Phil Lesh's side. As we started to climb the stairs, the band kicked in with this funky sounding tune I'd never heard before. Then Jerry started playing a grungy electric slide part on top of it. As I was climbing the stairs, I couldn't stop dancing while I stepping, if that's even possible. This was a strange, but fun, sounding tune. By the time we got to the top, Arien looked at me and said, "This is Bobby's new song. It's called "Corrina." They played it in Oakland."

"I like it," I said. Then we turned to our left, from the opening, and walked towards a group of familiar looking kids of all ages. Coming remotely from this section, was a kind aroma beyond English expression. There were a lot of faces I recognized only from the Haight. Spooky Rob for starters; he was the first bro to recognize me. He asked me almost immediately if I wanted to do some china white. Rob sat down and produced two very small bags of white dope. Arien pulled me over to her side, dragging me with her, and up to the right, with some bro, there sat Laura. Her face brightened up when she saw us.

"Oh Fuck! Brad, what's up?" Laura came running over, smothering me with kisses. "Sit down, sit down, let's smoke a bowl," she said. Arien broke out her fatty "Snotty," pulling it out of her corduroy pouch she made herself. "Snotty" meaning Bob Snodgrass. On the west coast, he was one of the first well known blowers whose name carried from one to another. There were two or three other pipes being passed around. I glanced at the stage enjoying the new Bobby song.

All of a sudden, I remembered Phil down there all by himself. I felt bad for leaving him down there all alone, but goddamnit, I hadn't seen these girls in forever. I'll meet up with him at the break, which was coming real soon. I filled Laura in with all my shit and she did the same. She was steady swinging on the Haight, and on tour. I don't mean to sound insensitive, shit, you know the gig. I was having good time being here at this moment. I did work a couple days to be here. Bobby was singing "Corrina, Corrina" over and over so I took it this was the end of the song. The band finally resolved to a close followed by, "We'll be back in just a little bit," from Bobby. The boys exited the stage, and the lights went up.

I told Laura and Arien about Phil, and promised I'd catch up with them later. When I walked all the way the fuck back, he was sitting down looking chill. "What's up man? I met up with some friends, and they puffed me out. Didn't mean to ditch ya." I laughed as I said this. He smiled as well. "Hey man, you wanna go up to the Phil Zone?" He looked at me expressionless for a moment, and I said, "Yeah man, you know where I'm talking about," and as I said this, I pointed to the upper section on the other side of the coliseum.

"Yeah, I've been up there and I like the view better here," Phil said. "Yeah, sure you're right, but I've got some friends up there, that's all."

"Well go hang out with them," Phil snapped. That alarmed me. We were friends too, and I wasn't trying to piss him off. Shit, plus I was riding with Phil, so you do the math. That sounds harsh, but that's about right. I didn't go back up to the Phil zone. I figured if I wanted to it make through this spring tour with less pain, I better not bite the hand that bakes my bread, so to speak. This was the first fucking show anyway. It was just nice to see everyone again.

After the show let out, I didn't do a fucking thing except be a kid. No fucking grilled cheese, no fucking anything, except enjoying the scene. I know I was a little younger than some of the other kids that I'd met in the south a few years back; however, where the fuck were they at? Oh, you will eventually bump into ghosts from the past. That's a given in any fucking culture. That wasn't an issue really, getting ready for the next city was. All the venders and swinger kids were working overtime to bring in the money. It felt good to relax, and watch it all happen. Time passes quick after a show. We went back to the car, cleaned up around us, and decided to go ahead and drive to Hampton tonight.

It was quite a ride leaving Atlanta. No tension, really, just both of us tired. Phil wasn't even listening to any dead tapes. That was all right with me. Phil handed me a pipe full of weed, and we smoked. I was going to try to get a little shuteye after we puffed. I felt guilty that I could do that. I turned on my side and slept. When I awoke, it was light outside. We were in a rest area. Phil was passed out with his Mexican blanket and pillow in the drivers seat next to me. Some old people walked past us heading towards the bathrooms. I got out of the car and followed them inside and used the facilities. When I got back to the car, Phil was awake. He said we were about ninety miles from the border of North Carolina and Virginia. "Damn, you drove all night didn't you?" I asked.

"No, not really. I've had a few hours of sleep," Phil replied.

"You want me to drive?"

"No," Phil headed off to the bathroom. When he returned, we got back on the road. There was still a little bit of pot left in the bowl so I smoked it without hesitation. On the highway there was a number of VW buses, cars, and trucks with dead stickers including ours. When you drive by each other the majority will wave. There's nothing quite like it. We stopped and got something real to eat at truck stop.

By the time we got to Hampton it was already getting dark. I suggested we go to the closest motel next to the coliseum, "There we can rage and get floor space. Maybe luck out and get a shower." We pulled into the Red Roof Inn. It was jam packed with Dead Heads.

We actually managed to find a parking spot. I got out and stretched, so did Phil. It was completely dark. We walked up to the well lit surroundings. It was not so much a bright white lighting, but it was more of a yellow light that surrounded the Red Roof Inn. And there, standing in a doorway, wearing a Hawaiian shirt, was Patches - still holding that huge fucking drum.

The Grey area

I saw this new kid bouncing around from room to room. His name was Stoney. He had curly blond hair at kind of a medium length. It hadn't reached the long hair status. Stoney was like many who came into the Dead Family throughout the thirty years, in and out quickly. He had done a few shady deals back in the Bay, so his presence wasn't liked by all. I liked him just the same though. He was just like me, someone who strived to belong, but the kids have very little tolerance for wrong doings. Anyway, Stoney was bouncing around from room to room, and I was looking for more familiar faces. Not to mention a place to crash. I didn't really want to crash in Phil's car. After running into more family, Phil and I eventually got some floor space.

There is not a whole lot to tell from this moment till we got to the Spectrum. When we finally got through "The Cap Center" in Landover, Maryland, we headed north to Long Island, New York. Nassau county, actually Union Dale, was the city name. The weather was brisk and cold as hell. My Coleman stove wouldn't fucking stay lit for shit. The wind was too fierce. It kept blowing the goddamn flame out, and every fucking body was huddled up in their fucking cars. So, there were no custys roaming around outside the Shakedown, and we were not even parked anywhere near the Shakedown. This was the moment in the spring tour I broke. Swinging grilled cheese was not making me shit, and I sure as hell wasn't having fun. Being that I knew a couple of people that I met up with from the family, they put me to work swinging doses. From that moment, I was swinging singles and sheets. This was the only thing I could do. I was in New York running out of money. I got in one night as a result of building my bank back up. The night I did get in was an ok night. Not a fatty show, but I was working so it didn't really matter.

These shows passed rather quickly. We went to the "Rectum" in Philly next, better known as the Spectrum. Now the Spectrum was nothing like it had been in 1988. They had us parked in a fucking concrete lot outside the coliseum. I wouldn't fucking bitch, but this was just one of the best fucking places to camp and vend back in the day. If you remember, we got to pitch a tent around the lake before fall tour '89.

I believe I got in; however, I don't fucking recall all that went down. That's why I call this "the gray area." I don't fucking remember much until Auburn Hills, Michigan. The thing is, after Philly we went to Ocean City, NJ to Phil's house. Why? Because Phil was swinging swag bud, and he had a quarter pound on him the whole time. Here and there he would sell a bag or two. Not enough for me to carry that much weight. You know Phil by now, he doesn't like to work at it, he just waits for the custy. His house was a small little place just perfect for a bachelor Dead head. We hung out for a couple days until the Ontario, Canada show was over and the boys were back in the states. Crossing the border and returning was a sketch, according to Mr. Lisi. The last stop for the spring tour was Auburn Hills, so we made our way toward the Great Lakes.

By the time we got there, the show was on in full force. The weather was a bit nippy and gray. I hadn't seen too many family kids for a few shows, as a result of hanging out with Phil exclusively. Finally, I ran into Laura and Arien that first night. They were hanging out with some bro who I'd never met before. As soon as we saw each other all of us jumped into each other's arms with big warm smiles.

Laura said, "Hey, I want you to meet this bro," she turned around and introduced us. He was scary to look at. His entire nose was crushed flat against his face. His face looked liked my face after I had my accident in Kansas. This guy obviously didn't have the means to have the surgery that I did. Very sad, it was, to see this bro in such a condition. It was like the girls were letting me know how fucking lucky I was. I was speechless inside, but greeted him with a smile on the outside. Phil was on my right, so I introduced both of them. I never saw that bro again, and this was the last show of the tour.

Yeah, a lot of this tour is a blank, but that's not because I was there at every fucking show. It was what it was, I suppose. I do remember this show pretty well though. They were playing two nights, the twenty third and the twenty fourth. There was this kid I saw throughout the whole tour that traveled with us, and was seen in and out of the Phil zone. I don't recall his name. He was thin and short and he looked, to me, like a young Chris Kattan. He was fucking cool, no doubt. I just can't remember his name. Well, the thing is, he did the whole tour, and he had friends with him. The friends had some box tickets they got through this bro. Phil and I were offered two tickets. These were for the first night. I never had box seats in my life, so Phil and me jumped on that deal real quick. And goddamnit, we deserved them! When you do a whole fuckin' tour, you rage it till the end, and thank fucking god you made it, let alone score box seats.

When we got in The Palace, we were led down a hallway that eventually ended up in actual rooms that had little fridges stocked with domestic and import beers, plus little mini bottles of liquor. It was a small living room with sliding glass doors that opened to a patio with outdoor carpet on it. The glass doors opened to a front view of the stage. We didn't get this box by ourselves. The people that we shared it with were the corporate type. I didn't fucking care; it was a rage to me. They opened the second set with "Victim or the Crime."

This was the last show on tour, and Phil was going back home to Ocean City. I myself wanted to catch a ride back to the city ... the bay of course. All the kids were hanging out in the parking lots of the main motels closest to The Palace. I walked around from bus to car to van to whatever in search of a ride back home.

Finally, I ran into a bro by the name of Hetzel. He was sitting in the drivers seat of his light blue seventies dodge van. The type with the extension on the back to make it longer, and in the back, was a bed. "You headed back to California?" I asked. Hetzel said yes, and then asked me if I had gas money. Being that I did, I had found my ride. Sitting in the passenger seat was a red headed dready. She said nothing. At that point, I told Hetzel I was gonna go tell my bro I caught a ride. Phil was happy I scored, and he helped me get my gear together. I sat my backpack down and turned to Phil. This was when you hug, and say goodbye. Phil never

was the hugger type, so he gave me a quick hug and wished me well. I
threw my pack on and walked away.

The Journey Home

There were three people in the van when I returned. I handed my
backpack to the bro in the back of the van. After he situated it in a place
that worked, he turned around and said, "What's up...I'm Mike."
"I'm Brad, what's up?"
The red dready turned around and said, "I'm Kathy."
I smiled, looked at Hetzel, and said, "Are these all the riders we got?"
"No," he replied. "We're gonna pick up two more in Chicago." With
that, Mike closed the door, and Hetzel started the van. Mike was known as
"China Mike" but at this point he introduced himself as just Mike. He was
half American and half Asian. His eyes were brown and slanted and he had
long straight black hair, originally, but at some point it had dreaded.
Leaving in the morning or afternoon is always kinder than at night, so
we made our way back to the interstate without any trouble. The painful
part came once we entered the Chicago area and tried to find their fucking
house. It seemed like an eternity. They were in the suburbs at someone's
parent's house. We found the place, finally, and pulled in the driveway.
Before we were completely out of the van, they were walking up and
greeting us. They were both hobbit-like kids, short in height and very
beardy. Turtle introduced himself first, then his bro gear, but we made it
work. We spent a little too much time at this place. That being, eventually
we got on the main road heading for the west.
We made it about two hundred miles before the engine stopped on the
highway. The next thing we knew we are all standing outside the van at a
repair shop. I watched Hetzel walk out of the front door of the shop with a
look of stress. "The engine is blown, and it's gonna cost about four hundred
plus the installation," Hetzel said. Somebody in the group suggested we
bail and just hitchhike. For Hetzel, that sucked, and Cathy was with him so
they were not down with abandoning the van. That was their house. Mike
asked me if I was in. I didn't hesitate to say yes. I knew what money I had.
It wasn't much granted, but I was in. Turtle and his bro were reluctant to
use their money. They kept talking 'bout the Greyhound and shit.
The feeling I got from Mike, Kathy, and Hetzel was very kind. I
wanted to stay with them. It was three against one, so we decided to put all
our money together and fix the van. Hetzel ran back into the garage to let

them know to buy the junkyard V-8 and install it. Then, he told him due to the situation, we would have to sleep in the van for the night. The owner allowed it. They couldn't get the engine until the morning so we were stuck in this little town, in the middle of nowhere, with nothing to do.

Everyone was getting hungry, and I did have the Coleman stove I used for grilled cheese. Luckily, there was still some gas in the tank. Kathy, ya gotta love Kathy, she had the smile. Her dreads were very long and very beautiful. She had the cute little freckles on her face like a lot redheads do. Her teeth were perfect. Her vampire teeth were just a hair bigger than most, and I thought she was so beautiful. Anyway, she pushed me aside with a smile, telling me how she makes the best bean and cheese quesadillas. We happened to have tortillas and all the makings. Kathy commenced cooking for the boys, and we all huddled around in a circle smoking camels.

It was getting dark quick, and we had only thirty minutes of light left at that. The shop people were closing the gates, and they were kind enough to push the vehicle, with our help of course, out of the garage and outside the shop gate. So we got out. We had a place to crash, but a lot of nighttime to kill.

Turtle suggested we walk around, so we did. It didn't take long before we figured there wasn't shit around that was even open. The little quick store in walking distance was all ready closed. What cigarettes we had were gonna have to last. We were all back at the van an hour later. An instant family we had become the moment we all decided to give what money we had to keep the van moving west. The problem was, now none of us had shit for money, as gas goes, but Hetzel told us that when all of our resources dried out, we can go to the local police departments and ask for a gas voucher to get out of their city. Cops want to get hippies out of their city, so the vouchers do happen. This I'd never seen before, yet I believed him.

Get this, there was this guy hanging out at the shop who had a van for sale for fifteen hundred and he wouldn't budge on the price. After all the workers left, he wound up giving us this swag that had been buried in the ground. Apparently the bag had busted and some earth had leaked into it. The shit would barely get you high. So he felt bad for us, and kicked us down like two ounces of this dirt weed…literately. Kathy found a fucking beetle shell in it. Mike wanted a beer. We had very little weed and we were a bunch of broke ass hippies now, that was for sure. But we got through it.

The mechanics were there bright and early in the morning. They took our money, picked up the engine, and we got out of their way. It took them all day to pull out the old engine and put in the "new" one. Well, the new junkyard engine. Basically, six hundred bucks it cost us, leaving us with very little gas money.

We got back on the road and an hour into the journey the engine started knocking loudly. We pulled over on the interstate, and found out there was no oil in the engine. They forgot to put the oil in. We were about a hundred miles away. Hetzel had a half a can of oil in the back somewhere. It was found, put in, and we got oil at the net stop. More money, more money, more money. We lost a cylinder as a result of the lack of oil and it still knocked loudly, but it ran.

Hetzel wanted to take the southern route, so we worked our way to interstate 40, and it was about this time that we were absolutely broke. This was when Hetzel pulled into the first podunk, Midwestern town, police station to get a gas voucher. They gave it to us without hesitation. Our goal was go to Boulder, Colorado first, the hippie central of the Midwest, and then work our way down to the 40.

In the van, we still had a lot of that dirt swag and some soapstone, plus a little bit of Minnesota pipe stone, which is a harder stone and a brick red color. We drove up the infamous hill, and hung out on the grass on the hill of the mall. As Kathy and I were sitting in the middle of the grass carving pipes to sell, the chubby guy from "Siskel & Ebert" walked by us. I noticed and called out to him, waving. He looked, smiled, and walked on.

Hetzel and China Mike were on a mission looking for the food boxes the Salvation Army would hand out. Once that was located, we all re-united at the van and drove there. They gave us a couple boxes, and since we were in the neighborhood, we decided to drive up the mountain to a little town called Netherland. I didn't know it at the time, but my aunt lived there.

When we got there, we parked. There's an obvious trail you can hike from that point, and we all did. So we climbed, we descended, and we got back on the road. We worked our way to I-40, and the desert life began. The desert, what a place to run low on provisions. We did have some food; however, we were hella broke and still needed to spare change at every stop. Somewhere near the border of Nevada we pulled off an exit coasting into a gas station. This was the type with two pumps only. Nowhere near a police station to ask for a voucher. At this place, they had an actual camel in a large caged area attached to this podunk store.

Everyone that passed through, we "spanged" them for money. Throughout this, we would walk over to the camel. He was tame and there was a feeder at hands reach. Kathy grabbed whatever was in the feeder, and the camel leaned down and ate from her hand. This was a very memorable moment to see a dreadlock beauty such as Kathy feeding such a foreign animal.

Believe it or not, we bummed enough change and dollar bills to get more gas and move on. The van was knocking louder and louder, the closer we got to Bakersfield, California, and that was scary, to say the least. That town was the new goal for us.

Hetzel and I sat up front quietly knowing the engine sounded horrible. Both of us were looking at the gas gauge with worry. The last sign said twenty-eight miles, and we were super close to "E." Mike and Kathy were asleep in the back. I truly didn't know if we were gonna make it.

As we entered the city of Bakersfield, on fumes, Hetzel asked where the police station was, and we headed that way. When we got there, they refused us, so we had no choice but to go to closest grocery store and beg again. As luck had it, Kathy got kicked down a twenty dollar bill in the parking lot. Girls have this talent ... well our girls did.

We didn't fuck around. We got back on route, and instead of going to SF. Hetzel decided to go to Santa Cruz, which is about twenty minutes south of San Francisco. That way we could all get one hundred and eleven dollars each in food stamps, and hang out in the park. The first thing I did once I got my food stamps was buy me some Ben & Jerry's heath bar crunch and a kiwi Snapple. I sat down outside the store eating my feast and washing it down.

Once finished, I walked back to the park. Joshua's spinner crew was there. Joshua was the leader of the spinners in '92. The Spinners would actually spin in one place, while the boys played, for an entire show. Josh had straight blond hair and always a warm brotherly smile on his face. Mikey had blonde hair and was wearing a white pair of overalls with no shirt. He was sitting in the middle of the park playing on a brand new white Epiphone guitar with F holes. He showed it to me with pride, and he knew I played. There was a lot family in the park.

The sun was extra bright and hot as shit! Junebug and his girl were hanging out, and we struck up a conversation about "Reuben and Cherise." I told him I couldn't play it yet. Junebug said, "It easy and tough, but I know you will get it." The next time I saw Junebug and his sister they were on a Greyhound bus a tour or two later. On that next encounter, he kicked me a JGB show on tape that had "Sitting here in limbo" on it.

As it started to get dark, China Mike and I walked down to the amusement park where they filmed "The Lost Boys" and we traded some of our food stamps to an essay for some cheeva (heroin). By this point, Mike felt like my best friend, so I just followed his lead. He led me back to a motel room that some other kids had paid for. I watched Mike remove a light bulb from one of the end table lamps, and break it appropriately so there was a hole at the top of the bulb. He cleaned it thoroughly in the bathroom sink. He opened the balloon that was tied in a knot. Then broke off a piece of cheeva, and dropped it in the light bulb. With a rolled up bill and a lighter Mike heated under the place it dropped and he inhaled the smoke. Then I did the same. That was my first experience with the real thing and not just some bunk ass violin resin or whatever bullshit. That night we got floor space in that room, and the next day the plan was to go to Greyhound Rock.

My last vision of Hetzel was of him sitting in the front seat of his van with his girl Kathy in the passenger seat. He was bailing with that look of, "and I ain't never coming back," and he fucking didn't. I never saw him again. That was his last rodeo. Kathy, I loved from the start, most brothers did. I didn't give a fuck that Hetzel wanted to bail, it was watching Kathy go that killed me.

I caught a ride with China Mike and the family to Greyhound Rock (near Santa Cruz) the next morning. There's a place you can pull off the road on Hwy 1 south of SF near Half Moon Bay. Anyway, this particular scenic pull over is unique. For years, a lot of bay family, as well as transients, would set up a tent and stay until they wanted to move on.

Later that night, I did some LSD that a bro kicked me. I forget his name. He ran up and down the beach, naked, all night. He suggested I collect alabaster shells and I did. I wasn't comfortable with getting naked like him. I enjoyed the Pacific Ocean at my feet while I was tripping. I watched the sunrise that morning from my tent opening. It was facing the ocean on the edge of a cliff. Mike and I finally caught a ride back into Cruz later on and were on our way back to the shitty.

There's nothing like the relief of having a fucking job again. Being that we were back on the Haight, we could work. I was swinging heighths, working to get ducats back in them dry pockets of mine. We all had to kill time. Spring tour was over, so all we had was the city and the west coast shows. Jerry Band at the Warfield and The Boys in the Oakland coliseum.

For the next month or so, I relied on my heighths, and Mail Order's, meaning Western Union. The people (from my home town or high school kids I'd kept in touch with) sent money for "L" or "Swag" and I would vacuum seal it and send it to them. I was constantly dodging officers Comfrey and Goff when they came to sweep up the swinger kids of the Haight. It was a job with the best co-workers. Outside of the legal aspect of it all, it was quite the journey. We made Malcolm X look like Brian Gumble. We were the goddamn Haight St. Posse.

I roamed up and down the street, trying not to think about Cathy, always keeping my eye out for Brandy. I had walked so much on my Milano Berks that the back straps had torn into my skin and the cork was deteriorating. China Mike got lost in the shuffle somewhere, and I starting running bags with Spooky Rob. He was a tall kid with brown hair who really looked "spooky," but in a nice way, if you get my drift. I liked him; he was very kind bro.

Spooky said he landed a job in San Jose, but it didn't last. He was telling me this as we were walking to his favorite place to shoot up. I helped him tie off, watched the needle register, and he pushed in the love. Rob felt well again. I didn't touch the stuff yet. Knowing he wasn't sick, we walked back to the Haight. Darkness was creeping in, so I had to figure out where I was gonna sleep.

As my family disappeared away from the scene, the late night crew started to surface. Kids like Raven, Morgan, Ragin' Rob, and the Wrecking Crew. Not to mention the runaways that flock to the Haight. You usually find them ducked away in a shop entrance with their shit laid out all around them. My goal was to get motivated quick or get stuck in the city under a porch somewhere. Just then, Angelo came out of nowhere with an acoustic guitar and singing Grateful Dead tunes. In no time, I found one to borrow and we were playing together. Angelo would always remind me that he was an illegitimate son of one of the band members of Kiss. Hell, I believed him; he was believable.

Now, Angelo and I had played together under the street lamp before. So if I'm repeating myself it's just that we would jam anytime we could, especially if we could get two guitars at once. Or we would fight over whose turn it was. Angelo wasn't into smoking hubbas, and, since I was surrounded by the finest, I was smoking before the night was through.

Yeah, yeah, there's nothing like walking among the living dead with a flashlight in the Golden Gate Park, tweaking. Why? 'Cause you might ground score a crack rock or something of value. Now, I could be wrong, but I believe this was about the time we had a scheduled Warfield show.

Zen Jim, Gretchen and Der had a school bus, and they would let me crash on their bus, as long as I wasn't tweaking. Zen Jim was about 5' 8" with very long, brown, dreads who lived on Der and Gretchen's bus. Der was a very short bro with dreads too. Gretchen was about Der's height, so they were a cute couple. Gretchen was very beautiful with brunette dreads and green eyes.

But the kids that weren't doing the hard stuff were frowning down on me. So I started to get to know the night kids better. The spring kids of '92 were still giving me the cold shoulder for not making a stronger effort to stay away from the "wrong crowd," so to say. My hunger for tweaking, up and down the Haight, started to take its toll. Quitting smoking crack was not an option. But walking to Waller to the free kitchen was. The Waller kitchen and the Hari Krishna's were lifesavers.

Eventually, Jerry played another show downtown in the TL on Market St. That particular night was insane. As you walk from the end of Haight, you turn left on Market and go several blocks to the Warfield passing The Regal on your way. This place had XXX nude shows and quarter slot video booths too. I frequently visited. Why? I love girl on girl porn. I have to admit it. But flipping through those channels to land on one of two grown men, one sodomizing the other, is a disturbing visual. At least to me it was. Sometimes you bump into those types of flicks when you're trying to get to what you really want: Girls, Girls, Girls. Anyway, you got to walk by The Regal to get to the show. What can I say, I'm weak.

Everything seemed normal at first. In front of the Warfield, a lot of the out of towners would huddle with their tickets in Tevas and colors (tie-dyes). On the same side of the street, where Polk and Fell come together, was us. We had a huge drum circle, and the air was filled with sage and ganja. I had made some money earlier, so I wanted to re-up on some crack. I walked to the area of the TL where the esses were swinging their shit, and immediately ducked in an alley. There I smoked. I didn't finish it all, and I headed back to the Warfield.

Sirens and loud commotion were all around me. Sounds of destruction... like someone throwing a brick through a window. People were looting left and right. On every side of the street, each garbage can was on fire. I was squinting my eyes to see in the distance, just to make sure I wasn't hallucinating.

While I was off getting fucked up on hubbas, a fucking riot had broken out. To the right of Wendy's, was a row of police officers or swat guys or whatever they were. They were all standing in a straight line with plastic shields covering their faces with protective helmets, blocking all traffic around the Warfield. Keeping the peace is what they were doing. A black guy came rushing up to me, and decked me in the jaw. Then he yanked off my peyote stitch necklace from around my neck. (I was given a choice of colors beads from what she had. I had chosen silver and burgundy red. It resembled a coral snake with a beautiful quartzite crystal at the head, and this was very special to me. It was made for me in Auburn Hills, Michigan at the end of the spring tour of '92). My fucking backpack I stashed was gone along with all my tapes in it. Yeah, I said tapes…not cd's. So all of my tapes, clothes, and sleeping gear were gone, but I had some crumbs left and the cake in my pipe.

The Warfield staff witnessed the incident, and came over to persuade me to quickly get inside. The mayor at the time was a wonderful lady, and she made sure the show would continue as long as all the family could be packed inside safely. Her plan was to run two buses, only for us, when it was over. The L–Travel and N–Juda (two buses that ran 24 hours a day in SF) were waiting right outside for all that needed transportation. They were instructed to take us wherever we needed to go.

When I got in, John was playing his beautiful bass line to "The Maker." That fact that I was tweakin' on coca made me less of a dancer, and more, "damn I love this song… now where's my push?" So I was standing up, swaying to the melody and lyrics, "Lord, have you seen the homeless daughter… standing there with broken wings?" Scrambling, I was, to find my push. When the second set was over, a guy got up on stage, and explained the situation vaguely telling us all to be safe. Those that have an audience recording of the show know this to be true.

I wound up catching a ride with some gutter punks in their van 'cause one of them was a tall redhead who I knew. I'm sorry I can't remember her name though. We all went to North Beach, and me and her snuggled together, keeping each other warm with a thin blanket that was kicked down to us. If she just happens to read this … Hey.

The next morning I woke up in the sand, lucky enough to be with this pretty girl. The beach was cold, yet beautiful. We drove back to the Haight. We found out some late night bro, probably a runner or hubba monster like myself, got stabbed. Our mayor set the curfew for eleven pm, and no one was supposed to be on the streets after that hour. All and all, SF had less damage than LA, and I was just grateful to have survived it. Definitely an experience to remember. If I'm failing to let you know that it was the Rodney King riot…now you know. The media (our right wing media) didn't want the rest of the world to know about the pandemonium that reached as far north as Seattle.

The fucking crazy thing is that the next morning it was business as usual. Just a little clean up was involved. I'd lost everything that I'd been carrying for months and months. All that was left was the Guati wool sweater on my back, and the cords on my legs. Oh yeah, my fucking Berks, of course. Separated from my closest friends, I was, and truly down.

So things looked bleak to me. All I had was the ability to sell nugs or do a mail order. Exhausted, I was, and the sleep on the beach wasn't exactly gratifying. We still had a lot of days left before summer tour began. If I had been smart, I would have looked for some clothes pronto. But I wasn't so smart, so off and running I went, making five bucks here, and ten there, and so on.

Once I got enough money to re-up, I looked for Rosco. He was a black man Brandy was known to run with. Rosco being her pimp and crack partner in crime. It was too early so I didn't find either one of them. They were probably working in the TL, so I took the Masonic bus down the Haight and made my way towards the hot spots the esses worked. I usually didn't have to go straight to Sixteenth and Mission … but that was later.

This went on for a few more weeks before I broke down and called home. Mom and Dad were still married and lived in Kansas City. At this point, I hadn't been taking many baths and still had the same fucking clothes. So I called home and asked if they could help me. Like most good parents they provided me with means to leave the city. I bought a Greyhound ticket one-way to K.C. I was as broke as possible with a ticket only. So, I made a few dollars as a runner, got some herb for the journey and headed downtown to the bus station.

When summer tour came around, I didn't do it in its entirety. I wound up living with my parents just long enough to save enough money to get to Chicago. One thing was for sure, my parents were not getting along. Getting some money and leaving again was my goal. With no car, I walked to the closest businesses and landed two jobs. One was a fast food gig "Sonic" and the other was at a movie theater. They were both in walking distance and, as time passed, sure enough it was summer. My plan was to get on tour starting with Chicago, buy some doses, then eventually go to South Carolina and sell them hit by hit to the custys of the south.

I hopped another Greyhound and headed for Chicago. Once I was there, it business as usual. I didn't even stay the night, after I bought some product. I got on a bus heading east. Once I got to South Carolina, my sister Michelle picked me up. She was living in a small piece of shit trailer north of Spartanburg. The first night we tripped together, while her daughter Melissa slept. Michelle was very depressed, and she seemed very happy to see me. She spoke of troubles and what was going on in her life. She had my old car so the next day we went to Jim Minchow's place and the following day we went to Donald Dorn's in Greenwood, SC. Donald is a tall and thin bro with brown hair. Not short, yet not long. He was living with Rene, my other blood sister. Donald and I lived together as roommates in '91 when he met my sisters. My blood sisters are fraternal twins.

I unloaded all the doses I had in no time. I was off tour, but with money. The Jerry Garcia Band came to Charlotte, N.C. just shortly after this. Both of my twin sisters went to that show, including Paula Scruggs, a friend from High School, Donald Dorn, and me, of course. Now get this, there was a jail underneath the coliseum. While Donald and I were walking around the lot, some bro kicked down a shit load of blank doses to Don. Why, I don't know. We jumped in the blue Honda to puff a bowl and gaze at the paper.

A few seconds later there were two sketchy fuckers tapping the window saying, "Hey, you got doses?"

"No," I exclaimed and that's when he broke out his badge and Donald and I were escorted to the busting grounds (under the coliseum). From the coliseum jail, they took Donald downtown since he possessed the paper. They let me go right about the time the show was over.

When everyone got back to the car, I explained the whole thing. All we could do was wait. Both Donald and I knew the doses were bunk, but Charlotte's finest did not. They analyzed them and still tried to give him a bogus charge but they couldn't. They had to let him go. He walked all the way back to the coliseum from the downtown police headquarters. Now, you have to remember concert security was clearing the lot and we were in the last car left. All of us were about to give up when we saw Donald walking toward us from a distance.

I didn't really do much on summer tour of '92. The big shock, for all of us, was that there was no fall tour that year. Apparently, Jerry was working on his health. Quit smoking cigarettes and started exercising. All I knew was I was out of a job, and I was fucking homesick. So I stayed on couches and bummed around for months until we got through most of the winter. The fall and rise of it all.

I got another backpack and more clothes thanks to Goodwill and prepared myself for change. Living with Michelle, who was also smoking crack as a result of her boyfriend, was bringing me down. Tired of the shit kickin' redneck, crack scene, I was. So I had to go, winter wasn't quite over yet, but I knew if I stayed, things would get worse. Michelle and I actually got in a fight and I wound up smacking her on her face. I had never hit a woman before. Yeah, it was time to go.

1993

I got on I-20 west, and the first people that picked me up were driving a stolen car. They had a gun they were fondling in the front seat, and they were smoking crack. You got to remember, I'm trying to pull a "geographic" to get away from the crack.

Getting picked up and then running out of dope by the time we got to Atlanta meant we had to re-up. They pulled into a crack area and asked for some hubbas. Poor guy at the window produced four or five little baggies filled with love. That's when the dude in the passenger seat pulled out the gun. The black guy didn't give a fuck and tried to grab his shit back, and the driver floored it. We dragged the man for a least a block before he finally let go. I'm just trying to get home. Why am I here? I think to myself.

They got back on the highway heading towards Mobile, Alabama. You might say I was a bit quiet in the back seat. As we drove, the sun started to come up, and his gas gauge was on low. An hour or so outside of Mobile, we pulled into a gas station to steal gas. They wanted me to distract them, so I grabbed my backpack yet left my Guati blanket, a gut feeling. Went inside, I did, to talk to the guy at the counter as they filled their tank. It all happened so fast they sped away leaving me without my blanket. I had to tell the clerk I was just hitching a ride and didn't know anything about it.

There I was, once again thumb in the air, waiting. It was cold as fuck that morning, but I was just grateful I was safe and closer to my destination. I walked miles, in the cold morning dew, on the side of the highway, with my thumb still in the air. Hungry I was. Eventually the classic thing happened, an old station wagon pulled over. There was an old man and his wife sitting in the front seat smiling. He told me to get in and I did.

They were Christian souls helping a Pagan. Not much talking was involved. They were wise. Took me as far as they could and gave me some money. When they let me out and went their way, I stood there and cried. I can't win for trying. I could have waited for tour to come to me. I was smoking coke too much. I thought if I left, at the very least, it would give me a break from the madness, what irony.

I trudged on ride after ride and changed course to go home to my parents in Kansas City. Once I got there, I rested for a few days. The weather was bad as well. My dad and I had our typical argument, yet I talked him out of some money and a ride down to I-40. Problem was, the weather was still bad. The drive down to the 40 was no picnic. An hour into it, the snow flurries became a fucking blizzard.

My dad says, "Look at this son, this is crazy, it's a blizzard and you want me to let you out on a exit"? There was no turning back. When we got down to I-40, we hugged and he let me go. It was zero visibility and I had my thumb in the air. Many miles I walked before somebody actually saw me through the snow and pulled over.

The folks that picked me up finally said, "Oklahoma City is as far as we are going."

I replied, "Thank you, that will do." They dropped me off five or ten miles outside the city and I walked on down the hall. I kept walking, with my thumb in the air, then the highway started to change.

As you enter Oklahoma City, the interstate is actually lifted above the city. Once this began, there was no room to even pull over and pick somebody up. My luck, that last ride lived on the east side. So I walked on the 40, on this bridge-like highway, through the entire city.

At least I got through the blizzard. Clouds were allowing the sunshine to poke through. The day was pretty, at least. Then I saw, first hand, the Federal Building that was bombed. Nothing was like seeing half a fucking building that had just been bombed. If you just stared long enough, you would see something fall off and hit the bottom. It was an experience, being there to see that, but for the love of God, I'm just trying to get off this elevated highway.

All I could do was walk and hope this madness would end soon. About an hour later the highway went back to normal as you left the city. Now, there was a pull over and a chance for someone to take pity on me and pull the fuck over. It was getting dark and it was hard for vehicles to see you of course. Like all things that pass, so did this. A truck pulled over. It was a single axle truck for smaller deliveries. The driver opened the passenger side, and said, "I usually don't pull over due to insurance; however, where you heading?"

I said, "San Francisco" and hoisted my backpack up to his cab and climbed in. When we got to Bakersfield, I had to look at my map and see what was best from here. Getting to Interstate 5 and going north was my goal. The driver set me out at an appropriate place to hitch. As I went from this point, catching rides wasn't so difficult.

I was in SF by the morning. I jumped on the Masonic bus and headed towards Ashbury. I found someone with weight to work so I started "making the donuts." My goal was to be with family in an Oakland motel, with floor space, by midnight. That's exactly what happened.

The boys were playing in Oaktown for a couple days starting the next day. So I was given some product to work. That being buds and doses only. I sold everything and felt rich.

Instead of doing the right thing, I didn't. The right thing would have been to get with the kids, find out where we were sleeping, etc. I had some money, so I left the Shakedown and got on the Bart heading back to the shitty. As I entered the train, to my right sat a beautiful girl. "Can I sit next to you?" I asked.

She said, "yes, of course."

"Why is a pretty sister, such as yourself, leaving a Dead show alone?"
She replied, "I lost my friends that I came with, so I'm going back to our hotel."

"Where is it?" I asked.

"It's off Market Street, dowtown."

Then I got smooth and said, "I've got a room close to your hotel. I'll walk with you. The TL can be dangerous." She said cool and we chatted on the ride back. We eventually got off the Bart, and I walked her to her hotel. Her name was Lauren. She lived in Tucsan, AZ on campus.

I gave her a hug and was about to leave when she turned to me looked me in the eyes and said, "You want to hang out with me tomorrow?"

"Fuck Yeah," I said.

"Meet me at the Fountain at 12:00, okay, on Market Street near Carls Jr's." That sounded cool. I told her I'd be there. Nevertheless, she was a summer tour betty, as they say, and I had an itch to scratch. I don't think she was into the hard shit like Brandy, I, and many others in our family.

I was hoping to bump into Brandy and party. She was the only sister, I knew of, that would have indulged with me. She was nowhere to be found on the upper Haight. I figured she was working lower Haight or the TL. She was still nowhere to be found. Even as I purchased crack, from some random esse working off Market Street, I looked left to right. I went into a corner store bought a pack of cigs and a couple crack pipes that were on the counter with brillo inside, all ready to go. I walked down the street to a GA (General Assistance) crack motel paid my twenty bucks and went to my room. Five minutes later, I was smoking.

That first hit was glorious, and the second one was like the first. I should have stopped there, just to test its potency. But I didn't, I kept on smoking like I was on death row. All of a sudden I got a deep pain in my chest. My breathing became sporadic. Fear set in. I thought "I'm having a heart attack."

Like a child, I balled up in a fetal position. My left arm and fingers went completely numb. As I laid there on the filthy ground, I concentrated on my breathing. Anytime I pulled too much air in, it hurt! So I tried to speak, breathing ever so slightly. And with every breath I asked God not to take me yet, at least not this way.

I laid there praying for hours, promising, "I'll never do it again. Just let me live." My left arm and fingers started to tingle and show signs of life. From the corner of my eye I could see the sun rising through the blinds. "How long had I been laying here? Fuck has it been four hours?" I thought to myself. I very slowing began to pick myself up. So I sat there on the bed looking out the window. There was still a good bit left on the table. Another hour passed. Didn't I just promise God I wasn't gonna smoke crack again?

Well, I broke that promise thirty minutes later. It was already nine in the morning, didn't I have some sort of date at noon? I was three blocks away from the fountain. Most of the money I'd managed to make on Oakland's Shakedown, I'd already spent. I checked out at eleven and walked up to the fountain. This was a day, in the city of San Francisco, that all those who lived there adored. Absolutely beautiful. The sun was shining, cutting its rays through a number of clouds, and then I saw her. There she was, an hour earlier than to be expected. It was an amazing site. No shit, the clouds shifted pouring rays of sunshine perfectly on her. She was sitting cross- legged reading a book, and at the same time the wind was blowing hair back. Man, I'm telling you, it was right of a Hollywood movie. "Hey, what's up," I said. She jumped up real quick and gave me a big hug.

Then she said, "I've got something for you," she reached into her Guati pouch and handed me a ticket. "Here is your miracle," she said. Speechless, I was, to say the least.

I told her, "do you mind if we go to the Haight? I've got to make some money." I mentioned a guitar was stashed, that was kicked down to me, and she could play while I worked. Her eyes lit up with a glaze and she said, "Oh really, lets go!" So we got on the bus to the upper Haight. We got out on the corner of Masonic. I took her to the squat where the guitar was stashed and led her back to the corner Asbury to play next to Ben & Jerry's. I worked my magic, made quick money in about an hour, and we headed back to Oakland.

Not to drop subject, yet my hair was very natty. I had dreads, some that were huge and others that were medium. No one had helped me separate the dreads yet. It can be painful. I'll get to that later.

When we got there, everyone was there. Lauren saw how I worked on the Haight; however, I did so well so quick 'cause all my friends were on the Dead lot working. She was impressed that I knew a lot of brothers and sisters. To her, it appeared I was well known and a needed member of the family. Fuck, I was just doing what I do and not going to jail over it.

That night, I traded a ten strip to some random for some great molly, ya know X. Santana got on stage that night with The Boys and played during "Stella Blue." After the show was over, Lauren met up with all her friends. We said our goodbyes and went our separate ways. She said these words to me, "I think you're my soul mate. Please come down to Tuscan and live with me." At that moment, I had a lot of money and I was really high, and girls on X will say such things. She gave me her number.

I called it a couple days later, after another coke binge. Now this girl had her shit together. I had to get out of the city and away from crack. So I got some LSD, "Shields" to be exact, and got on a Greyhound.

When I got to Tuscan, I moved in with Lauren in her co-ed dorm for a few weeks, just long enough swing all my doses on Fourth Ave. and find her in the arms of her old boyfriend who just got into town. Well, I started packing my shit, and Lauren's old boyfriend felt bad. Well, so did Lauren. Anyway, he said if I ever was in Wilmington, Delaware he would let me have his VW Bus. He gave his parents address where it was parked and that was that. So I got on a Greyhound again and headed to the city. My heart did hurt. Spring tour was right around the corner.

Once back home, I felt good. I had money and no intention of doing crack. It's a fucked thing to grow up on tour. All I wanted was that sister by my side going from show to show or wherever. That was my goal in Grateful Dead Land. Not to sell illegal substances for eight years, not to be a crack head, and so on. I'm sure I wasn't alone in this quest.

Brandy was always so unreachable throughout all of this. She was a carbon copy of my behavior. And yes, the family looked down on her and I. Yet in the spring of '93, it was all about moving forward. Brandy stayed in the city. Once the family turns its back on you, you really are alone. If I would have found her right then, I could have been the one to let her back in. Pretty simple deal, you come with me, I pay for it, she gets back to her roots and trust is built. Before ya know it, she's working on tour, not fucking up for her addiction in the city. Well, that never happened, so I went on another spring tour without a betty at my side.

Spring Tour '93

I ran into Phil Lisi in Ohio or Landover, Maryland and rode with him for the majority of spring '93. I threw my shit in his Honda; yes, the same Accord he had in '88. Basically, just pushed play, so to speak. As usual, Phil had some mid-grade Mexican herb and ice cold beer for sale. There was a Coleman stove on this tour with Phil. Basically, I just worked Roach's paper.

Everyone of the nineties kids were on this tour, in full force. There was Kelly Belly aka Kells Bells, The Virginia Crew: Jason Nance and Mariam ect., China Mike, Kathy, Tim(T-Dog) and Beth, Dready Kristy and Cypress, her dog. I'm not sure if Moon was with Kathy yet. I do know Hetzel was definitely out of the picture.

Anyway, we all had jobs, no reason to spare change unless you're the wrecking crew: Fast Eddie, Ira, Jackson, Artie, and Marlina. They would bring in the money. The time of groveling and hovelling was not a reality for any of us. Phil and I were hanging out together like old times. Things had changed drastically, over the years, for me. Phil still lived in Ocean City, NJ with the same haircut, the same tie-dyes, the same everything. Well, I had fucking ropes hanging off my scalp and Lauren in Arizona helped separate them and set 'em up, ya know.

The motel scene was going on before and after each show. No more campsites like back in the day. We stayed in some of the nicest suites across America. Easy to do that when ten people put their money together. Phil would still sleep in his car outside, instead of just grabbing some floor space.

I did a lot of my personal dealing, only with family, in these motels we all stayed in. Being a crackhead runner on the Haight for almost two years kinda hurts your credit in Dead Land. Now I was clean, so my credibility was strong. Kids would front me product, so I was working and making money, yet not as much as Roach was.

Then, finally, in the middle of tour, one of the oldest kids from my growing in Dead Land appeared. Her name was Lucky. When I was fifteen, and still in high school, (Spartan High) Lucky would hang out at DawGones in Spartanburg, SC (which was I believe was one of the last venues River Phoenix played at.) It was where I played out live, sometimes, as well. Anyway, out of all the fucking characters in this fucking book that were close to me, Lucky is the oldest. Rose, Mark Brantly, Mike Kyte, and Funky Phillips were also among the circle. None of these names were full timers except Lucky. She was the only one, besides myself, from the DawGone crew left.

Well, you can guess, she was beautiful. And was she alone? No...Fuck No, she hooked up with some bro from Ohio. I met him on the Haight with Lucky a year before. His name was John. He was a good looking bro, yet he was balding, and I was jealous. John was driving this huge GMC cab with a camper on the back. It was good to see them both. I would also like to say to John, "you got lucky, babe."

John had a connection, so I worked his fluff for three hundred fifty dollars a ten. That would be thirty five cents a hit. So me and Roach were a little competitive. China Mike was working with Roach and had been for some time. It wasn't a big deal. Just shit we got to get rid of. So for the next two tours it stayed that way. I definitely did not eat any more LSD and haven't since. Why? Well, when you play cards like we did with paper, it finds its way in your blood, whether you ate it or not. However, when we got to The Cap Center in Landover, MD, I did some boomers and they played "Dark Star."

When we got down to Atlanta, I met up with this a new sister than just stepped on. She was cute, and she asked Phil and I if she could ride with us. Phil said, "Only if she cleans up." Apparently, she hadn't taken a bath in awhile. She took a shower at the motel we were sharing with others; however, her clothes still smelled foul. Now don't get me wrong, I've had my moments. I usually don't give a fuck, but when you have to roll down the window for air, you say something. Despite her smell, she was beautiful, and I wanted to get laid. Well that's not entirely correct. I wanted to cuddle with a beautiful girl and maybe get a kiss. Just cuddling in each other's arms and sleeping would have been nice.

After her shower, her clothes stayed off, and we got in bed. No floor space that night for us. And we did snuggle, after the love making, I smiled at her and let her know how much I appreciated her company. The next day, we took off for Chapel Hill, NC. That was the next show. She put her clothes back on, of course, and Phil finally exploded. He turned around to the sister in the back and said, "You've got to get some clean clothes, this is fuckin' killing me." Phil was not a drainbro, he was a clean Deady. Like many others, she was as well, but without the extra clothes. So I could tell she knew it and didn't like it any better than Phil, yet she wason tour. Phil and I had done a couple of shows, so we usually had extra clothes.

She started crying and said, "I can't help it." I kept my mouth shut. I was thinking to myself, what sister wouldn't have an extra sundress? The drive with the windows rolled down the whole way sucked. Phil was irate, or jealous, or both. Looking over at him, through the ropes hanging off my scalp, I noticed he still had the same haircut as he did in '88. It was gonna be ok. The tension let up as soon as we puffed.

We arrived at our next venue in Chapel Hill that night. As always, we drove to the closest motels to the concert. We parked, got out, stretched, and started walking around the motel, checking out the scene.

Patches came running around the corner with a balloon in his hand laughing his ass off. "What's up?"

I exclaimed, "Patches!" We hugged, I punched him in the stomach he hit me in my eye…just kidding. I told him the deal so now he knew where to come if needed anything. Patches would get it cheaper through me, only cause I loved him and trusted him. It was good to see him. Either he had just jumped on tour or we kept just missing each other in passing.

That beautiful sister disappeared on us after NC. Then she resurfaced at the end of the tour, and she looked like she just went through a makeover. She had new rave-like clothes, less Deady and more conservative. It was a good makeover, the kind that could swing anything in disguise.

Nevertheless, I was hungry, so was Phil. So we were thinking maybe the nearest Denny's or IHOP. The fact that I had to locate John and Lucky in order to work, was on my mind. Kids were already asking for ten packs, but I hadn't seen them yet. No worries, I will, and I did. The spring tour was coming to an end. "Hellsaw" was the last venue after Abany, NY. Well, I mean Nassau Uniondale, NY.

Once we got to Uniondale, I met up with Little Mikey and Belue. Not everyone's' favorite venue, yet The Boys have played some fantastic shows there. I wanted to get in. I bumped into Michael P. Cohen. (You've seen his work. He designed some of the best Grateful Dead cassette covers for our live collections.) I also ran into Howard Frieberg who, in my opinion, was one of the best tapers we had. He had just installed a DAT player in his van because he purchased a portable DAT to tape with. Now, granted, he still had his Sony D6 cassette recorder as well. He agreed to bring both in and he would give me the master tapes coming off the D6 for the small price of a hook-up on the best nugs on tour. Howie said, "just remember where I parked." So, after the show, I got my masters. From that moment 'till the end, I stayed in contact with him to keep the tape trading flowing.

The entire family stayed in a huge crack hotel in Uniondale near the coliseum. That night I made a huge mistake. Little Mikey came to my room. Yeah, I was rich enough to put it in my name, two beds, ect, ect. Little Mikey was all excited and wanted to try some of this ready rock that was roaming the halls. The prostitutes were selling it. I told Mikey that I didn't advise it, and let him know I'd been clean for a little bit. "Come on Brad, I know you can show me. Don't make me do alone," He said.

"Ok, you twisted my arm," I said. Little Mikey gave me some money and I returned with what he wanted. We had no glass stem, so I told him to find a can and he did, I put a dent in it, made some holes, and put cigarette ashes on top of the holes. Then I placed a big piece on top of the ashes, took the first hit, and handed it to him. After his first small hit, I replaced the ashes with fresh ashes and placed a rock on top then gave it to Mikey. He put the fire to the rock, watched it melt into the ashes, and the smoke followed. It was a nice size, so I made him exhale. Apparently, he wanted to hold in every ounce of smoke. His eyes lit up, like I'd never seen them before and then he smiled. Please forgive me, those that knew him. From that moment, he was never the same.

"Lets get more!" he said.

"No thanks, I'm working, I've gotta keep my head on straight." Mikey left my room, and once he walked out that door, he forever was known as "Crackhead Mike" to most family. But he was still just Mikey to me. I suppose I created another monster, and I'm really sorry for that. I loved Mikey. I didn't mean it, but it just happened. No justification, nobody's fault, but mine. Being that it was the end of the tour, I was tired. I was tired of not having any wheels and there was a VW Bus waiting for me in Wilmington, Delaware. Most kids were scrambling on the last day to catch rides back to the shitty. Belue was willing to ride with me and Phil to Delaware. Phil agreed to help us get there, being that he lived in Ocean City. So, it wasn't too far out of his way. In the parking lot, we all hugged and said our goodbyes.

When we got to Wilmington, finding Lauren's boyfriend's parents' house was easy enough. It was just like he said it was, taking up space in their driveway. His dad was so happy we were there to take it. He kicked it down for free; however, I had money so I gave them two hundred dollars.

The battery was dead just like he told me it was. His father put a charger on it. While it charged, his dad offered us his shower facilities. We took him up on his offer, and I gaffled a clean pair of boxers out of his son's dresser.

Eventually, I went back outside where good old Phil was patiently waiting. The keys were in the ignition of the bus. I turned the key. The engine turned over a few times with a sputter here and there. It finally started with a bang. We let it sit there and idle, to let the battery charge. The tag had expired in '91. We put one of those black wraparound license plate covers and it covered the number just enough.

It was a great transporter VW Bus. It was a 1976, modified to fit the super upright single carb engine. So it had the small engine that everyone loves to work on, compared to the flat pancake series. Phil was happy to see this didn't turn out to be a nightmare 'cause it could have. I'm sure he was skeptical. Belue and I said our goodbyes to Phil, then we moved our shit to the new house on wheels.

I followed Phil out of the city and back onto the highway. I still had product to unload before we got back to SF, so we headed south. If you could have seen the look on our faces, it was classic. We had nugs, doses, and a new ride to go along with it. (Thank you Lauren for the experience!)

First we visited Jimbo in Spartanburg, SC and unloaded some "L" on him. I gave Jim a good bit for a good price and then we drove down to Greenwood, SC where Donald Dorn lived. He and my sister Rene lived together. When we got to Greenwood, Donald had met some girl who was moving out of her house and selling everything. She wanted to ride with us to the bay. She was cute and had gas money, so she jumped on the bus.

On interstate 40, in Tennessee, the engine blew up. We made it as far as Lebannon, Tenn. Luckily for us, just a few miles down the road from where we had the bus towed, was a VW junkyard. This kind owner sold us a rebuilt super beetle upright for four hundred dollars. Now, the mechanics at the Phillips 66 installed the engine. While they were installing the 4 main bolts to the transmission, I was having sex with this betty in the bathroom. When the bus was fixed, we payed the bill; however, they wanted us to replace the sink in the bathroom. (We kinda broke it.) I didn't know what the fuck they were talking about and off we went.

On the road again, we had less money in my pockets than I'd like. Had a new rebuilt engine and I got laid. I liked the "got laid part." We finally got home, I circled the Panhandle and eventually found a spot. She wanted to stay in the bus with me exclusively, yet she wasn't Brandy. Street smart she was not, and being my girlfriend wasn't part of the deal. Shit, I was just glad to be back. She had no idea I'd had my eye on another since day one. If I could only get Brandy to say the same words as this sister and stay the hell away from Rosco wouldn't that be great. How in the fuck was I suppose to tell her that I was secretly in love with Brandy, who now seemed like a prostitute, and she was my inspiration to keep pushing on, in hope of our uniting one day.

Well, I explained my situation, as best as I could, keeping us as friends. She kept her stuff in my van until another bro or sister came along. (That girl, I heard, is now married and lives on a garlic farm and is very happy.) Anyway, I headed to the bench near the bathrooms in the Panhandle. There sat Teddy (San Diego Crew). I bought some weight from him and went up the hill to the street. A lot of kids were just getting there as well. Fast Eddie walked by me without a word. The wrecking crew was near, obviously.

According to the kids, Vegas, Mountain View, and Cal Expo were next. After these events "Laguna Seca Daze" was next which had Blues Traveler, The Almond Brothers and others.

Later in the day, I saw Jason Nance and Mariam. We walked down to my new bus to puff. Just as we were entering the bus, a motorcycle police officer rolls up. He shifted his attention to Mariam and asked her to empty her pockets. She pulled out her personal head nugs so the officer just emptied the bag on the ground. Then, of course, he wrote her a thirty-eight dollar ticket and told her to carry on. We puffed, once it was clear, and they both asked if they could start riding with me in the new bus. All of us worked on the Haight for next week saving our money for the Vegas trip and then we left.

Vegas '93

To talk about Vegas would probably be smart. We stayed at The Marriott. All of us pitched in on a suite. While we were getting our gear out of the bus, a girl approached me that I didn't automatically recognize. Then, in a flash, I remembered her. She was one of Lauren's friends from Tuscan, AZ. The night I walked in on Lauren and her old boyfriend making out on somebody's random couch, I walked out immediately. I just got on the road and started walking. Well in less than five minutes, this sister picked me up in her VW Rabbit and took me back to the campus to get my stuff. She was very comforting and I was very grateful for all of her help.

But back to the present, there she was. So I told her of our adventure since I had departed and showed her the bus from the whole experience. We hugged and I told her where we were staying. Up in the room was a Glad garbage bag of laid paper. If you tied it in a knot it would look like its ready to be taken out. That's a lot of fucking LSD. Everyone wanted to go to Circus Circus 'cause they had seventy-five cent Heineken's. "Sluts of fun" is what all the kids were calling it.

Later that night, Belue and I went to another place just to get a bite to eat, and wound up sitting next to Vince Welnick's brother. Vince was playing keys since we lost Brent Mydland. Belue was feeding his face, talking shit about Vince and his song "Samba In The Rain." When his brother, who was sitting on my right, leaned towards us and he said, "Vince has been working really hard." He introduced himself, and Belue did his best not to look like a complete ass. He told us Vince had his whole family staying in the hotel above where we were eating. (Was it the Viking?)

What I did know was we had three days to be here. In Vegas, as all of you know, you can spend your money real easy. I didn't, I saved my ducats. I hung out around the blackjack tables with friends and drank cheap. Maybe I pulled a slot or two, but I mainly just handled business. I was sellin' ten packs to family for generally thirty-five to four hundred a piece. I no longer hung out on the lot looking for a custy on the Shakedown. We raged in Vegas, oh yes.

Then on to Mountain View, CA. which is the Shoreline Amphitheater. I wish I had more to tell. Cal Expo was when our bus became "Disco Bus Number 2." The first disco bus was broken into and their equipment was stolen. We used to dance outside their bus.

While in Sacramento at Cal Expo, I purchased a pair of twelve inch, box style speakers and an amp to go with it. We were given a lot of the tapes from the original bus, so it was on. Not only were we pumping out the jam, but I met up with Howard Frieberg again, who, as you know, is the shit. One of the best tapers we had. So once again I was helping Howie get the best bud for master tapes of the shows and we were breaking it off in the parking lot after the show.

One of the fun memories of Expo in the summer of '93, was this bro that had dry ice with Ben & Jerry's ice cream. It was a hot and muggy day. That ice cream wasn't holding up so they were selling pints for a dollar. The whole fucking family of the Expo's Shakedown were eating Ben & Jerry's. Hell, it was going to melt. Good times and Bobby played his acoustic during the first set on "Cassidy." Phil did a version of "Broken

Arrow" that is a favorite of mine to this very day. Jerry's "Deal" was nasty, nasty. Outside of that, there were good friends and family, especially at this venue.

Laguna Seca Daze

Until fall tour, there were no more Dead shows except Jerry playing downtown at the Warfield. There was a festival after Cal Expo that a lot of Deadheads went to. Blues Traveler, Phish, The Almond Brothers Band and many more were there. It was a full on amphitheater, kinda like Alpine Valley, in a way, yet you were allowed to camp all around it.

It was just like the old days with the Dead, up till '89 fall tour. Problem was, we were at a west coast function, not at an east coast festival. Laguna Beach has plenty of everything, apparently. Well they did when we went there.

Jason and Mariam plus Belue rode with me. We bought a fucking quarter pound of boomers and bagged it up. We walked around that whole scene from tent to tent hearing the same thing, "Don't need it bro already got some." Whatever that was. It didn't matter, I believe it cost more to experience this event.

I have one good memory that was cool, yet the more I write this book, the more I question myself. I sound like a whore. Why? Cause the only redeeming qualities of this venture was this: I'm sitting next to my van, blasting out disco, kids were dancing all around me, and I was rather bummed out.

Some random girl walked right up and offered me a beer. Ten minutes later we were fucking in the back of the bus while it's cranking out disco music. All of a sudden, it started to pour down rain. Jason, Marriam, Belue, and someone else jumped in the front and they started cheering me on. That poor sisiter wasn't expecting that, I'm sure, nevertheless, I had to finish. I hadn't had any sex since the sink episode in Tennessee.

See I am a fuckin' whore. Or I'm just your typical man getting it when he I can. I'm not certain for the whole population of men, but one thing is certain, I was looking for that sister that stands by you city to city and shitty deal to shitty deal. What I wanted wasn't attainable at that moment. So I suppose I did what most do, "love the one your with." And sometimes it can seem a bit sleazy.

Summer Tour '93

Like usual, before any tour, you round up a posse. Mine consisted of Jason Nance, Belue, Tim and Beth. Nobody wanted to go to NJ to start, so we headed for Hebron, Ohio, Buckeye Lake. This was a fun outdoor venue with grass. I met up with John and Lucky almost immediately. They were still in their old camper truck, and John told me we had a lot of work to do.

This venue was hotter than hot. I sold lots of "L" blah, blah, blah. The story will continue on, same as the tour before. The current family of the Dead was in full force. Mouse and Beth (I want to say Beth but I could be wrong), Roach, China Mike, the fucking Wrecking Crew (90-95), Kathy, The Virginia Beach Crew, Kelly Belly, Honduras Allan, my crew: Tim and Beth, James (Sparkle), Jason and Mariam, Crack Head Mickey, Dennis and Smiley Mike, Todd and Emily and their dog Dakota, even Abe, I believe, and so many others associated with us. You know who you are if your reading this.

There was lots of love on this summer tour. We went from Buffalo, NY to Kentucky. Then things started to unravel, or just get plain fun, around Chicago. Some locals had rented out the nicest presidential suite next to Tinley Park, so our little posse definitely raged that place. John and Lucky were parked near this hotel so that was convenient.

It was here that I opened up the future for Honduras Allan. I introduced him to John in that parking lot at their truck. Good thing for Allan. Now he didn't have to go through me. I did it mainly cause we needed the help to move the paper. At that very moment we had fluff. The print was Snow Men and Purple Jesus.

On the last night in Chicago, Tim, Patches, Jason, and I got a hold of sixty pound Nitrous tank at the Ramada Inn. The locals that had it did about half the tank, but they were sketchin' out about having it in their room. So Tim and the rest of the Jim Beam crew put a blanket on it and rushed to the elevator. (Tim talked us into drinking a whole bottle of Beam and decided, for the night, that's what we would be called.)

There was a room, a couple floors up, that we had a key to. So there we stood, all paranoid with this huge tank waiting for the elevator to get to our suite. Finally, we got there without getting caught. The rest of the night consisted of huffing gas until our lips were blue. We watched the sun come up. Hippie crack in full action.

Mouse was staying at another motel waiting for a Package (vacuum sealed full of Mexican swag) from Sky in So. Cal. Everyone somehow already knew of the package coming so picking it up was a huge sketch. I know something bad came of it, yet I don't have the details.

With no sleep that morning, we rounded up our crew and headed for Noblesville, Indiana, that would be Deer Creek. Indianapolis was south, a few miles, from the venue. So we checked into the Embassy Suites. Once settled in, all of us of loaded back up in the bus and drove down to Deer Creek. As we got closer to the entrance, like all shows, there was a huge and slow line of vehicles backed up on the road. We saw a couple friends walking along the traffic and they jumped on the side of the bus. We were already full, as people goes, but we did manage to get in the Dead lot, in Buckeye Lake, you have to be in a vehicle of some sort.

They let us in, despite that we had too many people. Unfortunately, all the fun we'd had and crazy shit we'd experienced, up to this point in life on tour, was starting to show in our behavior. The parking staff was directing where they wanted us to park, but everyone kept telling me to fuck them. We wanted to park on grass and they kept directing us to the gravel area. Well, to sum it up, they kicked us out. Well they at least kicked my bus out, so I went back to my presidential suite and relaxed while the rest of my family would come to me for ten packs or "gers" (a gram of LSD in crystal/powder form, not broken down yet.).

We had one more show to go to after Deer Creek. RFK stadium in Washington, DC was the last for this summer tour. When we got to DC, we did the same as we always did and before you knew it we were wandering the lot of RFK Stadium.

It was a concrete jungle. No grass, as parking went. Hotter than shit, it was blaring off the pavement. I re-upped with John, once I found him. We didn't have cell phones so you just wondered around until you found what or who your looking for. China Mike and I hung out mainly in Washington. He was swinging Roach's paper and I was swinging John's.

As we were walking on the gravel lot, Fast Eddie walked up to me and China. He said, "You are the next soldiers." Then walked off into the tie-dye madness. We were on our second day, and the last day at that, for the summer tour. I was just basically swingin' as much weight as I could, same as Mike for Roach, before we had to go back to San Francisco.

After exhausting all of our efforts to sell as much paper as we could, the day was over. Rick and Mike (who were head of Grateful Dead security) were on their golf cart screaming into their bullhorn the same words we always hear, "Time to go home! Pack it up!" I still had five or six ten packs in my possession and they were mine. So what I had was payed for; John and I settled up. At the motels, where most of the family was staying, kids going back west to the city were going through motions, as catching rides go.

Being that I still had a lot of product left, I decided to go to the south where I went to high school back in the day and unload what I had left. Mariam didn't like that, so she decided to catch another ride back to Chicago then the city. Jason Nance decided to stay and so did Belue. Jason must have gone to high school in Virginia 'cause he thought going south was a good idea as long as we stopped at Virgina Beach first. I agreed and we did just that. Jason unloaded everything he had and his people wanted what I had. I knew I could tax my people in Spartanburg, SC a little bit more, so I declined selling my shit. Plus it was a tradition for me. After any east coast shows, I would go to the southern region and sell my shit to my people just like Jason had done.

So we loaded up the wagon and headed for South Carolina. Once there, I checked into the Camelot Motel. It was June 29, 1993. Kim was one of the kids on tour with us. She came by and I sold her one of two ten packs. She had a friend with her, but I don't remember her name. Kim eventually dated Roach, later in life. I first met her when she dated Brad, who was also from South Carolina. When she invited me into Brad's brand new Blue VW Vanagon bus to puff some really nice nugs, she wasn't with him. Word was he got real tweaked out and ran home to be a Christian, just hearsay.

Jimbo came by my motel room and picked up the last of my weight. I now had a quarter of a single sheet, not perforated, that was used to mop up the last of the liquid LSD that was left in the glass pan.

Once my sister's boyfriend caught wind I was in town, he rented a room in the same motel. His name is Chucky Trent and he was one of the reasons I left that area in the first place. He was still smoking crack and he had Michelle smoking it with him. Being that I had some clean time from the hard shit, I didn't want to advocate the crack addiction, so I refused to sell to him. What I didn't know was he had been turning in people to stay out of jail; they call them a CRI (Confidential Reliable Informant). Hours later, after leaving my head stash on the night stand in the room. I returned with beer, only to have a gun shoved in my face as I opened my van door. Lucky for me, the day before all this happened I purchased a blue Chevy Van with captain chairs for a thousand cash, and put it in my sister's name.

Yes, I went to jail so did Jason and Belue. Yet, when I did get out I had a nice Chevy waiting. Chucky Trent sold my VW. My sister managed to keep my Chevy safe. Jason had probation he'd blown off in Virginia Beach. Belue had no warrants and was released.

I claimed my hits and Jason claimed his. He had about ninety hits on him but they were ALD, so when they did the LSD test, it was negative. So, if it hadn't been for that warrant in Virginia Beach, Jason would have been released with Belue.

They extradited Jason and gave me five years suspended down to nine months and five years probation. It cost me a lot for this deal. I hired a tough attorney. Jimbo walked into his office and payed him in cash. The product I gave him right before they busted me, I had fronted to him. He sold it in one day and had the money. So I lost my family, my VW Bus, but I still had a kick ass Chevy van with current tags. I had no money; they took thousands from me.

I could tell you how it was being locked up; however, this book isn't about how it is to be locked up. I wound up doing about six and a half months, then I was released. My parents actually moved to Clinton, SC so they could visit me while I was incarcerated during the last months and when I was released to do the five years probation, I started living with them. Great plan, right? Yeah, it looked good for a judge.

I could talk about how it was to travel with the personal crew and personal friends of The Grateful Dead, but I didn't travel with Rick and Mike (Security) and their staff. I wasn't backstage every show. What I lived, among so many others, throughout the years on the Haight and Dead tour, is all I have to write about. I'm pretty sure there was another Token Brad that experienced a lot of the same things, yet the story was never told of how it is to be apart of "The Family." The fucking family were those whom you've read about. Not people who partied with the band members after a show. Some Haight family got to hang out with Jerry and Bob, granted, but most real family members were on the Shakedown or at the motel closest to the venue, working whatever product they had. Those that had box seats at every show or back stage at every venue, I did not know. I had box seats once at the palace back in '92. However, this is the real story of "Grateful Dead Family" so listen up.

I still had a kick ass Chevy van with current tags. I had no money; they took thousands from me. I got a job at pizza hut in Clinton, SC. When I got my first paycheck, I cashed it and filled up the tank. I had about two hundred dollars. Whether it was enough or not was irrelevant. I had a little less than two bills in my pocket, right, so I packed a lot of bread, a jar of peanut butter, and some water.

1994

I took off heading west towards the bay. One, I was breaking my
probation which took thousands of dollars for me to even be free at that very
moment. Not to mention cutting off my dreads with a disposable razor
before I saw the judge. Two, I had a lot of unfinished business to attend to,
that would be my name. I cared what my people thought of me and I had
turned on no one. I did a small amount of time with a lot of hard core
probation ahead of me in this God forsaken state they call South Carolina. I
wasn't going to let them slander my name when I was true to the game.

I drove two and half days with no sleep. Urinating only at gas stops
or in a bottle, as I drove. Living only on water and peanut butter
sandwiches. I ran out of money in Bakersfield, Ca. and I coasted into the

Safeway parking lot on fumes. This the same fucking parking lot I've visited before under the same circumstances, but I didn't have a pretty betty bringing in the money, spare changing that is.

I was exhausted. I just sat there, in the drivers seat with the window rolled down hanging my head out of it breathing in fresh air. I must have really looked like shit because a couple that was coming out of Safeway with their groceries asked me if I was alright. They were parked next to me. As they unloaded I told them I was trying to make my way to the bay and I had just run out of gas money. I was super low on food as well but didn't tell them. From the looks of me they could tell.

The lady told the man with her to give me a twenty and he did. I put exactly twenty dollars in gas in the tank. I got on the 99 briefly until I could connect with Interstate 5 going north. Looking at the gas gauge, all the way up to the shitty. Miraculous enough, I actually made it into San Francisco around five or six in the afternoon with the gas gauge below E.

I found a parking spot on the Panhandle. Like a program, I climbed up the hill to the street. I'm broke for starters and I haven't slept for shit. Within minutes I was surrounded by all my friends, yet they were not looking at me as one of them. Mariam was the first to speak, due to the fact her boy got busted with me.

She said, "I heard you turned in Jason!" and then she flipped me off. Then some bro, also called Jason and from the Virginia Beach crew, started in on me. All my fucking hair was gone and I looked like a fuckin' custy or narc. That, of course, wasn't the case nor were these allegations true.

So my first days back were strange. I did just show up in a new van that was sweet, and I had to prove, by my actions, that I was being honest. Belue cut his fucking hair too, but it wasn't that long anyway. He was a part of that mob of hippies. He was looking good with new threads, new shoes, ect. He kept his mouth shut. He knew damn well Jason was extradited back to Virginia because his fingertips got him busted, not me. This was all addressed, believe you me, in the hours left of daylight. If I didn't mention it, all of this occurred in front of "The Coffee Zone" on the corner of Masonic and Haight. I'm sure the name has since changed.

After everyone lightened up, which they did, I showed Mariam the new ride. Belue had already seen it because he was with me when I bought it. So my story jived, bottom line, and I had a brand new Chevy Van with captain chairs. Not to mention it had a rocking sound system in it. By that night I was driving kids across the water to Motel six up.

I played the part of a runner and made some money by selling several heighths. It was good to be home. I ate well that night and smoked lots of good bud, some that I saved from being the middleman and other random ganja being shared in the room. Yeah, when you got wheels its funny how people can quickly forget, or at least suppress their inner emotions for the things they feel.

Things were different in this room with my old comrades on this night. Kathy, our sweet, red headed, dready beauty, was smoking cheeva off some tin foil from a crunch bar. They don't come with the aluminum anymore. (Cheeva is how it sounds. Spanish for heroin or black tar, more than likely from down south.)

In that year, in the San Francisco bay, Lollo was the big guy in the heroin world. Rumor had it that Jerry was doing the same dope as the kids. Rumors can get out of control; nevertheless, the main port and supply for the bay area seemed to be coming from one source. So you do the math.

I'm pretty sure I "chased the dragon" with Kathy that night. She showed me how to do it on the foil. Kathy did not shoot it at that point. I hadn't done it since that time with China Mike back in Santa Cruz in '92. So apparently, while I was gone for nine months, the kids had changed. On summer tour, and in jail, Jason would say he was dope sick, yet I didn't quite pick up on what was slowly going on around me. The family kids, that would give me shit for smoking crack just a year ago, were now smoking black tar or shooting it up, when I got back. Why this was more acceptable is strange.

There were a couple of Jerry Garcia Band shows playing at the Warfield downtown, and in a month spring tour would be starting. Getting back on top was my goal. Swinging heighths on the Haight was all I could do to get ready. With the new van I had riders for sure for spring tour '94. It was the same crew as usual. I don't think I need to mention names again.

Before we left for tour, I started doing what all my friends were doing...heroin. I just smoked it off tin foil until a day or two before we left. The van was parked at the top of Buena Vista West. That would be the park on your left as you enter the upper Haight before Masonic Streeet. It was that night Smiley Rob, while we were driving to Oakland to the Sleazy Eight Motel, shot me up with a needle for the first time. Mariam hated my driving and always gave me shit when I drove. She had good reason, I am near sighted. (I lost my glasses years before I even started touring.) At this very moment, Mariam was aware of what was going on, so she took the wheel and, as we left Buena West, Rob gave me my first intravenous experience. The van was loaded with friends as I sailed down the Haight in a euphoria I'd never felt before. I looked at Rob and said this, "Oh, I didn't know, so this is what I've been missing." That was the beginning.

Do you wonder why? You have to understand, I just blew off five years of probation in South Carolina and that would make it very sketchy for me to even visit my parents. Depression and deadication was the reason. Would you jump off a bridge if everyone else was? Yes, if you loved your friends like I did. My name was known and it was very important to me that all the allegations and lies were squelched. I'm aware I didn't have to shoot up heroin to prove shit, but I did anyway.

Spring Tour '94

We started out the tour in Oakland, then drove down to Arizona. Desert Sky Pavilion was the venue in Phoenix. It was a fucked up way to begin for me. Being that John and Lucky were not at this venue, I wasn't selling paper. That's due to the fact that they lived in Ohio and generally didn't go back to the Bay in between tour like the rest of us. So I was expecting to meet up with them at the next stop in Illinois. Rosemont Horizon to be exact. However, I had to get there first. All I had to work with was somebody else's paper and buds. So I sold nugs.

The problem was this fucking venue was in a zero tolerance state and the lot was swarming with undercover cops. I walked by a custy and muttered the words "Buds" and bro turned around. He told me he was looking, so I handed him a three gram eighth for fifty. He gave me a fifty dollar bill. Then immediately two undercovers grabbed me and the young man that I just sold the bud to. They walked him ahead of me while the officer held my arm. You could here them already working the kid with there tactics. While this is going down, the officer holding me said, "Don't even think about running, we've got you cold busted."

Well, I actually hadn't thought about it until he said it. So I do thank him for planting the seed. These undercovers were all wearing white Reeboks running shoes. So they were also ready to run themselves. Guess what? I pulled away from his hold with all the energy I had.

I managed to break free and took off running towards the Shakedown. He was so close I could feel his breath on the back of my neck as I ran. Yet he was in our playground now. As I ran harder and deeper into the crowd of the Shakedown the family of the Dead and the locals helped me out by creating congestion. I no longer felt his presence directly behind me. I knew he wasn't too far behind though.

As I passed the Tattoo school bus I ducked under another school bus parked next to it. Laying down on my stomach, I watched two men run pass the bus I was hiding under. The white Reeboks were a dead give away. I stayed under that bus crouched down next to a generator that was running and spewing exhaust in my face the whole time. Being that I had just gotten out of fucking jail two months back, I would of stayed there until hell froze over. An hour had passed, at least, and it was getting dark outside, so I was willing to risk coming out of hiding.

Quickly I climbed out from under the school bus and wiggled my way into the Shakedown among the rest of the sheep. Scared as shit, I was, and the Shakedown was clearing. Yes, I made it back to my van. There I sat in silence for another hour or so until everyone showed back up at the end of the night.

This was the second night in Phoenix, so when I explained what happened, I had no intentions of coming to this lot tomorrow. I stayed in the motel, on the third day, and looked forward to leaving. I watched some TV, smoked some ganja, and thanked my lucky stars for the ability to do that.

We got on the road heading east the next morning. When we got to Illinois, I finally found John and Lucky. It was business as usual. Nothing really spectacular happened until we went to Uniondale, NY. We did not check into the same crack hotel we did last year. On the island, we found a fairly nice motel with hot tubs. At the show the next day, guess who I ran into, that sister who rode with Phil Lisi and I in '93 (who was a little smelly) and bailed on us. .

Well she was looking good, to say the least. I didn't think she would surface again. Go figure. I told her we had a motel set up that had a hot tub. So the plan was she was going to stay with me after the show. She had a friend, same as I, so after work we all got naked.

Now the bro that was with her friend, I didn't know that well. Crackhead Mikey was in the room too. He wasn't naked. In fact he was smoking crack in the corner as we had sex in this hot tub. Not to be an asshole; however, the dude fucking the betty next to me only had one testicle. She was cool with it. I just never first hand actually saw someone with one ball. Anyway, it was fun. Beats smoking crack in NY like last year.

So we had to do even worse this year. Since eighty percent of the family, were either smoking, snorting, or shooting up heroin. Before you knew it, we were in Manhattan looking for Houston and A Streets. This is where you generally cop bundles of white dope. Yep, some things don't change. This is common knowledge to those that know, just like Haight and Ashbury is famous for hooking up with LSD or great ganja. Anyway, we located the hot spot and parked the van. Patches, Dennis, and I went to do the dirty. Let me tell you, hooking up with large quantities of china white at two in the morning isn't fun. Patches had a gun pulled on him in the middle of the deal, and the dealer demanded he do some. You didn't have to twist him arm.

We did get what we wanted. Each bundle of china white was forty dollars. There were ten individual bags per bundle. We got as many bundles as we could afford and bailed. Back at the motel, it was nod city. Each Baggie was labeled "Original." I did a little match head bump in my nose and nodded for hours. When it started to where off I did another bump this time a little bigger than the first. I threw up in minute's time. Not so fun when you overdo it. This shit was so pure it would kill a motherfucker. Patches did the right thing and stepped on it. If he hadn't, we would have had at least one or two OD's before it was over.

So NY this time around was different in many ways. My main product was LSD, yet I sold bags for thirty bucks a piece, once we got to Atlanta, GA. The Omni shows were always fun. We stayed at the Omni Hotel like usual.

Being that I was right next to South Carolina, I was a little nervous. I called my sisters that lived in SC as well as Donald Dorn letting them know I was there. I ran into Donald first. Then he led me to Michelle and Rene. I told Rick and Mike (Grateful Dead Security) my family from SC needed some tickets and they gave them all tickets for free. Very kind guys, I must say. All of us in my van, pitched in for a suite at the Omni Hotel. They were nice; each suite had its own fridge stocked with beer and liquor. They played two nights in Atlanta, and I'm not even sure if I got in. So many shows, so many shows. Had a good time hanging out with Donald and my sisters in the suite. This was after the show, of course.

I mainly stayed in the room. From the room, I could distribute the LSD easier. When someone needed a ten pack or china white, all they had to do was knock. I wasn't the only one burned out on the lot scene. Dennis, Honduras Allan, and Kelly Belly (Kells Bells) would come in and out.

Speaking of Kelly, she was definitely spicing things up that night. Our room had a balcony, same as the room next to us. We were on the second or third floor. The room next to us had a balcony as well, and its sliding door was open. Being that we drank everything in our little fridge, Kelly was drunk enough to stand up on the top of the railing of our balcony and jump to our neighbors balcony. Fucking crazy shit. That was a big leap. The fall alone if she would of missed the jump would have killed her for sure.

Kells Bells was no one to fuck with. She was a beautiful girl with a small belly from all the drinking, I'm sure. She was no small girl granted, yet she wasn't big boned, as they say. I liked her a lot and her inner strength and courage were impressive. We all begged Kelly not to jump, but once she set her mind to do something, she did it. Freaked us all out, it did; however, five minutes later she was in our room with every fucking thing from our neighbor's fridge. No one gave a shit about next door, due to the fact that they were there for The Boys. So we all loved on Kelly for her courageous stunt and consumed what she had gaffled.

To this very day, I still carry the wallet I purchased on the Haight in '92 that Kelly put chrome studs on. Unfortunately, they turned green years later so I removed them. When I pull out my wallet you can still see the small holes where they once were. So I'm reminded everyday of Kells Bells. My family from SC enjoyed themselves and I got to hug my sisters and brother Donald goodbye.

The next stop was Orlando, FL. They played only one night, so there wasn't a lot of excitement, other than Kells Bells starting a riot to get in. I heard about it while in the motel. I don't even remember if I if I stepped one foot on Orlando's lot.

The last venue was Miami. They played three nights there. Tim and Beth, Honduras Allan and Kristy and her son Harley, Dennis, Mike, China Mike, Cathy, and myself stayed at Hotel One Hundred, right on the beach. I don't remember much about the Miami shows other than this. We had all made a lot of money and this was the last show.

I did go to the Miami Arena lot. Regardless of how I felt, I still had to swing as much paper as I could before we went home. Roach and I worked together at this last venue. I helped him get rid of what he had and what John had left. Roach sold out, and then it was just me and Allan left working. When the shows ended, we all went back to the Hotel. Allan broke down a gram of LSD in the room with vodka and soaked each ten pack (one regular size of paper produces ten sheets) until all was gone. Then it was set out to dry.

While all this was going on, everyone else decided to jump in the Atlantic Ocean before we left. Tim and I swam way to far out and almost drowned just trying to get back to the beach. That sucked, won't be trying that again. When we got back in the room. We told our story of stupidity to Allan. He laughed of course.

That was my last tour.

Back To Cali

Aw man, we were tired. The road will take its toll on a body. We had a smooth journey home. No breakdowns or drama to speak of. Just simply back in the city. Being that I was back on the west coast, there's no china white in SF. Now why the fuck would I care? Well, that Manhattan run had launched a new addiction. I wasn't completely aware of how serious I had slowly become dependent on heroin. Little bumps here and there. No big deal right... I wish. I parked on the hill. That would be the top of Buena Vista West. Which was convenient, I could swing nugs easier, I guess.

I had money though and no reason to work at the moment. What I wanted was some cheeva. Allison and Kyle were bay residents that would come up to the Haight to swing the black tar heroin. Maybe they were from Canada, for all I knew. Most folks living in San Francisco were not born and raised there. Allison and Kyle lived in an apartment building a block away from Sixteenth and Mission. So, like I said, they would cop and bring it up to the Haight. Last year, this wasn't the case. I never met or knew of either of these people until now. I walked down to the street from top of the hill.

I asked Kathy where to get some cheeva, and she introduced me to them both. In which I bought a quarter of a gram, and Kyle gave me a clean needle. I had been watching my friends shoot up for a while, so I knew how to do it. Everyone had cleared out of my van besides their personal belongings. Having a place to keep your shit, when you live on the Haight is vital. So yeah, I let my friends store their shit with me. The fact was we'd all be driving across the bridge by dark thirty to sleep in Oakland later anyway.

There was no one in my van to bother me while I broke off a piece of glassy tar to place in a spoon with water. Sometimes it would be gooey, sometimes it would be hard as glass, or a little of both. This was glassy tar I had. I put a lighter under the spoon and it started to melt the tar into the water. I stirred it around with the back of the plunger. That would be the needle, on the push side. As I stirred it, the smell filled the van. The smell of black tar being broke down is hard to put in words. I suppose a real writer could explain it. You will just have to experience it yourself to know.

Now with most things in life, from my perspective, you try it and either you like it or you don't. The majority of people will tell you to never touch heroin. I myself disagree. Opium is a wonderful feeling. This I knew, yet, in the states, that wasn't easy to get. So heroin was the closest to a beautiful thing.

My arms were a junkies dream. Back in the day, I was one of those bro's that had rope like veins up and down my arms. This was the beginning. I could hit my mains on both arms where most professionals in the hospital industry do. It was really easy, just insert the needle in the main, pull back the plunger and watch your blood mix with the heroin. Then push it in slowly.

Yeah, its fucked up to put a needle in your arm to get high, yet it was much more gratifying than smoking crack. There was no crumbling on the floor searching for the piece of rock you swear you dropped. There was no looking out your window, and, of course, there was no telling people to turn down the TV or radio just so you can hear what the fuck is going on outside. I'm here to tell you the reason that so many great people have died as a result of heroin usage, is it's the best feeling this earth will provide, but with a price to pay for such love.

Aaron was a bro that used cheeva as well, and he lived at the corner of Baker and McCallister, which was a few blocks from the Panhandle. Aaron was moving out, and for the first time in two years, I finally had the opportunity to fucking rent an apartment. Guess what, I even had the money, seven hundred and fifty dollars a month. That was a good deal for an apartment on the upper Haight. It had the buzzer type entrance with speaker and doorbell.

So Aaron was bailing on his lease and offered to introduce me to the landlord to take his spot. Sure enough, money talks. All I had to do was wait for a week, and I was moving in. Just to make sure this was a done deal I gave my new landlord the month's rent Aaron wasn't going to pay. Then I headed back to the street to tell everyone. Dude, if you've read this far in this book, you would know how happy I was to finally have a pad.

Baker & McCallister

You know, you meet a lot of new kids when you have your own house in the upper Haight. Having a van to go with it makes it even better. For instance, the days of running around all night long on the streets to see the sunrise in the morning, and ending up on Waller at the free kitchen were over.

I stopped entertaining the thought that Brandi and I were ever going to be together. Especially since I stopped smoking crack and going for days without sleep. The times of running into her and sharing our shit seemed like just a memory. My feelings for her never really changed, I just tried to move on with my life. The only way I've ever been able to forget someone I love, has been to shack up with someone else, and if there wasn't a somebody else, I would just get high.

The new apartment became a haven for those that I cared about. It was a one bedroom apartment with a large living room and it had a good size kitchen. The first week I ground scored a futon, then turned the living room into my room, and I spread the word I had a bedroom for rent. There were a lot of kids that stayed in and out of my place for free; nevertheless, I needed a steady roommate to share in the rent.

Jengo and Erica wound up moving in. Jengo's father was a contractor that did renovations in San Francisco. So Jengo was one of the few kids that ran around the upper Haight that was actually a real resident of the bay. He would work with his dad, as a helper, and swing whatever he could when he didn't want to go to work. He seemed more solid than most because of this. Problem was Jengo and Erica shot up daily.

As I got more comfortable with the new place, I also got more comfortable using heroin everyday. Shit, I would wake up and shoot up immediately every morning. Jengo was such a good influence in my life. I had a good bit of money at that time in my life and I was tired of touring. My van wasn't in great shape, like it was the day I bought it. It started throwing oil on the spark plugs and causing it to foul out. So, I had to replace them every three months.

Before I go there, I will talk about how the summer of '94 began. The upstairs apartment was available, according to my landlord, and I told him I may know someone reliable to rent it. That someone was Honduras Allan and Kristy with her son Harley. So, once they moved in upstairs, new faces and friends started emerging from everywhere. In spite of the money I had saved, giving a big chunk of it just to have this place meant I still had to go up to the Haight and sell nugs. Which wasn't so bad in the beginning. I would get up, have my morning wake up and bag up buds to swing.

You may have heard of people that claim they could do heroin (intravenously) once in awhile without developing a daily habit. That was not the case for me. Unlike cocaine shooters, heroin will collapse your veins much faster and more permanently, in comparison. I still had a good six months, or more, worth of veins to continue on daily.

The word got around that I was somewhat a haven for close friends to crash at my place. Floor space I would provide, and so on. Tim and Beth stayed with me a lot until they finally purchased a VW Bug. They got a dog eventually so they really couldn't stay at my house anymore. No dogs (at least noticeable) allowed was the rule. Patches stayed with me a lot.

Then one day, while on the Haight, I was approached by a girl by the name of Stephanie Robinson. Apparently she was dating Nathan from Canada at the time. Nathan didn't have what I had, and their relationship had issues, I suppose. I remember Stephanie asking if she could have some floor space that day before the majority of kids went across the bridge to sleep in Oakland later.

Heartbroken I was that Brandy and I never had a chance to be together, yet no one knew my feelings. By that time Brandy was working lower Haight and the TL (Market St.) and I didn't see her much anymore. I didn't smoke crack with her anymore, so what good was I, in her eyes. She never got the chance to really hear about my little success story. Hell, it hurt my chest, so you didn't see me running around seven days a week like it used to be. Those were the days when we had a connection. The family of the Haight had turned their back on her.

My point is: love was an emotion I hadn't felt in so long, I was crying inside. Stephanie wasn't a replacement for anyone. At that moment, my intentions were only to give her a place to crash. I told Stephanie that, when I got done swinging the last of my shit, she could follow me to my place.

It wasn't hard to find me. I usually stayed up on the top of the hill of Buena Vista Park until all was sold. Do you want me to tell you how I did it? I would hide several cut up bags in the park and one under a tire of a parked vehicle. So when Goff and Comfrey would shake me down, I would not have anything on me. They called me by my first name, "Token."

"Hey Token, come here," and I would. They would pat me down and ask me to empty my pockets. It was like that. So I had perfected a system that worked for me, and others soon followed my way of selling pot. Anyway, I didn't get rid of everything that day and I was ready to go home.

Stephanie was nowhere in sight, by this point. Waited, I did, for at least an hour then I gave up and headed home.

As I walked, down the hill, there she was walking towards me. "I'm going home are you gonna follow me?" I asked.

She said, "Yeah, I've been ready for hours." So, we walked together toward Baker St. and then took a left and headed for McCallister. We didn't talk much as we walked. I didn't ask her shit like, "How long have you been touring?" or "How many Grateful Dead tapes do you have?" I assumed by her clothing and the way she carried herself she was like myself.

Stephanie was street smart. I noticed her here and there with Nathan. She wasn't a tall girl at all, and Nathan was about her same height. I'm almost six feet tall and she was definitely shorter than I. Her hair was brown, and her eyes were hazel with brown. "She is beautiful," I thought to myself, as we crossed Oak getting closer to the house.

When we got there, Jengo and Erica were in the bedroom fixing, and we went into my room (the living room with a futon). I had bought a nineteen inch color TV from somewhere. I don't fucking remember exactly where, but I remember I turned it on to Fox and the last Simpsons episode was on. The Fox channel in San Francisco would show at least three episodes, in the evening, Monday through Friday.

I watched the show from the corner of my eye, breaking out my cheeva I had bought from Kyle and Allison earlier in the day. Stephanie had her own as well and together we shot up. We didn't fucking share any needles granted. Well not on a first date. I'm kidding, I didn't consider this a date at all. Pessimistic, I was, by this point. After fixing, we sat on my futon feeling the high and watched The Simpsons and then smoked some nugs, once the peak of the heroin had passed. Most friends just slept on the floor with a sleeping bag when it came to floor space. She didn't have a sleeping bag.

We didn't talk about that part until later in the evening. Her intentions were unknown to me other than a place to crash due to the fact her and Nathan were having troubles. So I did what was expected and asked her if she was ok with sleeping in the same bed as me. Giving Stephanie a blanket and a pillow to sleep on the hard floor would have been mean and fucked up. I've shared beds with sisters without so much as a kiss, but maybe a little cuddle would arise during the night. So, I just wanted to be kind.

She said, "Yeah, you sure that's all right with you?" I assured her it was fine and let her know I would not try to fuck her, in so many words.

Once we got through that conversation, the tension was gone. We sat closer to each other on my couch/bed and eventually it was time to sleep.

During the night, at some point, we eventually were cuddling and come morning we awoke in each other's arms. This memory and moment was one of the highs in my life that no drug could compare to. The next morning we awoke to a chilled room, which was one of the reasons we were in each other arms, just for the body heat.

I would be lying if I didn't admit it was this particular experience that, for the first time in years, I unlocked my heart. I awoke before she did and I just looked at her face with her eyes closed. Maybe it was right then and there I knew I wanted her. Her eyes popped open and we stared at each other for a second, and I believe the feeling was mutual. I did not want to appear to be some sappy fuck that was on the verge of falling in love because of one beautiful and simple sleep over. So I gave her a firm hug and tried to get up. She stopped me from doing so and gave me a little innocent kiss, and then together we both got up.

I wasted no time getting my heroin in my arm, same as her and we walked up to the street to finish swinging what I still had left from yesterday. That day, at work, I saw her confronting Nathan on the corner of Ashbury with a few of his friends I didn't really know. From a distance I could tell their words weren't kind. I went about my day, business as usual. Sold out, bought some weight from Teddy, and went back to my house to cut it up. I was back on the hill in an hour doing what I do and sold every last bag.

It was kinda early to call it quits, so I just hung out at the top Buena Vista. About that time Angelo comes walking up to me and I hadn't seen him in a long while. He told me he had been hanging out in Berkeley (Bezerkley) off of Telegraph. I filled him in with what was going on in my life. We walked to the bench that's in the middle, top part of the park and we puffed some nugs. He wanted to play some guitar. I wanted to find Stephanie. I was feeling a little edgy and knew I needed another shot soon.

Now, believe it or not, I still hadn't felt the true pain of going without. Shit, I wasn't copping my dope off Sixteenth and Mission yet, Allison and Kyle were consistently taking care of most of the kids. I went to the street looking for them, and they were nowhere to be found. Luckily, Cathy was on the street, and she knew where they lived. She also needed to re-up. Kathy had a new boyfriend now, and his name was Moon.

She introduced us, and I drove all of us in my van down to Sixteenth and Mission St. Kathy was telling me Moon and her were planning on

moving to the same building. Moon was a blond haired bro with a ZZ Top Beard and was real fun to be around. I approved of him and they seemed good for each other. Moon made his money mainly with M.O.'s (Vacuumed sealed swag pot) Federal Expressed to the east coast through a bro, known as Sky, that lived in San Diego. So they still worked the Haight, yet they made much more money with a ten box.
That's ten pounds sealed and shipped. So the piddly change we made with good dank buds was no comparison. Like myself, their product and the work they did, allowed them to rent an apartment. Allison and Kyle told them of all the openings they had in there building, but at this moment they hadn't finalized the deal.

Once there, I parked across the street in a gas station from this huge, bland apartment building. We all went inside. They lived on the second or third floor. When we knocked on their door we heard, "Who is it?"

"It's Kathy," she said and the door opened. Kyle was a tall skinny guy that looked rather unhealthy. Allison was laying on her back, on the ground, in the living room.

I didn't know why until Kyle said, "hold on guys." Then he proceeded to inject some cheeva in the jugular vein on her neck. As I watched, I saw the row of track marks on her neck. The first time he inserted it, the needle it wouldn't register. Then I saw the blood come into syringe and he pushed the plunger. Seconds later she was on her feet and giving us want we came for.

If I had been smarter, I would have learned right then and there what happens to junkies when they run out of veins to hit. Little did I care, I was addicted to the shit, and I still had plenty of places to hit. I suppose I felt I was different and that would never happen to me. Sounds like a line from the back of The Big Book of AA, I know.

We left their apartment and drove back to my house. I found a parking space a block and a half above the small apartment building on Turk St. My van was in need of new spark plugs again. I knew this cause it was taking forever for it to start up

Jason Nance was back in the city. When all of us fixed in my place and went back to the street there he was, like myself, without his dreads. At first he wasn't so kind. It wasn't because he believed I was the reason they extradited him back to Virginia Beach. It was because he had did what I did, blew off whatever probation they gave him once he was released from shock probation. He knew if I would have sold all my product to his friends in Virginia Beach back in '93, we would have never gone to South Carolina, and none of us would have gone to jail. The fact Mariam was hanging out with me and the gang, meant he forgave me very quickly.

Mariam was so happy to see him again. She showered him with kisses and hugs. That moment was the happiest I ever saw her. So Jason and Mariam were back together. Kathy and Moon were a happy couple, and the dream we all strived for was becoming a reality. The dream of connecting with a Grateful Dead sister hadn't really happened for me. All I was thinking about was Stephanie.

While this reunion was going on, Stephanie was swinging nugs on the Haight. When I saw her I said, "Hey, where you been?" she told me Nathan and her were going their separate ways, and she had been talking it out with him. Now how accurate all this information was, I was unclear. I liked her, that was for sure. She wasn't known in the family, like others, and maybe she hadn't toured as hard as some. Regardless, I wanted what Jason had. I wanted what Moon had and so on. Where's my betty? As I listened to Stephanie talk, these were the thoughts in my head. She already had my heart, and she didn't know it. "While the fortune teller speaks, a door within the fire creaks. Suddenly fly's open and a girl is standing there." Doesn't that say it all?

We started as friends and became lovers in a few weeks time. Stephanie was a good girl, and she was good to me. Loving her was easy. Chasing Amy, metaphorically speaking, was over for me. She became the most important thing in my life. even more important than Grateful Dead tour, God forbid. When she moved in with me, I fell in love. All the hell I had been through finally paid off, in my head at least. It seemed she felt the same for me. Misery loves company, was what I was taught.

Living with Jengo and Erica was the scary part. In less than a month, Jengo started over doing it. His first OD on heroin wasn't his last. No, he didn't die the first time or the second and so on. When he nodded out and his lips turned blue we would throw him in the shower. First thing we would do was run the cold water while beating on his chest. It became a ritual in my apartment.

Erica would be hysterically crying screaming at the top of her longs, "He's fucking, dying call the ambulance!" All of us were prepared to do this, if our shower resuscitation failed. Believe it or not, we always seemed to get his heart and breathing back to normal. Hell, he was strong and young and his body just refused to die, at least in my house. Patches saved his life, at least twice, helping me carry him to the shower. Now, Allan upstairs was also using cheeva and so was Kristy. We had a house full of fuck ups.

Allan was very careful and he had to be. Abe was supplying him with LSD (Silver), at the time, so he had to have some control over the situation. John and Lucky were not Bay kids, so Allan and Abe were carrying the torch.

The whole house, as time went by, started getting their heroin from one source. Lallo was the big connection in city. He had his own people, like we had ours. Roberto delivered it to us most of the time. It was fucking '94 so there were no cell phones, just beepers. So, we would go across the street to the corner store and use the pay phones outside. The conversation would go like this, "Hey Roberto, can you come by?"

He would say, "How much?"

Whatever the fuck we needed, we would just blatantly tell him on the phone. His response was always the same, "Twenty minutes," with a heavy Spanish accent. He'd do twenty's sometimes, yet generally you had to at least spend forty dollars for him to deliver. For a dealer in death, he was very kind and good to us, and for that we loved him as a brother. I did at least. Why? Cause sometimes he'd travel across town just like I said earlier for small twenty. Most esses didn't do that. Most kids had to go down to Sixteenth and Mission for a quarter of a gram, and in the Mission, it usually didn't weigh.

Remember Crackhead Mikey? Let me tell you about the time he came over one particular night. I trusted him like a brother. I felt I owed him for being the one to introduce him to crack in the first place. Now I did not bring heroin into his life. He fell like me, everyone else was doing it, so he did it too. As me and Stephanie were sitting and watching TV, enjoying ourselves, we heard the doorbell ring. I got up and went to the speaker and said, "Who is it?"

He responded, "It's Mikey." So I hit the button that released the front gate. It made a buzzing sound when it unlocked the entranceway to the building. You could hear him as he climbed the stairs. We were the first door on the left, as you got to the top of the stairs. I let him in and we smoked some nugs. Both Steph and I still had dope; however, he didn't, and he asked if we could we called Roberto for him. Sometimes he didn't call back when we beeped him and this was one of those times.

Having a wake up was a must, you know, so when he volunteered to go down to the Mission for us if we bought him a twenty, I gave him a hundred dollar bill. I had my reserves, yet he was family and "honor among thieves" was our motto. Four hours passed by and we knew he was fucking up. Both Stephanie and I eventually gave up, did what we had, and nodded out.

We woke up about six in the morning to the sound of the doorbell constantly being pushed. It was Crackhead Mikey. He came running up the stairs and I let him in. He was all wired up to the max trying to convince me he got robbed. I didn't believe it for a minute. I was feeling sick already and listening to him tell me how he got burned did not fly. It escalated into a verbal fight, and then I just lunged at him. I started pounding on his face in a dope sick rage. All of a sudden he broke out some mace and sprayed my face with it. It splattered off me and hit Stephanie as well. As both us were feeling the burning he fled out the door. We jumped in the shower as quick as we could. Even though the water was running full stream it kept on burning. Finally, it simmered down and both of us regained our composure.

The street knew immediately of what he did that day. I chalked it to the game, bought some weight, and broke it up into heighths. It was very rare (at least in my experiences) that close friends stole from me. Cocaine is a hell of a drug. The things it drives people to do are unfathomable. I don't have any room to talk shit myself.

This particular month was a shitty one. A few weeks later another incident happened that left a permanent memory for life. My money was running out, like it always does in any addiction. Yet I trudged through it, working on the street swinging nugs. Trying to save my money one evening, I didn't re-up before I went to bed expecting I'd just call in the morning for my wake up. The next morning, Roberto was really late delivering the shit, and I was so dope sick by noon, when he finally got to our house. The doorbell rang and I pushed the button that unlocked the entrance. Roberto had several balloons in his mouth and he put them in his hand. Stephanie and I picked from the selection, thanked him, and he left.

As soon as I opened the red balloon that was tied in a knot, the tar shot out of it like a bullet. Where it went, I couldn't tell. I was so angry and dope sick I punched the living room door, the right side door (there were two doors) the other I usually kept locked in place. Little did I know they were once glass with framing around each other. Someone painted them white and they looked like just thin wood. My hand went right through it. A triangular piece of glass went right into my hand directly under the knuckle of my thumb. Stephanie, with pure terror, watched me do this. Her face turned white, as white as the door itself, horrified at what I had done. I carefully removed my hand from the hole in the door and she pulled out the glass.

The cut was over a inch wide and extremely deep. The bleeding was uncontrollable. Stephanie quickly found something to wrap around my right hand to stop the bleeding. I needed stitches, but I was dope sick. As soon as we got it under control, I immediately started moving all the furniture in the hallway looking for my quarter. Searched, I did, for at least an hour while

Stephanie begged and pleaded for me to calm down. She kept saying, "Brad stop! I'll split mine in half and we will look together." I wasn't listening, I had gone mad. When I cleared out all the living furniture, and it was crammed in the hallway leading into the kitchen, I found my piece along side the wall. The towel on my hand was soaked in blood. I didn't five a fuck. I just wanted to get well, and that's what the fuck I did.

I hadn't reached the point of hitting my jugular vein, yet I was running out of places to hit. The summer was long gone at this point, and fall tour was going on while all this shit was happening. I was a mess, and I can't say Stephanie had reached the point I was at. Either she began shooting up right about the time we became a couple, or I was just born with veins that collapse faster.

My arms, before I began shooting up heroin, were covered with ugly, large veins. They were easy to hit, and now they all had dropped. I did still have veins in my hands left. I had track marks all up and down my arms with bruises as well and a couple abscesses to go with the tracks.

My love for Stephanie had reached its maximum, yet our lovemaking wasn't so hot. I could still perform, but I could never cum. This frustrated her and I didn't blame her. One night, out of the fucking blue, I awoke with cum all over myself. I guess my body, one way or the other, had to get it out of me. Poor Stephanie was right by my side when it happened, and she witnessed it.

Time had passed, and I was getting worse. The veins in my hands were now hiding from me, and it was getting harder and harder to fix. I wasn't using my van much anymore, so I sold it to family for real cheap. Christmas was just months away. I had to get help, so James, aka Sparkle helped me get to the closest hospital.

We walked there only to find no help. I had reached a point where I was no longer able to go to the street and work. Coming back from the hospital, Stephanie sat next to me with my shirt off. We were sitting in the living room. I was going through the hot and cold flashes you've heard about. Somehow she was managing to stay well and continue to work. I was like the drunk, you would read about in the Big Book of AA, that could no longer provide for his family. She continued on like this for me for about three or more weeks.

Then she said, "Brad, I can't go through this anymore. I love you, but I'm going to have to leave you," and she did. How did I pay my rent? I had help from the family. Not money, granted, just information that was vital to keep me from being evicted. Rent was due, we had a house full of junkies, and no one had enough money to pay for anything except their next quarter of a gram. So James helped me again get downtown to the housing authorities, and its there we put in a writ of Habeas Corpus to fight eviction. This gave my apartment six more months before they could take any action to evict me in the city of San Francisco.

After I secured the place, I realized that the Free Haight Street clinic and Oz Detox couldn't fix me, so I became desperate. All the clinic would give me were Darvocets and that was like aspirin. Now down on Sixteenth and Mission, a few blocks past the Mission, was a produce stand owned and run by some Asians. They were selling Mexican Diazapam for forty-forty cents a piece in bulk. Each ten milligram pill was individually wrapped in a white colored wrapper that was perforated and connected to another and so on.

You would walk into the store, give the gesture to the counter person and they would send you to the back. There you were and they asked how many you needed, and they would pull on this huge wheel (like a movie ticket wheel back in the day) and you would get what you wanted. Crazy shit, and this went on for another couple of weeks, Valium mixed with the Darvocets. I was fucking miserable, and yes, I was still doing heroin, just less. I refused to put it in my neck and I don't know how people could hit between there toes, I sure as fuck couldn't. So kicking this shit the Haight way was not working.

I found out Stephanie went back to Nathan during all this madness. So I was heartbroken, strung out, and had finally reached the last house on the block, as they say. That's when I decided to pick up the phone. Serenity Knolls was the angel that spread their wings around me. I told Sandy, a staff member, my dilemma and she set me up with a bed in Salem, Oregon at a detox unit called Harmony House.

I had just enough money to buy a Greyhound ticket to get there and that was it. After I hung up the phone I went back to the house on Baker and McCallister and told Cathy what I was going to do. I asked her to watch my house while I was gone. In fact, I specifically gave her total control of the place. Now if I failed to mention Moon and her got a place in my building a couple months back, then I'm telling you now. So she had her hands full. Cathy, that's right, the same beautiful red headed dready I met in the beginning of it all. She assured me she would take care of it best she could so I gave her the keys and went downtown to the Greyhound station.

Detox Tour

It cost sixty dollars for a one-way ticket to Salem, which left me with about ten dollars to my name. The ride up there was uncomfortable in every way. Once I got to the bus depot I didn't want to spend all the rest of my money for a taxi, so I called the number of the facility. They said they didn't have the resources to pick me up, so I walked.

Once I was there, I checked in, filling out paperwork in pain. I should have taken a couple of Darvocets before I checked in, but I didn't know they were going to administer them to me as they saw fit. So, like I said, I was going through serious pain and withdrawal.

When all the paper work was done, I kindly asked for my meds that the Free Haight and Ashbury clinic had given me. They refused my request very coldly and told me to eat lunch. I remember very well what they were serving. It was cold ham sandwiches with lots of fat on it and bag of regular potato chips. I could not stomach the sandwich, yet I nibbled on the chips. A counselor was watching me, apparently. I threw most of the sandwich away and walked up to the staff, "Can I please have a Darvocet?" I asked.

The staff member I approached said, "You didn't even hardly touch your lunch and I don't like your attitude." I snapped inside. Not only had a left all my possessions back in the bay, but I had spent all my money just be in this moment. I looked at this guy and said, "Look I'm in serious pain and my appetite is horrible, give me my pills!"

"That's it your out of here" the staff member says. They practically prodded me out the door like cattle with all my stuff in hand that I came in with. So there I was in a town I'd never been in before in my life. So I walked back the way I came and eventually found a pay phone. I called Sandy's extension and thank God she was there to answer. I pulled no punches. I told no lies. I told Sandy from Serenity Knolls exactly what happened from beginning to end. Speaking of telling no lies, I'll let you know, I was crying.

Sandy worked pretty fucking hard to get me where I was and she was very disappointed. She told me to sit tight by the phone and call her back. Because I told her the complete truth, it collaborated with what she was told by Harmony House. Sandy was pissed about the way I had been treated, and she had a state vehicle drive me to a hospital in Salem.

They evaluated me and checked my blood levels, to see if I was honest, I suppose. Once they knew I still was on the right track, the doctor prescribed me an extremely high dosage of Klonidine (blood pressure medication). The doctor told me the state was going to drive to a motel in Salem next to a restaurant, and he gave me vouchers for food. I was awaiting a bed to open up in Portland, OR at Hooper Detox.

Three days I stayed in this low budget motel. I had run out of Darvocets the first night there, and all I had left was the Klonidine. This medication was so strong, when I would stand up I would get dizzy and my knees would start to buckle. Twice I blacked out and hit the floor, just from standing up to do the most simple things, like go to the bathroom. This stuff had my blood pressure so dangerously low I'm surprised I didn't bust my head open those times I blacked out.

When they finally showed up, in a four door vehicle with state tags, to drive me to Portland, I was so happy to see them. My facial complexion was almost white, according to one of the two men. I rested my head on the window as we pulled away. Through the grace of God, I managed to hold my shit together as they drove north on Interstate 5. Like Harmony House, once there they put me through the wringer in paperwork, unlike Salem, the vibes from the staff of Hooper Detox were kind and understanding.

Sandy, if you ever read, this I want to tell you I love you and appreciate everything you did for me. It's people like you and the staff of Hooper Detox that proves the system works if you want it. Thank you so much, and I do apologize for what I'm about to tell you.

After a few days they finally brought me to a stable point. You know eight or nine pills four times a day until you feel somewhat normal. Granted, I hadn't done any heroin for almost two weeks, since I left my house in San Francisco. So it was working its way out, while the pills were taking its place, and, like most addicted people, when you regain some sanity your old behaviors will surface.

There was a girl who had a meth addiction named Christina. She was a lesbian and her lover wanted her home, most likely to do dope with her.

To keep my attention away from myself, I started to hit on her. This only aggravated matters for her recovery. She realized, through me, how pretty she really was and men most definitely found her attractive. I'm sure her lover did all she could to keep this realization from happening. I got under her skin. I let her know what she may not of known at that time in her life. I'm sure she didn't need that. For someone that wanted it so badly, as I claimed, I still didn't want to deal with myself.

On the fourth or fifth day, they had a acupuncturist come in and treat the patients. This was my first experience with needles, other than putting them in my arm, and it did relieve stress. I was amazed. Christina was sitting across the table from me as they did this for all of us. She was my buddy throughout my visit to Hooper.

Then the next day, a lady came in who was a therapist in meditation. She played calm, soothing music and taught me for the first time how to meditate. All in all, I owe a lot of what I am today from these moments, and then things changed. There was a real nice black guy, a girl like me, and Christina that were buddies. Then another couple came in separately who were partners in crime on the street. They were not serious about kicking dope. The girl snuck in heroin and a needle in her vagina and some pot to go with it.

I was hanging out with a bro (that I can't recall his name) along side of all these wonderful people. Yeah, all of us had our shortcomings, of course, yet I believe for the most part every one of us had good intentions. Even if the couple that snuck the drugs in the detox were on "vacation" they were at least reducing their intake of heroin. Once they learned I knew of what they had done, to shut me up (like they had to worry) they gave me a little pinner joint. I really didn't want to get high to be honest yet, my stinking thinking told me, "It will make you feel well Brad ... go ahead and hit it a couple times, you'll see."

Yeah, I saw alright. That brother I was hanging out with talked me into it. He was the one that instigated the whole thing. He was the one that knew that couple from the street, and it was him they gave it to, not me. Let's get that straight. So as we've been taught, misery loves company.

The smoking area at Hooper in '94 was a room with a fan at the window. So dude and I hit a couple of times at the fan and that was all she wrote. No, it didn't help. It gave me a panic attack right after we smoked a cigarette to cover up any traces of pot smoke. As we were finishing our cigarettes four staff members walked in the smoking room and just glared at me, not the bro next to me.

The head staff member had an ID badge on her shirt. The name read "Sandy." Now probably coincidence of course, yet at that moment I figured it was the same woman. They gave me such a look that it pierced all the way down to my inner soul. Then they walked out. Not a word was said, but I knew they knew. I only thought it would help, and I was wrong. Please forgive me Sandy.

My heart was racing madly and I was upset at the bro for talking me into it and I was mad at the staff for mentally beating me up for it. I was mad at myself. I went back to my bed and rode it out. In about an hour, they gave me my hand full of pills. I don't know what the fuck I was thinking.

If I could have turned the clock back, I would have. If you haven't picked up on it by now, I like to have little crushes on pretty girls. That seemed to be my pattern. The next morning Christina had an argument with her lover, decided to check out and she did. That other couple (the black guy and white girl) got stoned as well, from what bro told me, and they wanted to check out. The only people that didn't want to leave were the junkie couple that were still on heroin and had weed.

The staff was no longer as kind to me that morning. Why should they be? I fucked up and I smoked a few puffs of marijuana. Yeah, Yeah, pot didn't bring me to this state of mind; nevertheless, the state of Oregon was looking out for me. Mutiny was happening right in front of Hooper's staff. So that morning, since my little buddy Christina left and I was upset at myself for failing, I gave up.

All of us had a meeting in the smoking room and decided we would all walk out together. To get down to the street, you had to take an elevator and after I refused their drugs; we all checked out and went down. Once on the street the light was blinding. The black guy and his new girlfriend went their way and brother man and I went ours. Christina was already home by this point with her girl. A bus stops right in front of Hooper and dude jumped on. He turned around and gestured to me to follow him. My legs would not move. "What the fuck have I done?" I thought to myself.

The bus driver said, "You coming?" and I just looked at him blankly.

Dude was like, "Come on man!" I couldn't say anything and the door closed. As the bus drove away, I saw the look on dude's face, and it was filled with confusion. Across the street was a coffee shop and I got a cup of java since I hadn't had a real cup in weeks. It tasted good and went down nicely. Then I walked over to a pay phone and called my Dad, collect. I told him what happened. All of it. He raised me differently than most dads.

I was smoking pot with him before I was even fifteen. You know what he said? I'll tell you, "You march right back in there and apologize, beg, or whatever and get right"

"I can't do that, Dad, I blew it. There's two cops staring at me Dad,"

"Well go over there and tell them what you did and get your ass back up there." Then I hung up. So there I was, in the middle of Downtown Portland, far from I-5, this I knew once I asked the policeman how to get to the interstate. They explained to me I had to walk the entire bridge to get out of the city and back on Interstate Five, and they did not recommend it. Nevertheless, that's what the fuck I did, coffee in one hand cigarette in other. My mind wasn't in such a bad place. I could do it I thought to myself. So I walked from Burnside Bridge to the highway.

The sun was blazing hot that morning, and in hour of walking, my sanity quickly dissolved. You can't catch a ride, even if anyone wanted to give a lift. There was no emergency lane large enough to actually pull over. So I was fucked again. My mind went from bad to worse as the hot sun mixed with carbon monoxide poisoning combined as one. I kept on walking, cursing myself for my stupidity. About halfway into it, the hallucinations started. I can't say I ever tripped on my own insanity like this before. Obviously, I was going through withdrawal from all the medication Hooper Detox had me on. "I'm not going to make it," I said to myself, and started to cry.

How I continued to push on, I'll never know. I looked down on the road and there was a plastic pitchfork from a devil costume on the ground. Then a song entered my mind, "I am the reaper man…yeah …yeah." You know the tune.

Just as I was about to pass out from heat stroke and exhaustion, there was a huge tree, the first I'd seen in a very long time. I saw it in the distance. "Just let me make it to the tree Lord, ok?" I said out loud. There was a fence in front of it, yet I could still touch the tree. I hugged the tree through the fencing and breathed in the oxygen it was producing. I thanked him graciously for its love, and he gave me just a little more strength to push on.

By this point there are no words to describe what I was feeling and seeing. I stumbled and almost fell to my knees. "Keep walking Brad…keep walking," a voice said to me. So I lifted my head and followed the orders, as a soldier. The clouds in the sky covered the sun and a cool breeze blew on my face. In the distance, I could tell the bridge was coming to an end, and there would soon be room for a vehicle to pull over. Low and behold as soon as I was on the I-5, on the fucking highway, not a bridge, a car pulled over. Before I even got close, the passenger door opened. I looked in and the driver said, "Get in."

The man was very silent and then he finally said something as he turned to his right looking directly in my eyes. "I'm sorry. I'm a not a religious man. My name is Gavin, and I'm going take you as far from this area as I can which isn't much but you'll have a better chance of getting a ride." I said nothing. I couldn't talk. I didn't want to talk. He took me to the next exit where he implied he himself was going to turn around, and head back to Portland. Gavin thank you so much, if your reading this, I owe you, and you will be payed. Much love, Gavin much love. He was right. In less than ten minutes an old Dodge van pulled over.

He said, "Where you heading?"

"South, back to San Francisco."

"Well, I'm not going that far, but I'll get you closer," and with that he merged back onto the freeway. The interior of his van was covered in stickers. Not Grateful Dead stickers, but stickers of all kinds. He started talking a mile a minute about his life. He claimed he was a Carney and worked Carnivals most of his life. He was extremely thin and his face sunken in. He acted like he was on meth or a shit load of coffee. I just sat there trying to listen over the hum of the engine. Which was inside the fucking van, between us, with an engine cover. A slant six, I'm guessing it was. While he rambled on about the places he'd been, it began to grow dark outside. That always worries me when it comes to hitchhiking. Our journey together soon ended, right about the time the sun set on the horizon. This was just enough light to be seen from a drivers eye. I thanked him for the ride and quickly put my thumb in the air as he drove away.

It would be dark soon. I was starting to shake inside and out. My health was shit. In thirty minutes, it was dark. That means zero visibility. I was coming apart and my hands wouldn't stop shaking. My luck with rides had run out, and I could smell death walking beside me...waiting.

An hour of thumb in the air and walking had passed. I couldn't go any further. "You win," I said to myself, and with that I walked off the highway into the woods just to get away from the stench of the road. In the woods, off I-5, I laid down on the cool ground and felt the true pain of my flesh. Shivering and hungry, I just laid there, surrounded by God's green earth. Thanks God, if your reading this as well. I'm not being sarcastic, I needed that rest.

My eyes never closed but my body shut down. I don't know how long I hid in the forest, but the trance I was in was broken by the sound of helicopters. Or maybe it was just one, I don't know. I knew this, it was looking for something. I could see a searchlight breaking its way through the trees. No shit, they were looking for something or someone. In my delusional mind, they were after me, and I was petrified. So, I cowardly hid until the searchlight moved on.

This definitely put a new light on the subject, no pun intended. So, with what strength I had left, I got up. I wasn't going to get off so easy and just die in the woods. I walked back to the I-5 South, and in the black of night with no streetlights, just the light of the moon, I put my thumb in the air. I don't even think ten minutes past before a Volvo station wagon with two bicycles mounted on top pulled over. In the front seat was a couple, both with dreads, and they said there were going to Eugene, Oregon. They took one look at me and the brother driving said "You look like shit, man, are you in trouble?"

I said no, not really, just trying to get home. I don't think they believed me. When we arrived they took me into town without a word. When the car stopped, the betty in the passenger seat pointed to a phone booth and she suggested I use it, and with that I got out and thanked them. I took their suggestion and called 9-1-1.

"What is your emergency?" the women on the phone said.

"I'm Token Jackson … I'm here, help me."

Getting the address of where I was must have been hard for the police department. I didn't know and I'd run out of steam. Being that I was nearsighted as it was I could not see shit. Hallucinating with exhaustion and fatigue plus withdrawal from whatever they had been giving me, was what was going on. I gave up trying to explain this and just dropped the phone and slid down the edge of the phone booth. As I sat there my mind drifted off. Thoughts of hopes I had, and thoughts of regrets were all spiraling together.

Then I heard the sirens. The sound was faint yet growing louder and louder. I opened my eyes. A white van with a bird on the side of it with two men were lifting me up putting me in the back of it on some sort of industrial mattress.

They drove so fast, like I was somebody worth saving. The van stopped with a jerk and both men were pulling me out and escorting me into a small building. They laid me down on a cot in a fucking room surrounded by a bunch other men. I stood up and looked around. The smell of this room was foul. Not so much the room, but the other fuckers sleeping and snoring stunk.

There was a huge glass window with a man behind it just looking at me. He pushed a cup of soup through an opening and told me to try to eat it. I tried but felt sick and nauseous. I laid it down beside me, and my heart started to pound hard. My chest hurt and I started to shake. The man looking at me started shifting around and pushing numbers on a phone next to him.

Then my sides started to vibrate, like a bad acid trip. Then my whole body uncontrollably started to contort or whatever the fuck you call it. In the background, I heard someone shouting, "Call an ambulance, we've got a problem!" I bounced around on the mattress and then some staff members came in, one was trying to put something in my mouth, telling me to bite down on it, the other was holding my head.

When the paramedics arrived, it was no white van, it was the real thing. I was put in the back of the ambulance and rushed to a hospital. While looking at the ceiling of the ambulance, my mind was a blank. There were no thoughts of, "Oh no, I'm dying." The mask they put on my mouth tasted sweet as I tried to breathe in the air. This was the real thing. All the years of drinking and of using drugs everyday had led up to this moment. Funny how someone can decide to live and then almost die trying to do it. At least, that's what I was thinking.

I was no longer biting down on anything, and my heart slowed down. As we were entering the hospital entrance my body and mind seemed stable. It's amazing what oxygen can do. Apparently, it's one hell of a drug.

Once I was wheeled into the ER, a doctor saw me immediately. "How are you feeling?" he asked.

"I'm feeling better," I replied.

He said my drinking, prior to heroin addiction, was a classic example of self-medicating. It made sense, yet I didn't like the fact that, one way or the other, I'll be on something for the rest of my life. I didn't completely believe him, and I wanted a second opinion. However, that second opinion was going to have to wait. How I was brought back to that room, I don't remember exactly. At least I was stable. Coherent may be more proper of a word for my state of mind.

I knew where I was now. The man behind the glass when I was brought back let me know I was at The Buckley Detox Center. His name was Ken, and he gave me another cup of soup and some sort of Gatorade drink. I ate it this time and drank whatever it was eagerly. They didn't keep me with the rest of the people, snoring all around me, for very long.

At this particular detox, the street people would check in and check out in the morning. The detox center would give them nourishment and a chance to get sober if they wanted it. This was God's beauty working through the minds and souls on Fourth and Jefferson Streets. It is here that I was shown that love is real and everyone has a chance. Now, whether you take this opportunity, it's entirely up to you. I wanted it. At least, I thought I did.

So they brought me in out of the drunk tank, so to speak. I sat down with Ken and started some paperwork on the desk at the big window. Whatever they did to me at Sacred Heart Hospital was working. I was told to strip down out of my street clothing and they gave me pajamas with matching socks. They were not exactly regular socks, on the very bottom was a white outline of a foot. I took a shower and then put them on. As soon as I got out of the shower, I was told to go to the nurse. They gave me Librium and a couple of other things. What they gave me didn't matter anymore; I felt well. One of the inside staff members showed me to my bed, and I slept.

They allowed me to sleep in the next morning, up until it was time for vitals. They checked my blood pressure and gave me more medicine. I went back to sleep. This was the kindest place I'd seen on detox tour.

When I woke up, lunch was already served, but the cook had a plate just for me. The kitchen cook was a wonderful man named Cleo. He wore a permanent smile and made the best pastry treats you can imagine. His cooking was absolutely superb. He was a thin black man with a heart of gold. The things he shared with me are not forgotten. The Buckley House was damn lucky to have him.

There is another man that I would like the world to know about. His name was well known in Eugene, Oregon…Tattoo Tom. You can guess from his nickname, he was covered in tattoos, of course. He was a short, big guy with a beard. Yeah, he had a belly, yet it looked great for his size and proportion. Jolly guy all round.

He would talk to me, as well as others, sharing his hope, strength, and experience. He inspired me. That first day, while in the shower, I hit my knees and asked God, as humbly as I could, for help, in tears. Sometimes the answer is "no" regardless of how much you ask. No one had told me that.

I got up, finished washing myself and got dressed in clean pajamas and went into the day room, which was very impressive. Lots of couches arranged perfectly. The atmosphere was filled with love and just good vibes the likes of which I'd never felt before. Some say I clean up well, and I suppose I do. There were a couple pretty girls sitting on the couches watching TV. I sat down alone and stared at the program everyone else was watching.

Then a pretty woman, in her early thirties, came in and made an announcement. "It's time for a recovery based movie guys," she said, and with that she put in a VCR tape. The movie starred Michael Keaton, and it was called, "Clean and Sober."

The woman that put the tape in was the director of this facility. Her name was Carol Crowe. She had beautiful eyes, brunette hair, and a smile that would light up a room. But at that very moment, the clients didn't see that, all they saw was, "In The Heat Of The Night" being turned off. I didn't care a bit. I hadn't been watching from the beginning. Carol said, "This is a good movie guys," and went back upstairs to where her office was. I hadn't seen it, and I loved Mr. Mom when I was a kid, so I didn't fight it. Carol was correct, it is a great movie. I never left my seat.

The one draw back, due to the fact United Way was funding this facility, was no smoking allowed. Somebody donated nicotine patches and they passed them out. I had one on my shoulder, and when it started to wear off, even with the meds they dispensed, I chewed on it. The fucking burning sensation in my mouth was unbearable, yet it took off the edge. I heard someone even snuck a lighter in and tried to smoke one of the patches. Next to the day room was the dining room where we all ate. Along side of the walls were shelves with books, games, puzzles, and miscellaneous stuff to occupy our time.

I was feeling better, and when I saw the new girl that just came in, I stared. She was very thin, and I would swear she glowed. Not to be a hippie fuck and talk about auras, yet I could see it. Her right arm was disfigured, a deformity from birth she told me. Her mother was a meth addict throughout the pregnancy, and she was born like that as a result.

Why was she here? Like her mom, she was also a meth addict. I took to her too fast. I didn't see anything but how beautiful she was, inside and out. So, being the jerk I was and feeling better, I approached her and poured on the charm. We were sitting too close to each other from that point on.

As we were practically cuddling on the couch, a very tall and thin, young guy came running in the day room straight to the clock on the wall.

Then he said, "We've got a short timer!" as he adjusted the clock to the proper time. I noticed one of his nostrils was considerably larger than the other. I didn't like him at all. He came across as cocky, arrogant, and full of himself. First impressions are everything generally.

I stopped focusing on my recovery and tried to hide my broken heart by making the same mistake I did in Portland. The staff was alerted of how close we were sitting and watched us put puzzles together. The next day we continued our little innocent crush on each other.

Stephanie had left me when I needed her most and I was licking my wounds. Now I meant no harm, I just liked her and she was helping me forget, and I believe I was doing the same for her. Well, the staff didn't see it like that, and they told us to quit sitting so close to each other and focus on ourselves.

They were correct, that's what we should have done, yet how does one not catch a ball when it's thrown directly in your hands. We tried to do that but we weren't so successful at it. I even fucked up by thinking out loud one day. I said to her as we were sitting in the dining room putting a puzzle together, "I like it here in Oregon. When all this is over maybe you and I could be together. I could take you away from this place."

Stupid, stupid, stupid. What the fuck was I thinking? I wasn't, stinking thinking was what that was. Maybe the fact I didn't see a problem with her deformed arm and other men had throughout her life did, I don't know. It affected her and she told on me. The fact that they dragged it out of her one way or the other, more than likely in tears, I forgave her. Nevertheless, the staff said, "If you pull another stunt like that, you're out!" and the honeymoon was over.

We were not allowed to sit next to each other. This beautiful place no longer felt beautiful at all. I'm sure it was for the best because I was full of shit. I was a California resident and taking her away back to my place in the shitty of the bay would have been fucked up. Especially when she was like so many other girls that get strung out, give their child to the grandparents and fight to regain what they once had.

So my last days in Buckley were terrible. Both of us knew we had to follow orders in order to get help. I was waiting for a bed at The Carlton House for men and she was awaiting a bed at the Willamette Family Treatment Center (WFTC) for women. So she got what she wanted and a bed came open. As she was leaving, all I could was wave goodbye from a distance with a smile and the hope that we would meet again under different circumstances. Meaning I get a bed, work the program and we see each within the program later down the road. That was what I wanted at that moment, to be free of heroin and see her sober with my shit together.

Well it didn't work out like that for me. Carol kept me in spite of my actions for eleven days, which was way over the norm for anybody. She was doing her best to help. I believe she understood how serious I was and how bad I wanted it. But I wasn't special. Nobody wants to be thrown back into the cold, harsh world without a net.

The problem was I was a California resident, and the state of Oregon could not pay for my treatment whether a bed opened up or not. This I was told on the tenth day. She was long gone and I was to be released tomorrow. Carol worked her ass off to find help for me only to find a possible opening in a halfway house. I didn't know anything about halfway houses other than the name says it all. It wasn't a treatment center, that's for sure and I now knew I had nerve damage, and was seizure prone.

So they really couldn't completely taper me off the meds, like others, due to the pre-existing condition I'd been self-medicating for years. They did lower the dosage down to a minimum and suggested I go to the mental department to treat my condition. It was the only thing they could do really. I felt hopeless and my world was crashing down right on top of me.

For the love of God, I knew if I returned to my house filled with junkies it would only be a matter of time. You've heard this before, and I was just another statistic. The day came when I had to go. They claimed they could help me and didn't. My only choice was to go to the shelter and get a doctor pronto. They explained to me about OHP (Oregon Health Plan) and so on. Yet all I heard was Eugene shelter and get a doctor ASAP. Well fuck that! I had an apartment with all my clothes in it and furniture. I saw what kind of people were in the shelters. Hell, I had a fucking seizure in a room full of them and most of them slept their drunk asses through it all.

Do you think I was mad? Stephanie dumped me. Brandy, I had already accepted was a pipe dream and impossible to reach. The only real solid reason to be a part of the family was to find her, wherever the hell she was, and settle down. That's how I saw it, from beginning to end.

So I looked like a whore myself, constantly looking for someone I've never met. Could have sworn it was Stephanie. I thought it was Brandy. Well those eleven days in Buckley gave me clarity alright. Clear as a bell, I was, on a very small dosage left in me of Benzodiazapines. All I saw was another dream crushed again. I didn't want to go back to San Francisco. I wanted to start a new life and never look back. Well living in the Eugene shelter sure as fuck wasn't my idea of a new life on the road moving forward. I'm sure it may have been. There's been thousands of cases where that did work, but a million that didn't. You do the math.

I walked out the door feeling jittery and scared. Lucky for me, the entrance to the highway was basically right above me. At least it wasn't miles of bridge after bridge. I hadn't smoked a cigarette in almost two weeks, and I actually pondered the thought of quitting. So I didn't light up as soon as I stood outside the Buckley Detox.

I got on the highway heading toward I-5 again going south. It wasn't right there in front of me, yet the walk wasn't too bad. As I saw the signs in the distance coming closer, I decided to walk off the interstate to a pretty clearing of grass with a beautiful tree that had my name on it.

I leaned my back against the tree and fired up a cigarette. They were filter less and strong. On the first puff I coughed and I'll admit it tasted like shit. They were stale. The second puff was a little tastier and so on. Unfortunately, it made me a little shaky and I had one hell of a head rush. It only seemed to aggravate my nerves, not help. So I put it out halfway into it. I sat there with my back against this old tree and looked around. It was a beautiful picture, and once my head stopped swimming, which is the appropriate word, I got up and walked down the entranceway to I-5 South.

I caught a ride rather quick. It was a beautiful day, so maybe that had something to do with it. Just a random ride, nothing to write about, they took me as far as Roseburg and dropped me off on the exit. Didn't catch another ride for hours and I was getting hungry.

The next ride I caught didn't take me as far, and I wound up walking for miles and then my mind started to unravel again. Exhaust and monoxide fumes, such a lovely mix with hunger.

Azalea was the area I was in, according to the signs I passed. "Fuck my head is hurting again," I thought to myself. Then the hallucinations started to creep back in. Not pink elephants and dumb shit people have lied about, just those little stars that move everywhere mixed with a blur. I would shake my head to make them stop.

"Shit, God what next?" I said aloud. I try not to say that anymore, but every time life gets tough, I fuck up and say it. I saw a sign that read "Heaven On Earth" exit something, another two miles. "Yeah, that's what I need. After all of this madness I've been through, that sounds really good," I spoke aloud.

I had to walk two fucking miles to get to Heaven. When I finally reached that exit, I walked up the ramp to this log cabin restaurant. It had a sign stating, "World Famous Cinnamon Rolls." I walked in. Well, stumbled in was more like it. I looked at the prices and stuck my hand in my pockets and pulled out less than a dollar in change. I didn't even have enough money for a cup of coffee here in Heaven.

I went to the back of this beautiful restaurant and there was a row of telephones separated between each by natural wood. The whole place was a natural wood color and the smell was so intoxicating. I mean that in a good way. This place was Heaven On Earth.

Heaven isn't cheap, not too terribly expensive, yet seventy-eight cents doesn't do much. So I called my parents. There was no answer so I just sat there resting on the high chair acting like I was talking to somebody.

When I milked that for all it was worth, I left this Heaven and headed back to hell. Breathing in all those wonderful smells of cinnamon rolls and good food mixed with pleasant air did help. I stuck my thumb in the air and walked on down the road.

Five minutes later, a red Saturn pulled over. I walked up to the passenger window, lowered my head saying nothing, and just looked in. The driver hit a button and the window moved downward, "hop in," he said.

I didn't argue with him. This guy looked strange. He was a tall man yet not too thin and he wore these ridiculous glasses. The kind with thick frames, thick glasses, you know the type. He was wearing a plaid shirt and he was balding. "So where are you heading?"

"I'm going back to San Francisco," I said.

"Well I'm driving to Eureka. I can take you as far as Grants Pass if you would like." I didn't know where fuck that was but I knew it was closer to home than here. This guy was a character alright. He said he was leasing the Saturn, and they were brand new at the time so he wanted to try one on for size. It only seemed like thirty minutes before he was telling me he was going to get off the I-5 and take the scenery route. "Its only way to get to where I'm going," he said. "You look like a Dead head. My name is Franklin. I would like to think Jerry Garcia named 'Franklin's Tower' after me," and then he started rambling on about something else as my mind drifted from the conversation. "You know, I can get you closer to San Francisco if want to ride with me."

"Where are you going again?"

"A little town above Eureka, CA, you could catch a ride probably from there just as easy," and he was right. I had never been there but a lot of real family talked about Blue Lake and it was close to where this guy was willing to take me. The fact that he swore Garcia wrote "Franklins Tower" after him seemed like he was alright.

So I said, "Sure, sounds good, thank you Franklin," and with that, instead of getting out at Grants Pass, we took the scenic route.

After about thirty minutes, around Cave Junction he says, "I want to pull over and smoke a cigarette," and he did. We both smoked and carried on. Franklin didn't like smoking in any confined area such as a car, house, ect. Now this mother fucker, once we got to the curvy part of 199, starts driving the car at top speeds around the sharp curves and corners, scaring the fuck out of me.

"I'm just testing the performance of this car," he says. I held on for dear fucking life while this tall fuck drove this new Saturn like a race car. I mean he was really pushing it to the limit man. I've never drove so reckless. He got my attention real quick.

"Why in the fuck didn't I get out in Grants Pass?" I thought to myself. Then he let up, with a shit eating grin on his face.

"I scare you?" he asks.

"Uh, yeah Franklin, you managed to do that."

"I'm sorry, this is just a prime opportunity to see what this car can do."

"Yeah and fucking kill us both in the process," I thought to myself.

It was starting to get dark outside when he said, "I want to stop by a friends house on the way if that's alright?" Now, he did not mention any of this when we back on the 5. What else was I supposed to say?

"Uh, sure man," I replied.

"Do you mind if we listen to the radio?"

"Not at all, its your ride man."

Then Franklin said, "Yeah, he's expecting me," and then he turned on the radio. The station he turned it to was faint, but it was rolling good tunes.

The reception got better and better as we went, then the radio announcer finally talked. It went something like this, "That was blah blah by blah and coming up next is The Grateful Dead with a song called 'Franklins Tower' dedicated to Franklin himself and a friend he's got with him."

Now that freaked me the fuck out. How in fuck did this crazy fuck pull that off? I was beyond terror and couldn't do shit about it except play along with my phony ass smile. Then the song began and the reception got stronger and stronger as he entered some little podunk town.

"Pretty cool huh?" Franklin says. I didn't fuckin' say a word, just sat still while my head began to throb and my chest tightened up. Then he pulled off the main road we were on and then we were on a dirt road.

"I don't like this, but it was exciting," I thought to myself, and at least he wasn't driving like a bat out of hell anymore. "Franklins Tower" had done ended by the time he pulled off on another road. We were in the fucking woods now and it didn't look too promising. He surprised me. He pulled into a driveway where there was house and tower.

The car stopped and he said, "Come on, I want you to meet someone." He opened his door and I did the same and followed Franklin. He didn't even knock, he just walked into the house.

The place was a wreck with electronic equipment everywhere you looked. Then we walked into this guy's personal studio/radio station. He introduces me to the guy and we shake hands. "This is Brad, I'm giving him a lift. He's going to San Francisco," and that's about all there was to it. We stayed about fifteen minutes and left.

It was dark thirty outside, and I was beyond calm. When we actually got back on the road, Franklin said to me, "I'm really tired, I thought we would have made better time. I'm going to rent a motel room and crash. Your welcome to share the room and I'll keep my promise and help you get closer to your destination in the morning." Now what the hell was I supposed to do? This guy looked like a psycho killer, and he definitely drove like one. But I didn't know where exactly I was and he did. I had been to jail before and I'd dealt with some heavy shit on the street, so I took a gamble and said ok. When we were finally inside this motel room he says to me, "Just a single bed is all they had, so I'll share it with you if you want."

I quickly said, "Franklin, that's alright I've had enough surprises for one night, thank you all the same, I'll sleep on the floor. If you wanna kick me down a sheet and pillow that would be great." He didn't fight me and acted like it was no big deal with a shrug of his shoulders and threw a pillow and top comforter off the bed. "This guy must think I'm stupid," I thought to myself as I laid my head down on the pillow and acted like I was going asleep.

I didn't open my eyes for hours, just laid there on the floor as far away from the bed as I could. My head hurt and my chest hurt as well. I could hear him moving around the room as I squeezed my eyes shut. Sometime during the course of the night, I drifted off. Then all sudden my eyes shot open.

Right above me was Franklin sitting in a chair just staring at me. Fully clothed, believe it or not, just staring down at me. I jumped up immediately and raised my fists, "What the fuck are trying to do Franklin? Fuck me in my ass or do you always just tower over your victims you pick up off the highway!"

I was so out my mind and ready to bite his fucking nose off, if that's what it took. I actually scared the hell out of this giant balding man with his freak glasses. "I'll kill you with my bare fucking hands mother fucker! Come on bitch, lets dance, you ever been to jail? Well I have, you picked up the wrong fucking hippie! Come on!"

Franklin cowered into a corner of the room, and I saw the terror in his eyes. My heart pounded painfully, but this fuck had pushed me too far. "What's up, big man! It's your time now!"

Then he started to cry like a child and, with sobbing tears, begged me not to hurt him. I was in control now. He had jeopardized my safety on the road, and obviously underestimated me. Now all I had to do was call the police. I made quite a noise and we were in a decent motel, so he was fucked, unless he had a knife or gun. I had so much anxiety and rage built up, I was willing to fight this big crazy fuck.

Franklin saw the seriousness of the situation, and he sat down in a red chair next to a small table. Then he began to tell me how sorry he was in a very calm manner. All I could do was listen as my heart pounded. His manner was quite calming, considering he appeared to be a sick, perverse man.

The longer he talked the more, I calmed down. I had to pull myself together and stay on top of the situation. All I had to do was call the police. He knew it, I knew it, and that gave me the upper hand. I don't remember his last name now, but I did then. He let me know while he was driving.

As the sun rose, pouring its light through the motel curtains, both he and I reached an agreement. He said he would take me to the local bus depot and buy me a ticket to San Francisco for all the trouble he caused. I no longer feared him at all. He was a pussy in a big shell.

So I agreed, and the bus depot in this little town was not exactly a Greyhound. When he walked out of the small building he was carrying a ticket of some sort. He gave me the ticket and told me it was a one way on a charter bus, not a Greyhound. Then he gave me some cash. Did I refuse? Fuck no. He was gonna pay for this cruel and unusual punishment he put me through.

So, I took everything he offered and watched him get in his car and pull away. I sat on the bench in front of this podunk outfit for about thirty minutes. I smoked my last cigarette and waited. Finally, the bus showed up. It was a strange site. Definitely no Greyhound, that's for sure. It had no lettering on the side. The driver opened the door and looked at me blankly. "Well are you coming?" he says.

"Yes," I said. I walked up the steps and gave him my ticket. He punched it and I sat right behind him in the front. Sitting next to me was a girl in her teens. As I looked around, I noticed there were only girls on this bus. "That's weird" I thought to myself. The driver pulled away from the depot. My head was swimming. Yes, swimming was the word. I sat motionless, still in shock from the all the trauma I had been through. I finally said something as I watched the trees pass by outside. "Why are there only women on this bus?" I asked the girl next to me.

"I'm not sure if everyone is like myself, but I'm on my way to a convent." Yeah, that's right, I was on a charter bus full of nuns, basically. I believe this happened before in the "Beavis and Butthead Do America" movie. Alright, so this bus takes me all the way into downtown San Francisco to the AmTrack station off Market St. I suppose these ladies now had to catch a train. I didn't care, I just wanted something to eat and get back to my apartment.

Back Home

Now get this, as I walked from the station up Market St, there was a group of people walking down a side street. You know what they yelled out? "Seizure!" very loudly. Coincidence? Only God knows. After what I went through I figured there was a cruel conspiracy going on. To those people that yelled that out I say, "Fuck You!"

I got on the Masonic Bus and headed up the Haight and got off near Baker. When I reached McCalister, I pushed the doorbell and I was let in. As I walked up the stairs, that old familiar smell of cheeva flooded into my nostrils. When I walked in, some random opened the door.

"Where's Kathy?" I asked and the brother told me she was in the bathroom. My hands were shaking and I was not doing well by any means. What benzodiazapines were left in my body had worked there way out and I knew it wouldn't be long before I had another grand mal seizure. I needed a Valium at the very least, and nobody had one. I didn't want to drink that's for sure. Just wanted a little piece of mind. I knocked on the door and the door opened.

"Brad your back! We are so proud of you," Kathy told me.

"Thanks Kathy, but I've been through hell and back." She hugged me and sat back down, reluctantly, on the toilet. She was smoking heroin off foil. A crunch bar was sitting on the sink.

"I don't want to do this in front of you Brad," she said.

"Kathy, you know I've got some clean time; however, I'm still miserable. Break me off a small piece of your shit."

"I've only got a little bit Brad, and I don't want to be the one responsible if you get back on this like you were. Besides you've got more clean time than any of us." She was correct. "Since you left to get clean a lot of kids started going to the Methodone clinic. Now most of them do half as much as they used too."

"Well that's great, do you have a Valium at least?" She said no and lowered her head and broke me off a small piece.

How she could stand to be in the bathroom I don't know. The tub had shit and urine in it because the toilet was plugged up or just broken.

Kathy looked at me dead in the eyes and said these words, "She waited for you Brad. She waited until Christmas Eve all by herself in this place." I had already gotten a new needle from Ozzy. Apparently, Patches and Ozzy had moved in permanently since I was gone, and as I listened to Kathy's story I found a vein on my left hand and was pushing the brown love in my body.

Now hearing these words, as I shot up for the first time in a month, was surreal. So as I relapsed, I was being told the girl I still loved, yet had already accepted threw me away like trash, still loved me. Fuck! I wished Cathy would have told me that before I put that shit back in my body.

Yet I don't think it would have mattered. I gave up way back in Eugene, as I walked out of those doors. I knew what was waiting for me, and I had given it my all. Know this, if The Carlton House would have let me in, things would have been different. So I'm high, not just well, fucking high. No shakes, no worries, no pain. Completely normal and I actually had a buzz. Only to find out all the emotions I had been feeling were wrong.

Stephanie did care. Man, I could have cried, but I felt too good for such things. Cathy smiled at me as I sat down next to her. She knew what I was feeling. I rested my hand on her leg and started to nod. I could feel her running her hand through my hair. I think she was crying for me in her own way.

"She's gone Brad and you just missed her. I'm so sorry." I wanted to cry but couldn't, I had lost the ability.

"What now?" I said.

"Well, I've got some nugs I've got to swing so I'll give them to you for cost, and we can go up to the street and get rid of them." She gave me a bag, and we both went up to the Haight.

The days that followed after this were business as usual. I lost in love, once again, and vowed to never put myself in that position ever again. "I'm not going entertain the thought of loving anyone for a long time," I thought to myself. So slowly, but surely, I built up my ducats and pulled myself together. While all this sappy drama was going on, Allan and Kristy upstairs were doing very well. Abe was helping Allan with laying down LSD, and he was mailing it to his people or Kristy's. So they had about ten thousand dollars to my hundred.

The housing authority still had the eviction on hold as a result of the writ of Habeas Corpus. Wes was doing pretty good with his M.O.'s and me, I was just getting by.

1995

One day I walked upstairs to cop some dope from Allan and he had company. There were two bettys sitting on his couch, neither one I knew, and one of them was a beautiful girl, American and Asian mix. She was very good looking, to say the least. Allan's Kristy introduced us. "This is Michelle, Brad." (I forget the other girl's name)

I said hey and didn't think much about it. I got a quarter of dope from Allan and went back down stairs to get high with a few new veins that had surfaced on detox tour. When I opened the door, Patches was there to greet me with a smile and a hug that almost knocked the wind out of me. Patches hadn't seen me since I got back and he always wore a jolly smile with a laugh that only Patches was known for. Then I heard the doorbell ring and Patches hit the button and said, "Who is it?"

"Its Dennis, China Mike, and Mike," the speaker blared. So he buzzed them up and we had a little reunion. Dennis was still tall and skinny and Mike (Virginia Beach Crew) had cut off his long straight black hair. He cleaned up good, yet even with his long hair, he was always clean. Now he looked less obvious, as drug dealers go. I liked his new threads.

China Mike looked at me with that shit eating grin he was so famous for and all of us hugged and did our hand snap. Then I got another knock at the door. I figured it was Allan or Kristy, but it wasn't. It was the girls coming downstairs from their apartment. Both were eager to come in and puff all of us boys out with their dank nugs. None of us fought them on it. So all of us went into my room and smoked.

After that was over, I went into the bathroom to fix. I listened to them as I turned on the tap water, cleaning my spoon and filling it with water. You know the rest, and I came back out. Apparently there was a Grateful Dead intervention going on behind my back.

China Mike was the first to speak, "Brad, we feel you need to get out of the city. We see you're starting to get bad again, and Michelle wants to fly you and me with her to Portland and then rent a car."

"Hey man, I just got back from that hell, no thanks," I said immediately.

"Brad we're gonna go to the beach. Michelle says she will take care of it all, and while we are up there we are going to stop by Christy's place. Then we are gonna stay at a condo on the beach."

I thought about all that was just said and replied, "Man, I'll go crazy if I leave the city, China, I don't want to go through what I just went through weeks ago."

China Mike said, "Don't worry man, I've got a lot of Valium still left from the produce store near the Mission."

Then Michelle says, "Yeah, Brad I've got a prescription of Xanax as well, so you will be fine." This was very unexpected. This is what showed me that I was loved. So I agreed, with a smile, as I felt the heroin do it's magic.

The next day, the three of us got on a plane (Southwest Airlines) round trip to Portland and back. On the plane, Michelle gave me a Xanax and China Mike gave me some Valium and I felt well. It was a relatively short plane ride to Portland. Michelle already had a rental car waiting for us at the airport. It was a blue Toyota Corolla stick shift. She wasn't too happy about that so Mike drove us to Eugene to pick up Christy and her dog Osiris.

We didn't even stay a day in Eugene, and that suited me just fine. When we got to her house, I was introduced to her and Osiris. Christy was pretty thin yet looked healthy. She was very happy to see us, and I thought to myself, "Why haven't I met her before?" I actually thought I knew everyone, but there were so many kids from '90 to '95. How could I know everyone? Well I sure as fuck knew faces if I didn't know their names.

So we all packed in the Toyota and, for whatever reason, we headed to Corvallis to do some buisiness. When we pulled in the driveway of this small house, all of us got out and Christy knocked on the door and we were let in. The house was a typical scene with Jerry Garcia posters, Bob Marley, and all the rest of what makes up a house rented by Dead Heads. I sat down on the couch by myself, just looking around. Everyone else was doing whatever in another room. Then eventually they came out and a bowl was packed.

We didn't spend much time there. All of us were hungry so we went to one of the well known local places to eat and drink good beer. This was the first time I had ever been served ice water with a slice of lemon in it. They gave all four of us this for starters without even asking whether we wanted water. Now my first sips were the best. How ingenious it was to add a slice of lemon to water. Who needed a soft drink. It was yummy, and to this very day I always make sure there's a lemon in my water when I go to a restaurant. I owe this to the city of Corvallis.

China ordered a beer and the rest of us did the same. Now I had to make it clear I was bumming and had no money really. This didn't matter, Michelle payed for anything I wanted. I was starting to catch on this sister liked me.

What she didn't know was Stephanie was still weighing heavy on my heart. To fall in love again was out the question, let alone letting someone into my life to open the door to another relationship.

Now I wasn't too bright, as I write these memories I'm aware of this. Michelle Gibby was her full name. Her father was American, and her mother was Japanese. They met when he was stationed overseas. That's what I know of her background, other than she was going to school in Berkeley. I did not know her from tour. She was brand new to our world as I saw it. Making mistakes one after the next seems to be what I do. This girl was giving me another chance or just letting me see Oregon again under kinder conditions. Or all the above, and I would like to think that's the case.

So we left Corvallis, and headed towards the coast. I just sat in the back most of the time paying no attention to my surroundings. We did finally get to the beach and Michelle rented a condo on the beach. It was a very beautiful set up with a fridge and a small kitchen. Complete with patio door opening out onto the Pacific Ocean.

The first thing we did was walk through that patio door after looking around the room. As I opened it, Osiris ran out to the beach first. The sky was a grayish blue and it was chilly, after all it was January 1995. It was in the low sixties, as temperature goes, so we were not going to swim in the Ocean. The Corvallis trip gave us more nugs and some mushrooms. After we walked briefly in the sand and got Osiris under control and back in the room, Christy and Mike started to make some mushroom tea on the little stove in the kitchen.

We wasted no time, once it was ready, and all of us drank our share. I myself was leery because I knew anything that was too stimulating might give me a grand mal seizure. Granted, I did have anti-seizure medication in me, yet it had been years since I had tripped. Sure, I constantly hallucinated just from the handling of the product throughout the years, but I stopped ingesting LSD when I became such a strong provider.

So I drank about a third of the cup and waited. As I could feel it twenty minutes later I drank another third and waited. The longer I waited the more it came on slowly and not disturbingly. I was aware I now had nerve damage, so I was scared. Seizures suck. When an hour passed I was tripping, very mellow like, and I finished the rest of my tea.

When the full effect of the mushrooms were at its peak I wondered off away from everyone asking Christy if Osiris and I could play on the beach. As I walked towards the Pacific there was a large log in the sand and I sat down it. Looking around at the colors and grey sky Osiris barked at me, getting my attention. He wanted to play, and I realized Kristy gave me a Frisbee. It was in my left hand and Osiris was very eager for me to throw it. So I got up and walked closer to the ocean and threw it. Not in the water just down the beach, for the water was to cold. Osiris eventually jumped in the ocean, anyway after he grew bored.

While he splashed around I walked back to the wood coming out of the sand and watched. The thoughts going through my mind were kind. It had been years since I'd had such a feeling of peace within and out. Life was worth living. Love is the answer. You know these thoughts, they seem to come hand and hand with boomers. Osiris came running up to me, looking very happy. I could see his smile. I loved that dog. This memory we shared together, I'll take to my grave.

So Both Osiris and I went back into our haven on the beach and joined the rest of the crew. They were all laughing about something. "How you feel Brad?" Michelle asked me with a smile.

"I feel great, and Osiris and I bonded." Christy smiled when I said that as Osiris went directly to her. While I was gone somebody went to a local srore of some sort and bought some groceries. Nobody wanted to stay in the room and trip all day. So we broke up in pairs. China Mike and Kristy also wanted to go outside and experience the beach. So they took off and left me with Michelle. We really hadn't been alone once. So there was a little tension in the room for a minute or so.

Then Michelle broke the silence. "So do you want to take a walk with me on the beach?"

"Sure," I responded. We walked out of the room and down the beach. Neither one of us seemed to have anything to say. So we walked in silence for at least five minutes.

"So how do you know so many people Brad?" Michelle asked.

"Well I suppose touring with The Boys for all these years would be the reason, Michelle," and she smiled when I said that.

"Well tell me about it," she says.

"What's to tell and where do I start?" That wasn't the best answer, I'm sure, yet it was a beginning. She did most of the talking as we watched the ocean splash against the shore. I let her know how I met China Mike, and I told her how much I appreciated all she was doing. Michelle was very humble and kind. She told me she was student at Berkeley and she told she envied the fact I'd been to so many places. That made me realize that there are so many people that just don't understand completely. Hell, at that moment I didn't have it in me to explain why. It just was. That is all I knew.

Some people live and some people just think they have lived. Finding that special someone to live with and live for is what it's all about, when you get right down to it. That's my opinion, of course. Wanting a family, a church, a fellowship of some sort is the other side of it. The shoe fit was all I could tell her without going into my whole life story. We had walked a good ways and she said, "You want to go back? I'm getting a little tired and chilly and its getting dark."

"Yeah, lets head back," I agreed. As we walked back, she grabbed my hand, and we walked side by side a little closer. Michelle was opening my fragile heart. I had my reserves, no matter how much money she possessed, I didn't care. I liked her a lot more than I let on, mainly to protect myself from another heartache. When we got back to the room, Mike and Kristy were there and they had that look of exhaustion.

"Let's do something," Kristy said.

"What time is it?" Mike asked.

"About Six," Michelle said.

"Well they have a bar connected to this place that looks pretty cool," said Mike.

"I want a fucking drink anyway," Christie said. So we ate some of the food we had. Then we smoked some bud and headed for the bar. When we got there, we were surprised by how packed it was. We started drinking and Michelle kept on paying for all my drinks. By eight or nine, all of us were feeling really good. The mushrooms had tapered off into the stoned alcohol realm. We had passed through the spirit world and came back to reality.

There was a lifted stage on one side of the bar with a huge karaoke set up, and we watched people make fools of them selves. Now I mean that in the kindest regards because Mike was tugging at my shoulder telling me, "Lets do it man!"

"Do what? From what I've heard so far, I don't think they will have anything I want to sing."

"Well, I'm gonna get the list of tunes they have," and with that Mike went up to the bar. He came back with a list of songs, and there was some decent stuff. Believe it or not (Mikes favorite Dead Song but that's beside the point) we decided on a Blondi song called "The Tide is High." I grew up on Blondie, same as most kids did, so we got up on the little stage and waited for the teleprompter to kick in.

The music started and the words followed on the screen. Mike and I started to crack up with laughter as it started. Both of us were pretty high. So we began, "The tide is high, but I'm holding on. I'm gonna be your number one…I'm not the kinda girl who gives up just like that, Oh No", and we both busted out laughing. The whole fucking bar was laughing with us as well.

There was a phone on the right side of the stage. Mike told Michelle to call Roach when we started, and she actually got a hold of him. Michelle held the phone out in the air while Mike and I made a fool of ourselves. We sang off key laughing our asses off the whole time. I would say it was the highlight of the whole trip. When the song faded out and crowd was clapping and asking for more. Both Mike and I had our fun and we got off stage. We washed down our smiles with beer and sat down at the table with a grin that was priceless.

Eventually another person got up and began singing a tune not so fun and we drifted away from the little bar back to our room. Michelle and I started to warm up to each other. After the mushrooms had completely disappeared from our minds we puffed some nugs. Mike and Kristy hopped in one of the beds and Michelle and I did the same. The TV was playing some random movie.

"Ouch!" Michelle cried out. Not super loud, just startling.

I said, "What's wrong?"

"I don't know, my side hurts," she replied. Then she cried out very loud.

"Fuck, Michelle, what's going on?"

"I don't know," she repeated. With another shout of pain she cries out

"Get me to a hospital!"

I called up to the front desk and they told me the closest Hospital was twenty minutes away, and they gave me directions. "Drive me Brad, please," Michelle said.

"Ok, let me help you up, I'll walk you to the car." I had no valid driver's license but I didn't give a fuck. She wasn't kidding around, and she definitely was in pain. So I drove like a bat out of hell.

When we got there, I carried her into the ER. They took her from me without hesitation, and no paperwork just yet. They gave her a shot of Demerol and she felt much better. After they got a urine sample the Doctor on call told her and I that she had a urinary tract infection. They gave us these packets of very small pills she was instructed to take, and they released her after she gave her insurance information.

On the drive home she was feeling much better. She had eaten one of the pills and it, mixed with the Demerol, put her in good spirits. As I drove back to the beach condo, she laid her head on my shoulder. "I really appreciate everything Brad," and then kissed me on the cheek.

As we walked in our room Kristy and Mike were eager to know what the fuck happened. Christy smoked us out and that made Michelle feel even better. All of us fell asleep as the TV did its thing. Michelle snuggled close to me on the bed. The next morning we ate breakfast at the restaurant that was connected to the bar. It was a large room with round tables with white tablecloths on each table with wrapped silverware. We sat at the window with a view of the ocean as we ate. I ordered eggs and hash browns. They were more like home style potatoes and they were good.

Michelle ordered some fruit and orange juice. "You stay with me and you can have anything you want," Michelle told me, out the blue, as I ate my breakfast.

"What do you mean?" I asked.

"I mean, you stay off the heroin, and I'll take care of you," she said.

"Just like that?"

"Yeah if you haven't figured it out, I like you," she said. I didn't know what to say. I just kept on eating. Michelle Gibby was absolutely beautiful. She could have any fucking man.

"Why me?" I said.

"Cause I like you," and she smiled.

"Just stay off the shit huh?" I said.

"Yeah and you can have whatever you want." It sounded like a reasonable proposal. I wasn't in love with her was the problem. I liked her and was growing with her every moment, yet I still had Stephanie in my head.

"I'm trying to get over a heartache, ya know," I told Michelle.

"Yeah, I know about it," and she reached across the table and took my hand. I looked up at her and looked directly in her eyes and stared for at least thirty seconds. She never looked away.

"Ok," I said.

When it was time to go and drive back to Eugene to drop off Christy, it was hard to believe any of this was real. We all hugged and said our goodbyes. The ride back to Portland was quiet. Once there, we returned the car rental and went to the terminals. The flight back home was just as quiet. I didn't seem sick. Mike had Valium and Michelle had Xanax so I was very well. Things looked promising and it appeared I was moving in a forward direction.

There was only one fucking problem: Stephanie Robinson. Why did she have to stay in my apartment up until Christmas Eve? Why couldn't she have just given up on me? These were the thoughts that would kill me. I had to let go and get over it. Sitting next to me was a beautiful girl that adored me.

So, on that flight back to the shitty, I made up my mind. I was going to love this girl and treat her good. Forget the whole year of '94 and move on. When we got off the plane we got our luggage and headed for Michelle's car. As we drove, China Mike sat in the back and he didn't seem to be too happy about that. He wanted us to drop him off on the Haight to do some business, and Michelle wanted me to go with her to her place in Berkeley. I did what she said.

When we got there, I was surprised to say the least. Her pad was clean and that's something I hadn't seen. Sure I knew people with their own places in the city. But most people I knew were like myself. I worked for everything I had from the gutter up. My parents were not rich. They weren't putting me through college and paying my rent. She had a small yet beautiful pad it was a reflection of her.

We did the usual bullshit, "Oh what a nice place." I said.

She says, "Oh it's a mess, I need to clean it up." Yeah, it was spotless, so it was just the typical conversation. She went to the kitchen and pulled out a carry out box of steamed white rice that had to have been in the fridge for at least a week. She ate it with sticks, and offered me a bite.

"No thanks, I'm still good," I lied to her. She put it away after I say that, and went into the bathroom. When she came out she walked over to me and started to kiss me. I follow suit and we find ourselves on her bed rolling around in each other's arms. I'm no fucking romance novelist. Hell, I can barely fucking spell. What you've read is what was, nothing more, nothing less.

The next couple of weeks we became partners in crime, as they say. I knew the people, and she had the money. But don't get me wrong I had genuine feelings for Michelle. She had me in her web. Hell, I had almost completely forgotten about Stephanie.

Until one day, some sister came up to me when I was on Haight, at the bottom of the hill, putting runners to work with weight I was selling. Michelle had bought a quarter pound of nugs and I was selling weight to family so they could bag it up into heighths. This sister hands me a small piece of paper with a number on it. I opened it up and it read "Stephanie" followed by a phone number written underneath it.

My whole world turned up side down. All the feelings I had been suppressing arose like a hundred people standing as the preacher says, "let's all rise." At that moment I had a calling card number, and I knew where the nearest phone was. Without hesitation I walked to that phone, called the number, and a familiar voice answered, "Hello."

"Is Stephanie there." I asked.

"That's me," she said.

"It's Brad," and there was a small pause.

Then she said, "I hear your doing well."

"I'm getting by, how are you?"

"That's not what I hear, you're doing better than getting by, congratulations Brad." Stephanie tells me. "I miss you."

I held back, as much as one can, who is still in love. "I miss you too, and I still love you Stephanie," I said.

"My nose is different, Brad," she told me. Then went on very vaguely why her nose was broken since I last saw her.

"I don't give a fuck, I just want you back in my life." However, I still had feelings for Michelle.

"Sounds like you already have someone in your life," she said.

"Yeah, your right, I do, yet I didn't go out of my way to get into another relationship. She came to me when I was down. Look, I'll fly you back out here. I've almost got the money together to do that," I told Stephanie.

The conversation ended finally and my life changed from that moment on. I'm not sure if she gave me a reason to buy some heroin or I was just waiting for a reason.

Shortly after that phone call, I bought a quarter of cheeva, and got high after weeks of clean time. After all, Michelle had one condition. That night I spent the night in Berkeley at Michelle's place and showed her what I had bought. Came clean, I suppose, that I wasn't going to be able to keep my promise.

She said, "Well, I would like to do it with you," and I gave her a low dosage to make sure she didn't overdose on her first experience with heroin. I'm not proud of myself by no means for allowing that to happen. Michelle leaned back on her bed, and enjoyed the ride. Then we made love.

As I relive these moments, I realize how unkind I really was in this adventure. I tried to contact her before she entered this book, yet with no success. I've used the search engines, that the internet offers, to find obituaries of Haight kids, only to find a couple late eighty's kids that were in the second to last family before our family of the 90's. While doing so, I thought about Jimbo and how it may affect him by telling this story. What I found out was he died in 2005. I've researched only to find very little of my family. With the help of Stephanie, I know some things now that I will reveal very soon. As Michelle Gibby goes, if this book ever hits the shelves she will surface as many others will, if they survived. That's my goal. I'm not supposed to be here, and I'll explain that soon as well.

Now to my knowledge she never became addicted, as many others did. This is not for sure, and I'm crossing my fingers. The next morning I went back to the hill (Buena Vista West) and hid my bags under tires of automobiles. This way if Goff or Confrey shook me down they would find nothing.

I had stopped selling LSD, and I was only swingin' buds. I can honestly say I'd retired from that. Nineteen ninety-five was my retirement year. I still had to make a living, so I sold the pot Michelle had bought. That quarter pound she purchased was diminishing. So I just sold heighths with the goal of flying Stephanie back to the city.

A couple of days passed, and I slowly got back into everday use of heroin. I don't think Michelle was going down the same path as I. When I asked to stay with her at her place, she said, "I've got some things to do." So it seemed the heroin use was affecting our relationship.

After that last conversation, I stayed at my place on Baker and McCallister. It was a fucking mess. Patches and Ozzy were running the place while I had been staying with Michelle. Patches didn't expect to see me that night. I could tell from his eyes and smile, that he wasn't all there. The next morning I got up and walked upstairs to Allan's apartment. He didn't have any cheeva to sell me, and I didn't have a wake up. It was alright, though, I wasn't so sick I couldn't go to the street and work. As I climbed up the hill I stashed my bags like always and the clock ticked by.

By noon the sun was very bright and the sky was clear. It was a beautiful day in San Francisco. I had sold one bag and things were little slow. At the very top of the hill were a couple of new kids swinging bags as well. Stepping on people's toes was a no no. So we all did what we could to balance out the business.

Since I'd been to jail in South Carolina for the nine months and had probation hanging over my head, that I blew off just to clear my name, I was extra careful. I can't say everyone was as cautious as myself.

Sure enough, it was time to sweep the streets again. Goff and Comfrey raced up the hill in a white, unmarked, four door sedan. Now, I didn't know it was them until they got out of the car. "Hey Token!" one of them yelled at me, and he asked me to come to them. I did and I had nothing on me.

I was padded down and then Goff says to me, "Aren't you on probation Token?"

"Yeah," I replied.

"You shouldn't be up here, looks like you're up to no good," he said. Now in '94 I was busted for having two bags on me. Which gave them a reason to take to me to park station and book me for possession with intent to sell. If I would have had just one bag, then that's just a thirty-eight dollar ticket. However, last year, that wasn't the case and they found out I was wanted in South Carolina for failure to report to the probation officer. Why? Cause I was so worried about my name, and I had turned no one in.

I felt I did the right thing. However, South Carolina did not extradite me, so they gave me a cool probation officer in San Francisco. He was a Rastafarian with dreads, and he only required I call in every couple of months to tell him of my status. If only the South Carolina probation officer was that cool maybe things would have been different, who knows. I remember the P.O. they gave me in S.C. only because his last name was the same as my mothers. His name was Mr. Wier. Spelled different than my mother's maiden name.

My mom's name is Roberta Weir, now that's she's divorced from my father. Not to jump off track from the facts, yet while I was waiting in San Bruno County Jail, I called my parents, collect. My mom answered the phone and after the small talk she said to me, "Well Brad, since you've been living in San Francisco for so long, I believe you're old enough and strong enough to know that I'm a lesbian and I'm leaving your dad for another woman."

Yeah, I was silent for a minute then finally said, "Ok mom", and didn't call home again for a year.

So I'll get back to the story. Sorry to jump around. So there I was on the hill just got shook down and Goff and Comfrey went to the next hippie. Who was walking away upward as he saw them shaking me down. Comfrey ran after him and for a moment it looked as if the bro was going to run. He didn't, in spite of the fact he was holding more than one bag to sell.

So I watched him get handcuffed, with sadness. As they put him in the back of the white car his girlfriend was in tears at the top of the hill. Like a dumb ass, I walked over to comfort her. She told me his name was Cheese. I assured her he would be out in a day or two, since she said it was his first time getting popped here in the city.

"They will OR him, as they say, by end the of today or tomorrow," I told her. "No worries, it's his first time he will be out in no time," and like it says, scribbled on the wall above the door in the waiting tank right before you go into the courtroom, "The judge will fuck you but at least he will use grease." I didn't tell her that part, that would be mean, they held him for pending charges or he was a flight risk. I left that part out because I didn't want to scare her even worse.

"Well, will you help me? They wouldn't let me get the keys to our car from Cheese so all I have is a hotel key of our room off Market St." She could have taken the bus. She didn't really need me, yet I saw it all go down and I could have warned him how it rolls, but I didn't know Cheese.

He wasn't a familiar face. He was shorter than this girl and very skinny. He was a small guy. I would have remembered his face from tour. So, obviously, he was the next generation moving in. It had been about four years of the same family. I have researched, while writing this book, and it appears that every four to five years, since the beginning of Grateful Dead Land, a new family would develop on Haight St.

So I hadn't had a wake up, and this girl wanted me to help her get down to the TL where Cheese and her were staying. What the fuck was I supposed to do? I gave her a bus schedule and that's it. No, I don't think so, she was a sister in need of help and I could afford to take a break especially since I was a little shook up myself.

I needed to cop dope anyway and get right before the sickness set in. I should have put her on the Masonic bus and been done with it, but if you want to kill me now, you know my weakness. We got on the bus together, reached Market St. and I prompted her to get off so I could get more cheeva, and walk her to her hotel room. Didn't I already do this before under different circumstance? Where did that get me?

At that moment, I was helping another damsel in distress. I got what I wanted and walked her to her hotel. She asked me to come up with her and I was hesitant. Why? Number one, I still had bags to left to sell. Number two, selling them meant one step closer to a plane ticket for the girl I was still in love with. They both meshed together.

One problem, I was getting those hot sweats and chills that let me know I need to fix. So the heroin prompted my sorry ass to go up to her room. When she opened the door, I went to the bathroom, and then realized I had no spoon. I had a rig stashed at the park that I had brought with me, but my spoon was at my house.

So I came out of the bathroom and asked her if they had a Coke can or beer can, and there was one in the garbage. I tore it apart and turned it upside down. Then put a little water in the bowl of the can dropped a piece of cheeva in the small pool of water and heated it up with my lighter stirring it with the plunger of the needle. It was a pretty big shot that hit me harder than I expected. I stumbled out of the bathroom and sat on the bed.

"What's wrong?" she said.

"Oh, I took a big shot, that's all, just let me chill hear for a moment and I'll go. What is your name anyway?" I asked her as I start to nod.

"I'm sorry, I thought you already knew my name, I'm Maria"

"I'm Brad," I said.

"I knew that already, Cheese told me your name on the hill," Maria told me. How the fuck does he know me? I thought to myself. So I say, "That's cool, Maria. I had crush, when I was Five or Six, on a girl named Maria I met at one of my parents live gigs on Corns Lake in Columbia, MO."

"Awe, that's so sweet," she said and then ran her hand through my hair (what hair I had). I'm not sure why I said those words other than the heroin talking. It has a tendency to do that. The next thing I remember, she turns my head towards her and looks in my eyes. Then she kisses me. Then her tongue is in my mouth.

It takes two I'm aware; however, I was vulnerable at that moment. Still feeling the high of the heroin mixed with the smell of her essence. She pulled me down on top of her. Fifteen minutes later I was no longer high and looking up at the ceiling half dressed. It was that quick, and I was powerless to stop what had just happened, yet it happened.

"What a shit head I am," I thought to myself. What happened in the next moments were classic. I came back to reality, filled with regret. "I've got to go, Maria, I'm so sorry about everything. This wasn't supposed to happen. Cheese will be released very soon, I'm sure. I suggest you stay here and call eight-fifty Bryant St. That's the police station where he will be booked and released. That's what I went through before. Maria, its only five or six blocks away from this hotel so stay put for your bro."

And I left, I went back up to the Haight and climbed the hill and it took the rest of the day to get rid of what I had to sell. When I sold my last bag, I headed home. When I got there, no one was there and that was odd. There was always someone there.

I ran upstairs to Allan's apartment and Kristy opened the door. As I walked in, their apartment layout was like mine, and I turned to my right and entered the living room. Sitting on Allan and Kristy's couch were Michelle and Maria. Yeah, that's right, both girls on the couch, talking with smiles on their faces, like all was well. I was speechless to say the least. What a fucking set-up! This girl seduced me and I'm aware it takes two; however, I was on a fucking mission. Looks like that mission just failed. Michelle smiled at me and said, "So I see you've met Maria already," she said still smiling.

"What's going on?" I reply.

"Oh nothing just girl talk. You got my money?"

"Yeah," I replied.

"Cool give it to me."

"I don't have all of it on me," I tell Michelle.

"Well get it," she says.

"Alright, come downstairs," I said to Michelle. She followed me downstairs and I got the money I had hidden.

"That's not all of it," she said. Where's the rest?"

"I haven't sold everything yet," I explained to her and let her know one reliable runner had a weighed quarter that I fronted to him.

"Okay, I'm going to take care of some business, and I'll be back later to get the rest." And with that I went back down to the street and get the money owed to me. I hung out a little on the hill to swing what little bit I had left, but no bites. I finally went home. I saw her car parked on the side street.

As I was walking up the stairs, she was walking down them. She didn't say shit to me, so I followed her to her car. She got in and opened the passenger door and I got in. "You fucked up, Brad. Where's the rest of it?" I gave her all I owed and we were straight. So after she counted it, she started up her car and pulled into the street then took a left on the corner in front of my place. "Get out," she said and I did.

That was last time I saw Michelle Gibby. I really did fuck her over. Shit, I could have done things differently. Maria didn't hold a gun up to my head. Using Michelle and her resources to sell buds in order to fly Stephanie back to the shitty was not honorable. I deserved everything I got.

I lost Michelle, a good friend and lover. It was fucked up, I cared a lot for Michelle, yet I was still in love with Stephanie. Why did I call that number? Because she waited for me till fucking Christmas Eve! At that moment, I reached down into my wallet to find Stephanie Robinson's phone number, but it was gone. The piece of paper with her phone number in Memphis was gone.

I had lost everything from the moment I called Stephanie. I got loaded on heroin after that. I fucked some random sister as a result. Yeah, I'm fucking blaming the goddamn drug! All I had to do was stay off the shit, like Michelle said, and I fucking didn't. One phone call is all it took to bring back all those emotions I had squelched.

It's nobody's fault but mine. It wasn't the heroin. It wasn't Stephanie. I fucked up, no one else. I should have stood by Michelle. She showed me her dedication by the way she handled herself. Calling Steph was gonna happen regardless, but it could have ended there.

The way I see it, I'm no kind bro. I'm just lucky Michelle didn't have me spun for my actions. I'm sure I would have been spun if I didn't give her all the money I owed her. She had the money to do it, and I would have deserved it. She knew Allan, so you can do the math. But to be spun over a lovers quarrel in our family is hard to justify.

I broke probation just to prove to my brothers and sisters that I'm real. I had five years hanging over my head as a result. This book is the story, I believe, for all those who entertain the idea of going to San Francisco, Seattle, or wherever, to find themselves, should read first. It's a miracle I'm alive to tell you what really happened to the last true family of The Grateful Dead. Turning people in, rolling on family, is not what this about. As you know, this is the first time I've ever mentioned to the general public what happened. So I'm going to finish this in hopes that my close friends will live again in the minds of those that read about their lives. I do hope that I've painted a picture clear enough for the reader to visualize each and every person in this book. For this is the only way that I know I can bring them back, here in this world, if only just for a moment.

I walked back in my apartment, sat down, and counted what money I had. There was definitely not enough for a plane ticket. I was in shock. Not only did I insinuate I was going to help Stephanie, and I couldn't even tell her how things went wrong.

I truly felt terrible for playing both sides of the field, and a third party as well. (That would be Maria.) Forgive me, Michelle, for loving you with a broken heart, and not being a hundred percent honest with you. Forgive me, Stephanie, for being immature and being comforted by Michelle before I had gotten over our relationship. Forgive me Cheese for not being strong and for sleeping with Maria while you were in jail. Heroin or no heroin there was no excuse for any of these things I did. I didn't roll on anyone, but I sure as fuck wasn't the kind bro I was supposed to be. Nobody's fault but mine, kids. I love all of you still, and I failed.

I was feeling sorry for myself, and I was on my pity pot. Oh poor Brad ... Well fuck that! So I went upstairs and Allan without saying a word sold me a quarter of heroin. I did this for a week solid, not going to the street much. Just sat there and tried to nod all of my mistakes away.

There was no family intervention. If anything I deserved to die, and I had once again run out of places to hit. I tried to hit my feet and that hurt like fuck. So I pushed the plunger into my nose trying to snort it like old times. As it drained down the back of my throat and hit my stomach I threw up violently. As I sat there holding the toilet bowl with sweat dripping down my forehead I knew a change was coming. What I just pushed in my nose was the last of what I had. I was broke again.

I went upstairs and begged Allan to front me a quarter, telling him I'd go to the street and pay him back later. He did, for he knew I was the one who launched his career in the sale of LSD. Abe was his knew connection and John and Lucky retired for all I know. Hell, I'd retired and let Allan carry the torch. I'd come too close to going back to jail so many times.

Selling marijuana in San Francisco was safer, by far, but not as profitable. When I came back down stairs I managed to get I a good shot in my body through one of the last tiny little veins left on my left hand, and, thanks to Allan, he gave me a new rig.

While I was nodding out Patches came in and went to his room and then I saw him adjusting the thermostat in the hallway where the gas heater was. I awoke hours later choking on a house filled with natural gas in the air. Whatever Patches did must have caused the pilot light to go out, and as a result the house was polluted with gas. If I would have nodded out throughout the night I'm sure but it could have killed me. Don't quote me on that. I haven't done any research on gas leaks, other than people that close their garage doors and leave their car running.

At the moment, I honestly thought he tried to kill me by gassing me to death. I wasn't in my right mind, so I won't believe that entirely. I shut it down completely opened the door, and the place did air out. It was late already and dark outside. I promised Allan I would go work the street and I didn't. However, I still had half a quarter and once I was breathing clean air again, I used that new rig and managed to hit that same little vein again, and then I nodded out. I awoke abruptly, by Allan screaming, "You got my money? Where's my money!"

Now I exploded and jumped on Allan and blackened his eye. I screamed at him, "Don't you ever come into my house without knocking, waking me up telling me give you money! What the fuck is wrong with you? I know you have thousands of dollars as a result of selling "L" that's fucking silver. Not even good product, and Abe and you can go fuck yourselves! Oh, I'll get you your fucking money that's a promise."

That night, I hardly slept. Allan woke me up and I was having trouble getting back to sleep. I didn't have anything left but a spoon and cotton, and as hard as it was to get it in me, I wasn't about to stab myself to death for small traces of cheeva.

When morning finally came, I was up and out the door. I headed for streets with a vial of water I was willing to pass off to a random custy as a vial of liquid LSD. Now I hadn't burned anyone for years. That was the one thing most people new about me. My word was golden. So I had reached the point of no return. A couple of hours passed, as I stood on the streets saying, "doses" to anyone that looked like a buyer.

Right as I was about to give up because I so dope sick and the sun was killing me, three kids turned and said, "You got some acid?"

"Oh yeah man, beautiful stuff I got some liquid LSD," I tell these guys. They looked about twenty or so. "Well we need more than one vial, and I'd rather have paper."

So I put on my poker face and said, "Suit yourself I only deal with the best. I'm sure if you keep on walking your find someone with paper." And as some other prospect passes by I say, "doses," and ignored them like they just missed out.

"Alright we will take it, but we need more," said the leader of the pack.

"Hey man, I've only got one vial and its super clean, and it's on a front. Tell you what, walk with me to Buena Vista Park, to the top of the hill where he is, and lets see how much he's got."

They followed me to the top of the hill where other kids were swinging buds and I said "Ok, I need eighty for this one and I only make ten bucks on the whole deal so how much do you need?"

He said they had a hundred and eighty dollars were looking for at least four sheets. I told them ok, and walked over to someone, I knew who was swinging nugs and acted like I was negotiating.

Then I walked back up to the hill and said these words, "Yeah guys, I kinda fucked up by walking over to my man in front of you and he saw you were watching him. He's sketched out selling you vials of family 'L' for family prices."

The kids automatically said, "Dude, we're not cops, come on."

"Yeah, I know, but you're not known here so this is the deal. Give me your money and I'll give you one vial, and you can taste it at the same time while I give my man the money. He won't front me three more vials," they hesitated so I gave the guy that was doing all the talking the vial I had on me, and we walked up the hill.

This random guy pops the lid and tasted it. Now, I was a little nervous when he did that, but he turned to me and said, "okay," and handed me the money.

I told them all to sit on the bench and let me give this money to my man. They did just that and I walked down the hill to the bro I didn't even know him in the first place and acted like I was doing a deal. I even showed the money the guys on the bench gave me. I acted rather open about so they would see I flashed their money.

What was really going on was I told this bro I wanted a weighed eighth, and I wanted to walk down the hill so the custys sitting on the bench wouldn't see me tax them a big bud so bro said cool and we walked down the hill and around the corner. I did buy an eighth from him, then in a second's time I bolted across the street. I ran down towards the panhandle and crossed both streets on both sides of the park not stopping for traffic. Ran like a devil, I was, all the way back home to Baker and McCalister. I thought I was gonna have a fucking heart attack. I passed my door on the second floor and kept climbing the stairs to pay Allan and re-up. When he answered the door, he stepped back like I was gonna punch him again.

"It's cool Allan, I'm so sorry I hit you man, I didn't know who you were at first and it freaked me out. You shouldn't wake people up like that, ya know. Shit, here's your money," and I handed him what I owed. "I need a half a gram, Allan," and he said nothing just went into the other room and gave me a half a gram of cheeva.

Allan said he was sorry for going about it wrong last night and we hugged. He had a little shiner on his left eye where I had hit him. I felt bad for what I did. We both felt bad for behaving poorly to each other. That was the last time I saw Allan.

I went downstairs, got myself well, and grabbed what I needed and walked across the street to the pay phone. I called my dad. My mom no longer lived with Dad, they had separated by this point. I told Dad I needed help and I'm coming home if I have enough money to pay for a one-way ticket to South Carolina on a Greyhound Bus. I was wanted in South Carolina, yet I was leaving California, knowing I burned no family. So I was willing to turn myself in on one condition, I had to go to detox first.

So Dad wired a few more dollars by Western Union because buying that eighth set me back fifty dollars. It was weight, Mendocino Indo, to be exact. So, I was only thirty dollars short for the ticket, yet I didn't have food money so dad covered what I needed, and I got on a Greyhound with one black backpack with very few clothes, a bag of new rigs, a bag of dank nugs, my one-hitter and a half of a gram of Cheeva. The journey was three and a half, almost four, days long from San Francisco to South Carolina. If I was well I could smoke, if not, I would have a panic attack.

By now, I'm sure you know (whether you once were a heroin addict or shot anything period) how fucking painful and maddening it is to run out of places to hit. Once you've collapsed all your veins your pretty fucked. Kurt Cobain I'm sure was a prime example of that. However, try hitting yourself on a moving bus in the bathroom when you've collapsed all your veins. Man I missed eighty percent of the stabs until it ran out. My arms were yellowish and purple with an abscess here an abscess there. Fuck man, I painfully stayed well, mainly just missing the whole way. Yeah, I still refused to hit my neck, feet, and my dick. I still had my limits, no matter how much pain I was in.

One thing was clear to me through all the madness, if I was willing to face five years in prison just to get off dope; my mom and dad must have done something correct raising me. It's right up there with willing to blow probation off and become addicted to heroin with all my closest friends just to prove my innocence. People who claim they don't care what others think are full of shit. They are not the kind of people I want around me. Honor and Valor are words to live by. We were the last family of the Haight before Jerry died, and that's a fact.

So I'm well, running low on heroin, and I've got some nice herb to puff so I would go to the back of the bus just like shooting up yet a lot less painful. There is always a small window on the Greyhounds; nevertheless, this little window had a latch on the outside and every time we would stop I would walk around the back of the bus and unlock that little latch. Some stops were impossible to get away with it so what I would do is take those wipes they would provide and shove them in the window so fucking hard it would wedge that little window next the shitter open just enough to inhale and exhale with a little one hitter. Now I know I'm not the only one who has done it. The first thousand miles wasn't so bad. It was the last three hundred to Denver that things turned to the worse.

If you thought my bitching about missing left and right was bad, that ain't shit compared to not having anything to miss with. I ran out of heroin on the fucking bus before I even got to Denver, Co. When I got there, I was dope sick, yet one of Gods angels was waiting for me. I was so sick, and I got off the bus and went inside the terminal. Who do you fucking think was there? Remember Little Mikey?

Yeah, the same Mikey that became Crackhead Mikey thanks to me. He was inside, we saw each immediately. The last time I saw Mikey was when I gave him a hundred dollar bill to cop some dope for Stephanie and I. We didn't even have to say a fucking word we just hugged, I started to cry.

"Mickey, I'm sick."

"I know," he said. "I have something that will help, its not cheeva, but it make you feel a little better. Follow me Brad to the bathroom."

"I'm right behind you Mikey." So we walked into the bathroom and went into a stall together. "This is Ativan and we can break it down and shoot it."

I said, "Ok Mikey." He produced a spoon and put a little water in it then dropped a small pill in the spoon that didn't break down very easy, but eventually did. I don't know how sick Mikey was, but I did know what I was. As Mikey was stirring it up in his little spoon. He asked me if I had a cig for the cotton. I did have cigarettes, I was too sick to smoke them. So I tore off a filter, and they were Camels so it was all cotton.

Unless what I was told was a lie, Little Mikey shared his last Ativan with me. He even had a new needle he gave me to use. My hands and arms were a mess, so I didn't even know if I was going to be able to find a vein to inject this into. Luckily, once again that last little vein that was barely visible allowed me to register and push it in. I can't say I felt good immediately. It did seem to help a little. "I'm sorry Mikey for how I acted back in the city," I said when we were done.

Mikey said he was sorry as well and told me to forget it. We walked out of the bathroom separately not to draw any attention to either one of us. "Brad if you got money I know where to get some," Mikey told me.

"Mikey, I've got a little money, that's mainly for food, to make it across the America, but I'm willing to spend ten dollars."

"Well we can try. I know where to go come on," he says.

"I'll miss my bus if I'm not back in forty minutes."

"Don't worry, it's close," and with that we walked down the lighted streets of Denver. It wasn't that close, I thought to myself, or my pain just made walking twice as hard. I was struggling to keep up with Little Mikey. He was walking so fast. When we finally reached the corner where there were esses swinging, Mikey approached them with my ten dollars in his hand. I watched as one of them shook there head no. He continued to work his magic, but these guys wouldn't budge. I had less than eight dollars left in my pocket so even if I gave them every dime it still wasn't enough. Felonies aren't for free, I was told once, and that is why they denied Mikey, more than likely.

He walked back to me and said, "I know another spot, just follow me Brad." I was too sick to argue and only had twenty minutes left to be back before my bus was leaving. The fact that we had a lay over in Denver was a blessing. The bus needed to be fueled up, and its toilet emptied and whatever else. I was almost running it seemed to keep up.

Once again Mikey had my money, and it wasn't a hundred dollar bill this time yet it might as well have been. When we crossed the street and rounded another corner there were another group of esses swingin'. Mikey started talking right as he walked up to them without a drop of fear. No matter how hard he tried nobody was going to give us shit for ten bucks. I walked over to Mikey and said my shit is on the bus, Mikey, I've got to go now.

He saw in my eyes how serious I was and we both walked as fast as we could back to the depot. "Brad across the street is a liquor store with a drive through window. You can get something there that may help. Come on I'll walk with you," and he did. I walked right up to the drive through window and asked for a half pint of Jack Daniels. I payed for it with the money Mikey gave back to me. My bus was scheduled to leave in five minutes so I had very little time to prepare a drink.

Both Mikey and I ran across the street together and I walked into Denver's Greyhound bus depot. There was a Burger King inside, so I bought a Coke to mix with the Jack. Then I gave Mikey a few dollars for his help, and I hugged him tightly knowing it was our last hug. I almost started crying. "Hey you get out of here," he said in a commanding voice. He showed no emotion other than a stern look that seem to say "Get off your ass private! Move it! Move it! Move it!"

I knew he was full of shit, and he wanted cry too. I just felt it, and I knew right then and there this was the last time I would ever see him again and it was. Little Mickey was my brother with so much love in his heart. That morning he showed up at my apartment after spending all the money I gave him, he was in tears. Now I was the one in tears choking it back as he ordered me to push on.

So I followed his orders, as the soldier I was, and got on the bus. I was in so much pain, as I walked down the isle of the bus, and took a seat. I waited 'till we were moving as I sipped lightly on my chaser then went to the bathroom. I dumped out a majority of the drink. I filled it back up with Jack Daniels in hopes it would make me feel better. When I returned to my seat I began to drink. It did make me feel a little better.

A hundred miles had passed, and then I began to feel really awful. My sides started to vibrate like a bad acid trip filled with poison. I rested my head on the window without thought. Trudging through the mud is what it felt like, with a fever of a hundred and five. I was confused that I now felt three times worse than I did just an hour ago. I twisted in my seat from side to side moaning out loud. I tried not to let it be known to others around me how bad I felt. I stank of whiskey and death. Jack Daniels was not a good idea. Somehow it had only made me worse.

How I made it to the morning was a miracle. The hours on the bus were an eternity in my mind. As the sun started to rise, I realized I was on the floor of the bus curled in a ball in a fetal position, and the bus was pulling off an exit.

The driver made an announcement, "We are going to make a stop for breakfast." The driver pulled into a McDonald's. I managed to get off the bus with the rest of the passengers. I had very little money, and all I wanted was something I thought would make me feel better. I choice to buy one orange juice, and got back on the bus. As I was walking toward the back one of the passengers said, "Your face is yellow," and I sat down, ignoring the comment, I drank the entire cup of orange juice. It went down easy and I drank it very eagerly.

The bus pulled away and as soon as we were back on the highway things got worse. I began to feel very nauseas. I tried to hold it down as hard as I could in the seconds that followed. Then I knew there was no stopping it. I quickly got up to head to the bathroom, but as soon as I got up all hell broke loose. I vomited pure orange juice in a projectile manner on the floor at my feat where I was laying down hours before. I stumbled my way into the bathroom and dry heaved into the pool of blue. There was nothing left in my stomach to come up.

I grabbed as many wipes and pieces of toilet paper as I could to try to clean up the vomit on the floor. My hands were shaking, my sides were vibrating, and I was hallucinating. Not pink elephants and that bullshit. My vision was blurred. I wiped upped my puke as best as I could. The bus stank of orange juice and vomit. While I was in the bathroom one of the passengers had notified the driver.

I sat down in a different seat while my body vibrated from the inside out. There was no holding on anymore, I had reached a point in my heroin abuse that I'd never experienced before. I looked like hell and felt like I was burning up.

Another passenger looked at me, knowing all that just happened and said, "You're as yellow as the sun," and she opened her purse and pulled out a little mirror. As I looked in the mirror, I was horrified to see the reflection. I was yellow, and in all my episodes of being dope sick, I had never turned yellow. Something was definitely wrong. "You need a hospital, you better tell the driver." I took her suggestion and worked my way towards the front of the bus. The first seat on the right of the driver was open and I sat down.

"Sir, I'm very sick. I can't go on anymore."

He looked at me, and his eyes widened with genuine concern, "We are thirty miles from the next town, can you hold on Son?" the driver said.

"I'll do my best Sir. I need to go to a hospital, I think I'm dying." He pushed down on the accelerator and the bus picked up speed. He looked terrified, and I so grateful that he was there. It could have someone else who didn't give a rat's ass about me. Maybe he didn't, yet he sure did show that he cared.

"Just hold on, when we get closer, I'll call it in", and he did just that. The bus pulled over on the side of the highway, twenty minutes later, behind an ambulance that was waiting. I was carried off the bus and they layed me on my stomach, and then strapped me down. The ride to the hospital was a blur, yet I remember being wheeled in the ER. The lights were so bright. I was crying out loudly because the pain was so fierce.

They injected me in the butt with Vicaden but it still didn't stop the pain. An hour later I was still crying out. Then they gave Demerol, and it only felt like Tylenol. This was more pain than I ever felt before. What was so different now than before? I shook and trembled as nurses and doctors took blood and exchanged words. Then I was wheeled into a room feeling no relief from this agony. "What did they give me?" I asked myself. "Was it sugar water?" All of the pain was still there. It just reduced it a little. My back hurt so bad, I begged the nurses to help me. One did and she rolled me over on my side and massaged me carefully. Bless her for sympathy. It did help a little.

Then the doctor came in. "I'm doctor Koke," he said. "You have Hepatitis A, and your liver has been scarred. I'm aware you also have opiates in your blood. I have no choice but to give you Delada because your liver can't handle anything else for the pain. This is not what I want to give you; however, I have no choice."

You better believe I knew what Delada (Morphine) was. When he left the room I saw my black backpack sitting on a table. I rang the buzzer for the nurse.

Her voice came through the speaker attached to the bed. "What can I do for you?" she replied.

"Can I have a can of sprite please?" and in less than five minutes I had a can of sprite with bucket of crushed ice with two or three plastic wrapped cups. As soon as she left the room, I wasted no time. I was in too much fucking pain to go on like this. All I could remember was trying to squirt cheeva in my nose the last time I was sick, and the results were bad. So I took a little sip from the can itself poured some ice in a cup and filled the cup to the top. Then as fast as I could, I hovelled toward the bathroom and emptied the rest of the sprite in the sink. I tore the can in half, expecting they were going to bring me a little pill that I know for a fact breaks down in water in a snap.

After preparing the can I opened my backpack. I went through what clothes I had, searching frantically for the brand new bag I had filled with insulin syringes. I found the weighed eighth still in the shirt I wrapped it in, but I didn't hide my needles as well. I was running out of time. I knew they would return very soon. I looked again and again, and then finally gave up. They fucking took my rigs out of my backpack. This hospital had a smart staff. Before things got worse I crushed the can as quietly as I could and went back to my bed expecting no relief.

Well at least they let me keep my nugs.

Not a moment too soon, in walks a nurse with a tiny paper cup in her hand. "Here Mr. Jackson, this will make you feel much better. It has been crushed up in jello, so eat all of it please."

So they were on to me. I did as I was told and waited, expecting nothing. Why would it lessen my pain? The Vicaden and Demerol did nothing. Shit, I was still in pain and I'm very aware of those drugs. Then a feeling of warmth slowly came over my entire body. The back spasms were no longer talking to me in less than ten short minutes.

An hour later, yellow as hell in the face, I felt just fine. What the fuck I am doing here? I feel fine now. Oh, that's right, my immune system was so low I got Hepatitis A. How? I'm not sure. Doctor Koke entered my room and asked me how I was doing.

"I feel a lot better doctor," I told him.

"We had the nurses remove the bag of insulin needles from your backpack, before I decided to treat you with Morphine. I'm sure you understand why? It goes against everything I've been taught as a doctor to give Morphine to a heroin addict; however, there is no other drug we can administer to you for the pain. Morphine doesn't damage the liver or kidneys compared to Demerol, Vicaden, and other pain relieving drugs. Until your liver has healed, you must be given Hydromorphone. Your liver is permanently scarred, and from this moment on you will have to be aware this. That means treating yourself better, and being aware of the damage you have done to yourself.

We have contacted your mother in South Carolina and she is driving here with Barbara Garrison to pick you up, and drive you to the Greenville Detox in Greenville, South Carolina. Since your mother is an LPN she will administer the Delada. By know means will you have this medicine in your possession. Now we here at Boonville County Hospital have done all we can for you Mr. Jackson. They are on the road right now and should be here in two days. Do you have any questions?"

I replied, "Is Hepatitis A an STD and something I'll have to live with forever?"

The Doctor replied, "No you can get it from food or just casual contact. Its not B or C, so consider yourself lucky and good luck." He went into details of Hepatitis B and C, but I won't bother quoting every fucking thing Doctor Koke said. Doctor Koke, what a world.

I just learned that I was conceived in this city, and of course my home fucking state. A little coincidental, wouldn't you say? So over the next two days, I had time to think about the decisions I had made that that up to this moment. Laying in that hospital bed was just what the doctor ordered. No pun intended, just the truth.

Why was I here? Well truthfully, I felt good in spite of the damage I had done to my liver. I was well, by all means, no longer in pain. I felt quite good. So I didn't jump into the "What am going to do now?" shit. So I turned on the TV. There was nothing really on that I wanted to watch, until I turned the channel to MTV. It had been years since I watched Music Television. I stopped surfing the channels right then and there. Maybe it was VH1, I'm not certain. It was one or the other. They were toasting "Kurt Cobain" in so many words, but it was more like a documentary of what little they knew of his life.

As I watched, I knew why he pulled the trigger. If I had a gun, I might have done the same thing, who knows. To run out of veins, as a heroin junkie, is beyond words. The pain you suffer from is unbelievable. I knew there was a good reason I didn't resent Kurt for what he did. You have to live like he did, to truly understand. All the doctors, psychologists, psychiatrists, or whoever they may be, they don't really know. Money cannot buy veins. Maybe in a couple years, but not yet, and I'm not a special case.

Why I couldn't bring myself to hitting my jugular, my feet, between my toes, and so on is unknown. All I can say is: I wasn't allowed to. Like a program pre-installed before birth. Or maybe my grandmother Eleanor Jackson who lives in St. Joseph, Missouri had something to do with it. Just maybe that Methodist church she would take me to at the end of Francis Street had something to do with it. Maybe it was Susan, that girl I had a crush on, that attended that church, and kept me coming back just to see her beautiful face. I don't know.

What was certain, is that deep within me, is a governor of some sort; it only lets me go so far before my survival instincts kick in, or so it seems. After watching Cobain's story, I cried. Ever since that day in that hospital bed, I've had dreams. One dream I had stands out, and it scared the shit out of me. In the dream, Kurt was standing by a tree which all the leaves had fallen off of, and he was waving his arms in the air around him, for he was blind. When this image became clearer, his eyes were missing. I awoke covered in sweat from this nightmare, and didn't want to go back to sleep that night.

The Morphine was nice, yet, like I mentioned earlier, it masked some emotions. Covered it up like cat poop basically. So I enjoyed my stay in the hospital. I was recovering from the Hepatitis A. It wasn't lethal or life threatening, so that was cool; however, they gave me an AIDS/HIV test which I got the results back in South Carolina while in the Detox. All the tests came back negative, which gave me good reason to possibly make a change in my life.

Mom and Barbara eventually made it to the hospital. Mom walked in with tears streaming down her face, and Barbara just smiled. Anyway, Dr. Koke gave my mom a prescription for Delada K2's, to be exact. Not Cancer level dosage, yet a kind form of methadone for the journey to South Carolina. So they released me, and I said my goodbyes and thanked the doctor and the staff for such a wonderful job they did. After she went to a local pharmacy and filled the meds, we got on the road. In less than thirty minutes, while on the road, I was feeling quite good with the first dosage so I handed Mom a Grateful Dead tape and asked her to play it.

She said, "Brad, you got any Jerry Garcia Band? You know I do prefer that over the Dead," and I had a Garcia/Grisman show on tape that had a one of my favorite songs on it. That song was called, "The Wind And The Rain" or something close to that title. These ladies were both pot smokers back in the day; however, both of them had long since stopped smoking pot.

I said, "Mom and Barbara, can I smoke some weed? It would make me feel less nauseas" which was bullshit, I felt great. Surprisingly enough Mom and Barbara, allowed it and for the first time in years my mother smoked, as well as Barbara. I did warn them it was Mendocino County Indoor and quite strong. The fact they didn't take it from me at the hospital was fucking great!

So we are trucking down the road listening to Jerry and David Grisman, baked out of our minds. I was feeling really groovy. The morphine and the dank nugs was such a beautiful mix. Fuck yeah, I'm glorifying it. Sorry folks, if it was all bad, who would smoke pot? Who would get addicted to heroin? Right, so marijuana isn't a physically addictive substance, but opiates sure are. So kids, don't try this at home.

We had great time driving from Missouri to South Carolina. Mom and my new step mom were reliving their youth just for a day. The journey to South Carolina almost made up for all the pain I had suffered. Now I'm aware of where I was going; to a state that I ran from as soon as they let me out of jail with five years hanging over my head. Just to remind you, the only reason my mother and father were there was the original bust from June 30, 1993.

So the plan was to turn myself in after I got out of Greenville detox. I had accomplished my mission. My name wasn't slandered to shit, unlike Fast Feddy, Grasshopper, and other so called "kind brothers" who did roll on Grateful Dead Family. It was just a fucking shame I had become addicted to heroin in the process. All of those that read this and have one moment of doubt that these word are lies. Go fuck yourself! I'm done proving myself and that's how I felt in the drive home. After living the life I have lived, going to jail to finish what I started didn't sound so bad. I know that sounds crazy. You must realize how dedicated a lot of us were.

When we finally rolled into Greenville, South Carolina I was checked into the detox immediately. I stayed there for five or six days, and was released. They tapered me off he K2's with Klonipin. When I was picked up, I was taken to my Dad's house. The same house he moved into just to be able to visit his son in jail in '93. I stayed overnight there with the intentions of turning myself in the next day. I had talked to Mr. Wier on the same fucking phone right after I talked to my Dad when I was back in SF. So they knew I was coming as well; however, Mr. Wier didn't want me to go to a detox first, it appears, or stay one lousy night with my dad. They wanted me to kick dope in a cold cell without a staff of nurses trained in the detoxification.

The next morning, on the way to the store to get some cigarettes, before turning myself in, Dad let me drive his Eagle Talon Turbo. I had no license, and that he knew, yet his only son was turning himself in. So dad broke a little rule to give one last joy ride in his new sports car. That fucking car was so fast I was at seventy before I knew it heading toward the town of Clinton, S.C. (Laurens County). When we both heard the police car siren go off. Now this was a little coincidental as well. Obviously, if I'm turning myself in they go a little easier on you right?

Well they were there waiting, and when we told them we were on our way to turning me in. The cop said, "Sure you were."

I said, "No, really call Mr. Wier, my probation officer," he just booked me and took me to Laurens County Jail. My parents were outraged by the situation so once again they hired the same lawyer that got me out of it in the first place. His name was Rick K. Harris.

Well in spite of their efforts to railroad me, they did and they didn't. They knew who I was and how I didn't play ball so I did twenty-two months at Cross Anchor Correctional Facility with five fucking years of probation hanging over my head again. Now that's called one foot in and one foot out.

Like I said before, this book is not about how it is to spend time in jail, it's about what real niggas go through that are true to the game. My bad ... real Dead Heads. Just know that you don't get fucked in the ass by inmates and convicts, the judge does all the fucking. All that shit is pure propaganda. It's a fear tactic, like Christianity's heaven and hell. I got news for you, religion is for those that are afraid of hell. Spirituality is for those who have lived it.

1997

So I did my twenty-two months, which is what a nonviolent crime usually does on a five year bid. Problem was, when I got out, I had to live with my father. That was a major problem. For starters, back then he grew his own marijuana in the bathroom that was supposed be my bathroom and was connected to my room. Of course I couldn't puff, so it was a living fucking nightmare. We eventually got into a big fist fight, and I actually broke chairs over his back like in a bar brawl. Insanity at it's best, so I freaked out, took all of his weed, and bailed in my Caravan. I'd worked for it by riding a fucking bike up to Pizza Hut for months.

Yeah, I reported to Mr. Wier for at least six months. I paid all the monthly payments and so on. Living with Dad, when you're not allowed to puff, is too difficult so I loaded up my Caravan, started paying payments, and headed back to San Francisco.

Why? Well I had kicked heroin, and I told Allan I was going back to South Carolina. He was the last person from the city, other than little Mikey in Denver. I suppose all that time in jail left me wondering. How many of us were still left? The reason I left was not clear yet. Sure, I fought with my dad everyday, yet to return meant I was going to use. Or just maybe I'll find some family and take them back east. Taking all the nugs we had growing was a fucked up thing to do. I wanted some money to rest on in case I needed it. Selfish is selfish.

Well, I left and drove across the United States again and alone. It was in the fall. I always seem to have a driving force that moves me in autumn. When I got to California, Bakersfield area, it was about two in the morning. A police car turned on its lights behind me. I grabbed all the jars of nugs and started throwing them out the window. By the time I had thrown all the buds out the window there were two cops in pursuit. I wasn't speeding, just evading until I had gotten rid of all pot. When I pulled over they came to my van with guns in hand shouting, "Get out and get on the ground!" I did and they handcuffed me. Then as they searched the van they soon found there wasn't anything to find, except a small nodge that had flown back in the window. So they had two charges evading and simple possession. Not the best charges when you've called for back up. So they dragged me around (handcuffed) the side of my van and a officer threw a bag on the ground.

"What is this Mr. Jackson?" the officer said. This scene is right out of Hollywood, classic bullshit. The guy cuts into the package complete with duck tape around it and a white powder emerged from the cut.

"Hey man, that's not mine! You guys planted that on me!" The police squad said their typical statements when they are trying to terrify someone young who is bringing pot into their state. After I had hit my knee's, with the tears to go with it, swearing my innocence, they eventually told me they were just trying to scare me. Their goal was to scare this young looking kid bringing in marijuana to a state already filled with it. That's basically what the head officer said to me. I was brought down to the small outpost station and the two original officers were sitting in a small room with me thumbing through a book.

"What is the least we can charge him with so he can go get his van out of the impound station," the main officer said to his partner. They did scare me, and I lost all my pot so they felt they had done something noble. So, they released me with a simple possession ticket and minimum evading charge. The kind you got when your radio is on to loud to hear. Walking back to the impound station and paying the eighty-six dollars to get it out wasn't fun. They said they wouldn't have pulled me over if I didn't have those, "I support my local police officer" stickers. These cops said the majority of people that buy those are doing something wrong or will.

Well, I got the Caravan back and went toward the bay, plans slightly changed. I crossed the Golden Gate Bridge and entered the Bay. I reached the Panhandle, found a parking spot around the park and headed up the hill to Haight and Ashbury. All I found were new faces. Same clothing type, just different people, all doing the same as I once did. You could stand there for fifteen minutes, anywhere, smoking a cigarette, and you'd see what apparently always was.

We were the last Haist St.Posse, when Jerry's kids were really "Jerry's kids." The '92 crew to '95, three solid years we all were together. I was a late '91 going into the spring family of '92 and on. Every four to five years, at the very most, a new Haight St. family would develop. As new ones came in, others left. Like one of the original members of "The Oxford Groups " (Acron, Ohio area) told me at the Buckely Detox, "Son, when you sit down in one these chairs, someone gets up out of their's." That's what it looks like happened in San Francisco's Haight families.

Maybe since Jerry had died, things had changed to a certain degree. If you look at it one way, some have said, "Jerry Garcia was King in the church of The Grateful Dead. All of his soldiers (The kids) kept the King alive. Apparently in this church there is a hero all right. A Hero within. A Heroin, becoming a part of a group of ill-treating people, refusing to pay for a decent burial of a man in debt." That is how the folk tale goes. Not to twist the whole wonderful tale; however, my family was alive and well in the beginning.

As I looked back in the past of my Haight St. family, there were also kids I heard about that overdosed on heroin in the very beginning. Every four to five years, a new family developed, as kids goes. Fast Eddie came into the scene around '86, word has it. He was Wreckin' Crew material that out lasted the norm. Scotty, one of the original crew members, now drives a sixty thousand dollar Silverado and lives in Eugene, Oregon. The Wreckin' Crew spare changed and sold product carefully, and they out lived many for the "King." Their poison was alcohol, and Jerry's was heroin. When I returned after '93, the entire family was using the same dope as Jerry. That main connect was Lallo, I'm sure he had to deal with the politics, nevertheless, he still had the same product one way or the another.

So here you got this loyal family of kids, who always stayed close to Jerry. From staying at The Fireside, in Marin county to just living in the shitty motels in Oakland, we all stayed close to Jerry in those last two years. Eighty percent of us were shooting heroin. We were quite the church. We drank from the same wine, and kneeled before the King. I write this because, whether its delusional thinking or not, like the hundred and one year old man from the Oxford groups said to me, "one gets up, another takes its place." A theory, not a kind one, just a theory. From the moment I stepped into that first show on September 18, 1988, there were kids strung out on heroin all around me. I didn't see that then. All I could see was the Hollywood side of it all, that is, until I became full time.

My friend Morgan was an inspiration to me. He taught me how to play Crazy Fingers, and was one of the first "brothers" I had met who was trying to kick heroin. He passed away with Hepatitis C. There were many strong soldiers, in the end, that decided to kick heroin, where others didn't. Crazy as it seems, I had influenced some. It seemed the last family was probably the strongest there was.

When there are less people to take the bullet for you, your chances of living are reduced. For every child that was taking the bullet for Jerry and lived to tell about it, I'm left wondering, were we responsible for Jerry's death? If I would have continued on for a few more months, might I have been the one to die instead of our King?

Conspiracy theories are something I don't want to touch. I'm Lot, the one who didn't look back and get turned to salt. Every fucking time I hear "Gomorra," by The Jerry Garcia Band, that thought drives each word in this book. "Tell it so others don't have to go through what you've been through." Can't say I would want to try what I've done and expect a different result. That would be the definition of insanity. Whatever you get out of this book, will be just that. For me to say, "If you're looking for yourself in San Francisco, just look inside yourself. It's all there to be seen," would be bullshit. It may be true for those that take your word on it.

I drove down to Sixteenth and Mission. I parked my Caravan a few blocks away and walked towards Mission St. There were lots of people on the corner, esses working left and right, but no sign of any familiar faces.

As I walked across the street, I noticed a bro with his hat pulled down over his eyes, sitting crouched down, sleeping. As I walked closer, I noticed a poncho on him. The sun was blazing hot on this San Francisco day. I leaned down to get a better look. In spite of the burly beard, if you call that patchy look a full beard, it was Patches! It was like the day I first watched him walk up the hill to the corner of Haight and Ashbury, with that fuckin' red drum and leather jacket, mixed with the man he had become. His eyes sparkled in the sun when he looked up at me, and he said in that crackly, yet cheery, sounding voice, "Brad!" I helped him up and quickly briefed him on the current situation. "Why did you come back?" Patches said.

"For you," and with that he told me about a couple of new kids, who had come in and taken our place, and wanted to leave the city. Whether or not anyone I took from the city actually stayed off the shit or not, this was there opportunity. I assured those Bakersfield Police Officers, I would go home as soon as I finished visiting, and it was time to go. I've been known to tell a lie, yet you can count on what I say. It was time to leave, and I had stayed only a matter of hours. We were on the road heading east. Patches had a plan. He said Ozzy had his own construction company in Colorado Springs, Colorado.

So that was where we were going to go first. My passengers consisted of a young skater girl with blond dreads, her partner, another young bro (I forget his name or anyone except Patches), and Patches and I. They had money, I remember that. When we got to Colorado Springs, Patches got on a phone and called Ozzy. He and his girl eventually showed up, and we followed them back to their house. We were there in less than five minutes and Ozzy was breaking out this huge pill bottle filled with Delada K8's! Shit, Doctor Koke only prescribed me K2's, let alone K8's. Patches, Ozzy, his girl, and myself were all in the bedroom. Clean and fresh needles were being passed around, and all of this in moments time.

Wasn't I on a mission? Well this stuff is pharmaceutical, at least I won't overdose. That was my reasoning. I hadn't shot anything since early '95. Why now? Why did I even go to SF in the first place? I'm not certain; however, I did a shot with Patches and Ozzy at his place in Colorado Springs. After all that, I decided it was definitely time to go. Patches wanted to stay. Ozzy offered him work with whatever he had going on, construction of some type, this I remember. But let's not fool ourselves, Patches stayed mainly due to the fact that there was an entire bottle of K8's. That's a pretty large amount of pure morphine.

So we said our goodbyes with a lot more care involved than some. Wished him well, I did. We both knew, as we looked at each other, it was the last time we would see each other. This was more casual, with less drama, than Crackhead Mickey and I. Patches was always good about that smile he wore till the end.

I loaded up with the rest of the crew that I didn't even know, and they didn't even know where they were going. Just away from San Francisco and the dope it provided, whatever that may be. You can run, but you can't hide. It's the oldest expression in the book. Eighty-eighty percent of everything in the city, is in every town in America. The difference is, it's not on every fucking corner or every other corner. The availability of what you want is in such abundance in San Francisco, you reach a bottom faster because you don't have to wait for whatever you're fucked up on. Most places I lived there's usually a down time for whatever your addicted to (outside of New York, of course.)

Anyway, with these unknown travelers, we set out east. We went through Missouri and dropped off the two girls in St. Louis. That was a quick decision on their part. I was trying to get back to the forty route from St. Louis, when I eventually got too tired to drive. So the only bro in my Caravan offered to drive, and, like a dumb ass, I took him up on it.

When I awoke, the glass from the side sliding door had burst open as the van was scraping against a fence off to the left of the highway. I told dude to get out of the driver seat and drove the van back onto the road. We were lucky, it was just cosmetic damage, yet the fucking window was gone. The pressure in the van was so unbearable.

We stopped at the first exit we saw, and luckily there was a truck stop with a restaurant. We pulled around back to look for some cardboard to place in the hole. The only thing we found were lettuce boxes in bad shape. That's all they had so we went to the gift shop and found some strong tape. I taped this stinking cardboard to my van and looked at the missing passenger side mirror. The whole passenger side of my van wasn't too terrible considering how bad it could have been. I was pissed, yet I know he was just as tired as me.

I got on the forty and headed to my Dad's house in South Carolina. I was sure Donald would be pissed and dad as well. But I was certain I was on a mission from God. Once back on the forty, I had no need for maps. The bro hanging out had no plans other than heading to New Orleans.

He asked, "Can I catch a ride from your dad's place so I can get a shower and a nights rest?" I said yeah. There were lots of pretty pictures to take on the forty, but I'll just take you to my dad's house.

As he looked at the van and heard why in the hell I went there and back he said nothing. Donald was more pissed than dad. I tried living with my dad for three more months. We eventually got into one of our fights and I pawned his Less Paul Gibson that was his cherry for about four hundred dollars. I had reported to Mr. Weir, my probation officer, just days before this happed. My plan was to just give up. I wasn't strung out on anything.

Living alone, attending AA and NA meetings in Clinton S.C. wasn't to cool. I couldn't puff. My dad always had herb on him, and it was just an impossible relationship. I didn't drink but my plan was to go to Eugene, and live in the surrounding mountains and drink myself to death. It sounded fun, really. Just live in the woods with a tent and be free. Whether I died or not, freedom was the goal, the freedom to walk into town without reporting monthly to somebody about shit that happened years back.

1998

    I got on a Greyhound in February '98 and went across the US again all the way to Eugene, Oregon. I took a bus to Wal-Mart and bought all the necessary camping gear. Got back on a bus and rented a room on Franklin Blvd. I started drinking as soon as I checked into the room. I hadn't drank in long while, but living alone, without all the friends and family I grew to love, drove me to this point. Who knows if Brandy and I would have connected, things could have been different. If Stephanie and I would've worked out maybe she would be my wife. That's how I saw it. They were both dead to me. I did find out while in Clinton, South Carolina that Brandi died.

    Kelly was the only person that I had managed to get a phone number for while I was in the bay, that's, aka, "Kells Bells and/or Kelly Belly." She told me that Brandy died of AID's shortly after Jerry's death. There was a funeral on Market St., put on by all the homeless and street people, like myself, who loved her. Kelly said it was beautiful. I was in prison while all this was happening. So I knew Brandy had died. Mariam was in a wheelchair and living in Chicago from a gunshot wound that paralyzed her. A bad drug deal I heard. Crackhead Mike got killed in a bad drug deal in NY, rumor has it, and Patches died under the same circumstances. So these are just the very few I knew that had fallen.

    Giving up with dignity was what I was doing. Alone in this world, as a criminal, I was. All my running buddies were gone. I was three beers in, when I decided to call my mom in Missouri. When she answered, I filled her in with the typical drunken babble of my great adventure. After listening to me, she calmly told me to find a Yellow Book and look up that detox I went to the last time I was here. "Mom, I'm not strung out on anything, just drinking and moving to the mountains." That was true, I hadn't been chemically dependent on drugs for over two years.

Mom said, "Look, I'm saying you just check yourself in and give yourself a few days to think it through…ok?" Well I was tired, and I remembered Buckley Detox well from the last time I was there.

"Mom, I'll make no promises, but I'll call to see if there is a bed." Now there was a lot more talking me into this than I care to write. I called and sure enough they had a bed. So I took a "Jerry Cab" from the motel with all my gear and headed toward Buckley on 4th and Jefferson.

They stored all my shit and took me in immediately. No drunk tank, just sit down, fill this out, and get in pajamas. It had the same smell. Carol was still there, but that cool black cook no longer worked there. I stayed there five days, and then Big Bob from Phase II solutions picked me up. He ran the halfway house, and he was a tall, old, Indian named Bob. He had the typical gray beard. I stayed in that house long enough to move across the street in the Campus Quads next to the University Of Oregon.

I met a girl, while living in "Phase II Solutions" on 16th and Alder. I gave love another chance in this new world of the AA and NA culture, only to find, once again, a broken heart. While I was in the "Carlton House"(In-House Treatment) I asked her to watch my apartment. While I was trying to get my head on straight, in a twenty-eight day program, she was fucking this guy in my apartment. So I bailed on the treatment place, and with the help of my sponsor, kicked her out of my apartment. I fell in love again, that was the problem. There was no love, there was no girl for me in the world of "The Grateful Dead" I had lived in since I was fifteen, and then in the culture of Alcoholics and Narcotics Anonymous, I also fell.

Then one day, while I was walking on 13th Ave., I ran into Dready Christy. Her eyes lit up and she gave me a big hug. "Where have you been?" she said.

"Doing fucking time in South Carolina for an old LSD charge," I said.

"Well come with me, I'll show you where I live." I followed her to a little truck that looked brand new. "Get in," Christy said. I got in the passenger side and shut the door. As soon as the engine started the radio came on very loudly. The song playing was "Scarlet Begonias" covered by Sublime, live.

We parked and got out, and as we walked closer to the house, I could see Osiris tied up to a tree with a good size chain. Christy was buying dog food and some grub for herself when we ran into each other. So as I walked closer to Osiris, he started getting really excited. "Hey buddy, long time no see, huh?" I tell Osiris as he jumps on me.

Christy opened the bag of organic dog food she just bought for him, which isn't cheap, she always gave Cypress the best she could. Once his bowl was filled, she gave him a hug, and we walked up the porch stairs towards the front door. When the door opened, she walked in and took my hand as we climbed the stairs. It was narrow with poor lighting. And that's how you entered her place. The kitchen was large and very white. She was sharing this house with others, so one fridge can be tough. She started making herself a vegetarian lunch. There was a knock at the door downstairs. She went down the stairs and opened the door. When she came back up there was a bro with her.

"What's up man?" he says when he sees me. "I'm Phish."

"Right on, I'm Brad. I'm a old friend of Christy's." Christy and Phish walked into another room without me and returned shortly.

"You wanna puff?" Christy said when she entered the kitchen.

"Yeah," I replied. We smoked, then Phish went on his way. After she fed me and Osiris, she dragged me down to some bar where we played pool.

After we both got tired of that, she said, "Lets bail, Brad."

I said ok and followed her. As we walked back to her truck she asked me if I wanted to hang out at her place. I said yeah, and we went back to her house. She had a real job, at the time, as a telemarketer for a company called Venture Data. She told me she could get me a job there. Phish worked there too. As we walked up the stairs, she turned left and showed me her room. It was probably one of the best Grateful Dead bedrooms you could imagine. From tapestries to posters you've never seen before. I was impressed. Now what she did next did surprise me. She pulled out a spoon and a needle from a dresser. Then she dropped a piece of cheeva on the spoon.

"Can I have a hit?" she said yeah and gave me a brand new needle and I fixed with new cotton from one of my own cigarettes. As we lay there on the bed, side by side, we eventually nodded out and woke up in the snuggle position the next morning. When we started to wake up, I asked Christy if she knew where China Mike was.

She said, " I hadn't heard from him in awhile Brad." I expected that response. I had a good time with her, and we didn't have sex. What we did was stronger than a meaningless one-night stand. As time passed, I developed a habit again. Phish would usually cop the dope from the esses and sell it to me and Christy. Phish also sold nugs, so you got the best of both worlds.

Then one day I ran into Kelly (Kells Bells) at 5th and Blair at the Astro Station. She was buying a pack of cigarettes and dressed in a black Addidas jacket with matching pants. She was wearing a brand new pair of White Adiddas. She looked good.

Later that day, I went over to Kelly's place and bought a eighth of nugs from her. I asked if she knew of other kids that were still around. She said a lot of our family had fled like myself. She had no news of Kathy or China Mike. We hugged and she gave me her number and we said our goodbyes real cool like we were expecting to see each other again. That was the last time I ever saw Kelly.

Once again, like a broken record, I went back to the AA's to clean up, and, in the process started dating a girl named Sarah Douglas. Kelly and Christy were the only two people that were left of our family, that I'd seen, and like myself they'd moved to Eugene. Christy was on dope and Kelly was still drinking. Both friends were off limits in the world of recovery. So of course depression hit me hard, and I was tired of being dope sick.

I lasted maybe two weeks, tops, before I was back at it. I called Phish and he sold me half of a gram. I spent all my money. On August 15 1998, I wrote out a suicide note, signed it, swallowed twenty Klonapin pills and then locked the door. I waited for about twenty minutes, and then I injected about a quarter and a half of good, brown dope in my arm. I layed back on my comfortable Lazy Boy recliner and listened to Roger Walters CD called "Amused To Death." Those were the last moments before I drifted off. Darkness came over me.

As I lay there, slowly dying, Sara Douglas was walking up my steps, coming by to see me. I was sure I had locked my door, so I don't have an explanation for being alive. Or she used a credit card and opened my door, and she just didn't want to admit it. She found me in the Lazy Boy, and, according to her, I didn't seem to be breathing. So she called 911.

My entire life, as I knew it, was a failure. My soldiers, my friends, my family had all died by the sword, poetically speaking. I felt like Lieutenant Dan in "Forest Gump." I wanted to die in battle. It was a war we were in. I knew enough to know that. For three years after Jerry Garcia's death, I had this feeling that it was kids like us (that shared the same drug addiction) that kept Jerry alive.

I was taken out of the game and forced to quit in '95, and I was one less person in the vicious chain to take the bullet. And somebody has to take the bullet. We all did the same heroin, from the same connection in San Francisco. One way or the other we were all connected. If I would have died in '95, like so many other kids had in the past, Jerry may still be alive. So, in theory, you could say its possible, all of Jerry's kids, that used the same dope as him and died with it in their arm, kept Jerry alive for so many years. Theories should at least be vocalized.

As I've written this book, its become clear to me that the dedicated kids that find themselves living on and off of the Haight and Ashbury, eventually are called family, and a majority of them die of heroin. The ones that made it out alive are those that got locked up or realized the danger and got the fuck out. There's that turn over, every four to five years, as people go.

Before the ninety's crew, the eighties and seventies crews had heroin deaths that were not publicly announced, just random kids that died from a heroin addiction. This tourist attraction, that has funded the shops since the sixties, has an unspoken tale that I hope was just told. My story is the behind the scenes of how it was really like to be called Grateful Dead Family, in my opinion. Killing myself was not a desperate cry for fucking help. The majority of my fucking friends and family have died. I joined the army of the dead in the beginning for the girl and the music. I got the music and lost in love.

Epilogue

I awoke after a three-day coma in Sacred Heart Hospital. The doctor said I had brain damage as a result of the amount of time my brain went without oxygen. Three days later, I was admitted to the loony bin as a result of that suicide note. My doctor's name was Doctor Saxman. He was my primary care physician. They arranged a one-way ticket to South Carolina from Portland. I eventually did another twenty-two fucking months in prison and they finally released me without probation.

So after I got out of prison, for the third time, I was in no hurry to go anywhere. I started a band named "Token" in Columbia, SC and we played some nice venues for four years. I decided to come back to Oregon. I'm now retired from the music world, and I work as a computers tech. I'm still a swinger kid, my product has just changed. Instead of "buds, doses, mushrooms," it's now "computers."

This book was written for several reasons: so hopefully others don't have to go through what I've been through, and so that the real truth of the last Grateful Dead family is told. China Mike was the brother I never had and Kathy was the sister that you wished you had. I'm hoping the people that are in this book and survived the last five years may read this and find me on myspace.com/tokenbrad.

THE END

Token Jackson, Author

Heather Stillinger, Editor